Just Call Me Faye

A Novel

Phillip D. Demarco

First Edition

DS Publishing

New Orleans, LA

Just Call Me Faye is a work of fiction. The names, characters, businesses, places, events, and incidents portrayed are products of the author's imagination or are used in a fictitious manner. Any similarity to actual persons—living or dead—or actual events is coincidental.

ISBN 979-8-9866183-6-4 (hardback)
ISBN 979-8-9866183-0-2 (paperback)
ISBN 979-8-9866183-1-9 (digital)

Printed in the United States of America.

CONTENTS

CHAPTER 1

Never Mind, I Just Do

In the 1989 movie, *Field of Dreams*, Burt Lancaster, in his role of Dr. Archibald "Moonlight" Graham, stated, "We just don't recognize life's most significant moments while they're happening."

*****

The start of each new academic year was still exciting, even after teaching for over a decade. When the first day of classes arrived, it often appeared as collective chaos after a long summer of relative quietness. This chaos arose from students rushing to class, looking for their classrooms, adjusting their schedules, and greeting friends they haven't seen in months. Sometimes, a few of them would stop by my office to say hello or tell me about their recent adventures. This excitement, always undeniable to me, showed I was ready to begin another year of a job far more demanding than most people understood. My enthusiasm resulted from several notions: what my classes would be like, who my students were, what challenges I'd face, and how my classes would compare to others I've had in earlier years. How everything would unfold was unknown, but not knowing was the best part of the excitement.

At this point in my academic career, I had become a seasoned professor. Tenured and promoted several years before, I was very comfortable in the classroom. I knew how to manage a large class and handle the challenges presented to me throughout the semester. The courses were no longer new to me as I'd taught them all before, and a few of them, multiple times. Also, since I'd seen many types of students during my career, nothing surprised me anymore. Or so I thought.

Before classes began, I selected the topics I wanted to cover, generated the syllabi, and printed the student rosters. I never covered new material on the first day; instead, I conducted the administrative duties required at the start of a semester. These included taking roll, going over the syllabus, discussing the grading policy, and reviewing classroom rules. I also discussed the keys to success in the course.

During the first class meeting, I asked the students to complete student information forms. These forms requested things such as their academic major, year in school, age, hometown, hobbies, extracurricular activities, the name they wanted me to call them in class, and their plans after graduation. This information helped me get to know everyone on a more personal level. I always enjoyed reading the forms, and the students appreciated my knowing them as more than a number.

Even though I prepared for my classes, the fall semester of 2006 turned out to be different because of a late change in my teaching schedule. This resulted when a colleague asked me to take over a course he unexpectedly couldn't teach at the last minute. Since I had taught it before, I was happy to help, so I adjusted my schedule to accommodate my added responsibilities. I felt unprepared before meeting his class later in the morning because I didn't have much time to print off the student roster and other handout materials. This increased the excitement so befitting of a new academic year. My additional class was an undergraduate course in engineering mechanics called dynamics, the study of applying engineering principles to solve problems involving moving objects. After gathering the material I needed, I walked down the hall and entered the sterile-looking classroom through the door at the front. The room had seven rows of long, gray bench-like tables with six blue plastic chairs to a row and a green chalkboard on the front wall. There were doors from the hall to the classroom at both the back and front, and windows filled the outside wall opposite the doors. A podium stood left of the chalkboard and opposite the front door. The cinder block walls were painted white, and the white tile floor was speckled with gray-and-black markings. The room was almost full, with over thirty students in the forty-two-seat classroom, and most of them were male. It was noisy but became quiet as I entered, walked across the room to the podium, and introduced myself.

"Good morning. I'm Dr. Phillip Demarco, and this course is EGM 3400, Dynamics," I announced.

Everything went well as I moved through my first-day administrative tasks. As I spoke, a few students came in after I began and found seats in the back. After completing my discussion of the course details and answering a few questions, I collected the information forms and dismissed the class. A few of the students who arrived late continued to complete their forms while I talked with a small group afterward. When I finished, several remaining students were standing in line to turn in their forms. As I reached for the last one, I looked up to see a striking female student. She had long, thick blonde hair, which extended to her waist, and emerald-green eyes I could almost see behind, and she was tall— five feet, eight inches at least. She wore long golden earrings, a loose-fitting cotton top, and hemmed denim shorts. She appeared thin, but very well built—not the typical female I had in my classes. This student was quietly beautiful, with soft, inviting eyes. When she handed me her form, she looked at me and smiled. The sight of her took my breath away and made it difficult for me to even mutter, "Thank you."

All the other students had already gone as she turned and walked toward the door to leave. I watched—or perhaps gawked—at her as she left. After a few steps, she stopped, glanced back at me over her shoulder, and smiled once more before exiting the room. I may have smiled in return, but I couldn't be sure. As I looked down at her form, I learned her name was Laura Faye McDonald, but she went by "Faye." Faye, I read, was from Nashville, Tennessee, was twenty-one years old, and was a junior studying electrical engineering.

*****

With all due respect to the esteemed Dr. Graham, I somehow recognized this very moment as a significant one in my life. I just didn't yet understand why.

*****

I was not twenty-one. I was a married forty-five-year-old associate professor of mechanical engineering at the University of Florida. My wife, Sophia, was a successful stockbroker and taught finance part-time at the local Santa Fe Community College. She often said she enjoyed teaching more than her regular job.

Sophia and I celebrated our fourteenth wedding anniversary a few weeks earlier. Although our marriage wasn't perfect, I thought it was a good one. We faced challenges over the years, as most couples do, but we worked through them. Our difficulties stemmed from our collective pursuits of educational and professional goals, which resulted in time spent apart and required solitude even when we were together. I suppose our relationship wasn't as strong as it could have been, and maybe I was vulnerable because of it. I know relationships change for many reasons, but I believed we still loved each other.

The major problem in our marriage was that I always wanted children, and Sophia did not. She thought she wanted them at first, but as she became more successful in business, she didn't feel her career pursuits left enough time to raise a family. I felt we were missing out on an important part of life without children, but Sophia disagreed. She was more focused on her job and was interested in climbing the corporate ladder. Another problem we had was that I was a very sexual person, and Sophia was not. Nor was she passionate. Our sex life was more important to me than it was to her, which resulted in adequate but routine and uninspiring sex.

My wife's background and mine differed significantly. She came from a wealthy German family in McLean, Virginia; was an only child, and attended private schools. When she turned twenty-five years old, she inherited a large trust fund from her maternal grandfather's death a few years earlier. But Sophia was an anomaly; she didn't grow up spoiled and was always a kind and generous person.

I grew up with three brothers in a middle-class Italian family in Bethlehem, Pennsylvania, and attended public schools. My father worked for Bethlehem Steel, and my brothers and I worked in the same steel mill during our summer breaks from college.

Sophia and I met as undergraduate students at Princeton University in New Jersey, where she studied finance and I majored in mechanical engineering. I was fortunate to have won an academic scholarship to attend Princeton; otherwise, I never could have afforded it. While there, we dated for two years and often discussed having a future together. After we graduated, Sophia attended Columbia University in New York City to work on a Master of Business Administration while I stayed at Princeton to study for a master's degree in mechanical engineering. I made the short trip to New York often to visit her during her Columbia years. After we finished our degrees, Sophia stayed in New York and worked as an investment banker, and I moved to Atlanta to pursue my doctorate in mechanical engineering at the Georgia Institute of Technology. My specialization was structures and structural analysis. I first became interested in structures after an accident occurred at Bethlehem Steel that killed two employees. When I completed my PhD three years later, I accepted a faculty position at the University of Florida to teach and perform research in structures and related subjects. Sophia left New York two years afterward to join me in Gainesville, and we married in 1992.

Sophia is a beauty, with shoulder-length, jet-black hair, brown eyes, and the prettiest smile I'd ever seen. She's five feet, five inches tall, thin, and very athletic. She played lacrosse at Princeton and is a strong and confident woman. I also thought myself to be attractive. I am six feet, two inches tall, with an athletic build, dark hair graying at the temples, and blue eyes. We often received compliments about how good we looked as a couple. But I wasn't sure Sophia was happy living in a small town. I always believed she'd be happier back in New York or Chicago—cities she visited often for work.

My wife's description of our marriage may have differed from mine. She was less concerned about our relationship than I, and she appeared accepting of its quality and its shortcomings. Perhaps her outlook was because of the reasons I've mentioned, or others of which I was unaware. She was never interested in discussing our marriage or ways to improve it. I remember trying to voice my concerns several times over the years, but Sophia always resisted my efforts for reasons I never quite understood. Perhaps it was because we didn't communicate well. We were fine talking about life's everyday issues, but any relationship talk or discussions about sex seemed off-limits. Those matters created a chasm between us, which led to feelings of insecurity on my part. Regardless, that was the state of my life and marriage at the time I met Faye.

The semester began in the usual way. Faye would sit alone in the middle of the last row during class, focused on taking notes. Whenever I'd glance in her direction and catch her eye, she would smile; it wasn't quite a flirtatious smile but one hinting there might be something more behind it. It just wasn't a normal smile. Sometimes, it was more of a grin that made me curious about her, and then she'd continue grinning as she looked back down at her notebook to resume writing.

As the days and weeks passed, I collected, graded, and returned homework and gave exams. Faye appeared to be an outstanding student. She earned As on everything she submitted—grades assigned by my teaching assistant and not me. Each time I handed Faye her graded work, I received a warm, inviting smile.

We had no other interaction until one day about a month and a half into the semester when she came to my office, during office hours, to ask questions about the course material. As I worked at my desk one afternoon, she knocked on my open door. When I looked up, Faye was standing in the doorway. I greeted her by saying, "Hello, Ms. McDonald."

She smiled as she answered, "Hi, Dr. Demarco. Do you have time for some questions about class?"

"Sure I do. Come in and have a seat," I responded as I gestured toward a vacant chair next to my desk.

My office was in room 302 on the third floor of the MAE-A building, an older red-brick structure in the mid-campus area. It was near the end of a long hallway, close to a rickety old elevator and a stairwell. It was a rectangular-shaped room, more long than wide, and had white walls and a gray tile floor. There were three windows at the far end, extending from mid-wall to the ceiling overlooking a courtyard two stories below. The courtyard was enchanting, complete with towering palm trees and a splattering of live oak trees, each dripping Spanish moss from their many branches. My desk was wooden and dark brown and positioned against the wall to the right of the solid oak door and near the windows. A matching computer credenza and wooden bookcases were against the left wall behind my chair, a high-back brown leather one on rollers. To the left of the credenza and bookcases were four gray, four-drawer metal filing cabinets, the tops of which held stacks of technical journals and research reports I intended to read someday. Next to the filing cabinets and nearest the door, I kept a small, dorm-sized refrigerator for drinks. A second chair for visitors sat on the right side of my desk. There was a five-foot-by-seven-foot black chalkboard mounted on the wall next to the extra chair.

Faye came in, sat down, and began asking questions. As she did, I remember thinking her questions were rather trivial as they were about the material she appeared to already understand from doing well on the homework. In answering them, I drew sketches on a notepad at the edge of my desk so she could see. As I explained my drawings, Faye looked at me, nodding and smiling, oblivious to what I was saying or writing.

When I finished my explanations, she responded by saying, "Okay, I understand now," and she smiled again. I soon realized Faye didn't come to only ask questions about the course because after I finished, she stayed seated.

I responded, "You already knew this material, didn't you, Faye?"

"Yes," she replied meekly.

Sometimes, students in distress will come to professors to seek guidance about other problems or other issues they're dealing with in their lives. I wondered if Faye was struggling with something other than schoolwork and needed to talk to someone about it. In such cases, I always try to be helpful and offer my best advice about whatever problem they may have. In the past, I had even referred students to the University Counseling and Wellness Center to help them address troubling matters, something the university encourages all faculty members to do.

So I asked Faye, "Then why did you come in to ask questions? Is there another problem or something else you're going through that I can help you with besides the course material?"

"No," she answered. "I just wanted to talk to you. I hope it's okay."

"Yes, it's fine," I replied.

So we talked. Faye told me about growing up in Nashville, about her family, and about her parents who divorced when she was seven years old. We discussed her likes and dislikes and how she spent a year studying at Vanderbilt University in Nashville before transferring to Florida to be closer to her boyfriend, Alex. He was in the military and stationed at Moody Air Force Base in Valdosta, Georgia, about a two-hour drive north of Gainesville. I told her about my career, my wife, and a little about me as a person. Faye didn't drink, smoke, take drugs, or curse. Water and Dr Pepper were all she drank. She never even tasted coffee. She didn't display the silliness of some women I had in class and impressed me as being wholesome and mature for her age and more of a woman than a girl.

I could tell Faye was nervous as she twisted the ends of her long hair while we talked. I found her a delight to talk with, although our discussion was odd for both of us because Faye didn't enjoy talking about herself, and I seldom shared details of my personal life with students. We appeared to draw that behavior out of each other from the beginning for some unknown reason. For me, it may have been because of her warmth, openness, or her gorgeous smile. Or perhaps I was just an overzealous older man being flattered being around a beautiful young woman. Regardless, our conversation was pleasant. It surprised me because with Faye being twenty-four years younger, I assumed we wouldn't have much in common. But the more Faye and I chatted, the more we found that wasn't the case. We both loved classic sports cars, traveling, working out, and similar types of food. We were also liberal-minded, and not religious. We viewed life in much the same way, and we both loved to joke and tease.

Our discussion must have lasted forty-five minutes before she needed to leave for her next class. When she stood up, she smiled and said, "I need to go now, but I'll be back. And, Dr. Demarco, please don't call me Ms. McDonald anymore. Just call me Faye, okay?"

"Okay, Faye, I will," I responded.

After she left, I wondered how I could have so much in common with such a young woman, and I looked forward to seeing her again. Two weeks later, Faye returned to my office, again during office hours, but this time, she didn't use the pretense of having questions about class material. She said she'd like to talk if I had time. I was happy to make time for her, and we talked for quite a while again. We didn't talk about anything specific, but we discussed many topics, and Faye smiled nonstop throughout our conversation. We were getting to know each other better, and we were both enjoying it. At first, I thought she might have only wanted to improve her grade in class, but she didn't need any help as she was already performing at a high A level in a difficult course. Although I remained puzzled by it all, I enjoyed whatever connection we shared and didn't feel chatting with her was at all inappropriate.

Faye's visits continued throughout the semester. She soon began coming outside my office hours, often popping-in whenever she could. Faye explained she didn't want to take my office-hour time away from other students. Although to me, it felt more like she didn't want our time together interrupted. Regardless, our discussions were always interesting, and her visits flattered me. Through our conversations, it became clear she had few close friends on campus. She spent most of her weekends either visiting Alex in Georgia or with him driving to Gainesville to see her. She told me they were getting engaged over Christmas and planned to marry during the following year.

Faye possessed a dry sense of humor and loved jokes and puns of all kinds. She viewed herself as an expert on the television comedy show *Seinfeld*, which created fun for us as I considered myself to be an expert on that show, too. I would often tell her jokes, and we always laughed a lot together. Colleagues in nearby offices often asked me about the laughter coming from my office during Faye's visits, and I never had good answers to their queries.

Our mutual attraction became obvious the longer Faye and I talked. Mine was easy to understand, but hers was much more difficult for me to comprehend.

One day, I asked Faye why she kept visiting me if she didn't need help with the material in class. She replied, "Because I like you, can't you tell?" Well, I thought I could, but arriving at such a conclusion would have been far too presumptuous or a pure figment of my imagination.

I responded, "But why do you like me?"

Faye answered, "Never mind, I just do."

Then in my most dignified, professorial tone, I replied, "Well, I like you too, Faye." After a short pause, I added, "Now you realize us liking each other won't affect your grade in my class."

Faye appeared amused by my statement. She commented, "I know that. I wouldn't expect anything else."

"Okay, as long as that's clear," I responded. We both laughed and stared at each other for a few moments in silence before she needed to leave.

When Faye stood up, she said, "You won't be getting very much work done from now on ,because I'll be visiting you all the time." Then she giggled and walked out.

As the semester progressed, Faye developed a pattern of coming to visit me every Monday, in addition to other days, so she could tell me about her weekend and hear about mine. Faye was always excited to see me on Mondays, and she soon appeared sad when she left on Fridays, already looking forward to us reconnecting the following week. It wasn't long until I had those same feelings. My confusion at these unusual circumstances continued, but I thought I would let things play out and see how it all unfolded. Since Faye was in a different curriculum and taking dynamics as an interdisciplinary elective, she wouldn't be taking any more of my classes. Because of that I expected that her visits would end when the current semester concluded.

The semester was over in early December. I always looked forward to finishing up such a long and busy period, but this time, I had mixed feelings. I needed a break from school, but it also saddened me because I assumed my time with Faye would be ending. But even though I wouldn't be seeing her anymore, I was glad we had become friends. I expected nothing more to come of our friendship, although neither of us could deny our attraction to each other. I knew it would be difficult saying goodbye to her when the semester ended.

After our last class meeting of the semester, I didn't see Faye again before our scheduled final exam time. Being the outstanding student she was, she always focused on her schoolwork first and studied hard for all her exams. She had a high grade point average, which she intended to keep, so it didn't surprise me we didn't interact the rest of the week. When she came to say goodbye before leaving town for the holidays, we chatted about the grades she expected to receive in her classes. She already knew she earned an A in my class as I posted the final grades a few days earlier. Faye finished with the second-highest average of the thirty-five students in the class and ended up earning four As and a B for the semester.

I thought seeing Faye on the last day would be sad for both of us. But Faye seemed very upbeat, making me curious about her demeanor. We chatted about our holiday plans, including her pending engagement over Christmas. She told me how much she liked my class and how she enjoyed the time we spent talking. I told her it was fun having her as a student, getting to know her better, and that I enjoyed all the
joking and laughing we did.

Then Faye said, "Well, I won't have you as a teacher next semester, but I still plan on visiting you a lot." Then she added, "And I can't wait to see you when I get back after the holidays!"

Surprised at her comment, I replied, "I'll be looking forward to seeing you again too, Faye." Then we just stared at each other, with neither of us able to stop smiling.

Soon, the time came when she had to leave for her long drive to Nashville, which took about nine hours, depending on traffic. It wasn't easy to say goodbye, knowing it would be a month before she'd return. As Faye moved toward the door, she stopped, then turned around and walked back to me. While I was still sitting at my desk, she reached toward me and, with the tip of her right index finger, gently touched the back of my hand as it rested on my notepad.

Smiling, Faye said, "I just needed to touch you once before I left." And this enchanting young woman mesmerized me with that one simple touch!

CHAPTER 2

I Had No Idea

Vacations were always fun regardless of what Sophia and I did. This holiday break, we flew to Washington, DC, to visit Sophia's family in Virginia for a few days. I had three weeks off for the holidays, but Sophia could only be away for a week. During my time on vacation, fleeting thoughts of Faye in Tennessee teased my mind. I soon found myself eager to get back to campus, as I was looking forward to seeing her again when school resumed.

I returned to work a few days early to begin my course preparations for the spring semester of 2007. When the first day of classes arrived, I wondered if I'd see Faye. Later, on my way to my office from a meeting, I found her waiting at my door. She looked bright, cheerful, and beautiful, dressed in jeans and an oversized light-brown turtleneck sweater. We talked for an hour, telling each other about everything we did during the break. As expected, she got engaged to Alex and showed me her engagement ring. It was a beautiful, three-quarter carat, opal-shaped diamond mounted on a thin golden band. Faye told me they planned to marry the next fall. When I congratulated her, she whispered, "Thank you." I must admit, while I was happy for her, I was also sad because of it.

We discussed the upcoming semester. She mentioned she was taking a heavy course load and thought she'd be very busy.

After I glanced at her class schedule, I agreed. As a result, I didn't expect her to be available for many office visits.

When I told her so, she looked at me and replied, "I don't agree with that at all." Then she added, "Well, even if that's the case sometimes, we'll always be able to talk through email, but I'll still come to visit you whenever I can."

As Faye stood up to leave, she reached over and touched the back of my hand with her finger once more, smiled, and said, "It's nice to see you again."

"It's nice to see you again too, Faye," I replied.

The thought of having a relationship with Faye beyond a friendship never entered my mind. That would have been rather ridiculous on my part. A few years earlier, a colleague in another department became involved with a student, and it surprised me to learn that no university policy prohibited it. In fact, those relationships weren't uncommon in academia. I've never been involved in one, and I often wondered how they might occur. Although, after knowing Faye, I now understood how they could.

As expected, Faye's busy schedule affected the time she had available for visits. She stopped by once or twice a week, sometimes only for a few minutes, but she kept her promise to email me. I always enjoyed her visits, but I also enjoyed her emails. One reason was emailing seemed to allow us to say things we might be hesitant to mention in person—which was especially true for her. She didn't seem as nervous in her written word. Likewise, I felt I could approach topics that would have been more difficult to discuss face-to-face. It was as though we were each talking to someone behind a curtain, free to be more open and get past our inhibitions. Faye's emails also helped reveal her true self and what she may have wanted from me. When we got to visit, those email discussions made our in-person talks even more fun. And they still included joking and teasing, which we both enjoyed doing.

We found that the limited time we could spend together wasn't enough for either of us. One day, I joked that perhaps we should have lunch sometime. To my surprise, Faye agreed. So we planned to meet at the Reitz Student Union food court the next day at 11:30 a.m. I chose a very public place because we were having a harmless lunch, and it wasn't uncommon for professors to have open lunches with students.

But the weather didn't cooperate. Springtime in Florida brought a horrific downpour that drenched us both by the time we arrived. Once we found each other in the crowd, we laughed when we saw each other dripping wet. We got our food and drinks and sat next to a group of students eating with the campus minister of St. Augustine Catholic Church, where I was a member. I wasn't a very good member, but a member, nonetheless. Father Tom, a new priest at the church, didn't recognize me but Faye and I both thought it all to be ironic and amusing.

Having lunch gave us a chance to spend time in a non-academic environment. We could ignore our professor/student status and act more like friends. But we were both nervous about being together in public, Faye more than I.

During our short walk back after lunch, Faye teased me about sitting next to my priest. That opened the door for me to tease her about being nervous whenever she was around me. To my surprise, Faye admitted it, causing her to blush.

She said, "I don't know why I get nervous around you. I just do." We met for lunch again two weeks later and ate at the Subway restaurant, which was also in the Reitz Student Union food court. This time, there was no rain and no priest, but once again, it was fun. We sat outside on the patio and enjoyed the beautiful spring weather.

During my discussions with Faye, we seldom mentioned Alex. Nor did we talk about Sophia. But after our lunches, our relationship changed. Faye was no longer my student, and we became friends. We still found each other attractive, despite the circumstances and our age difference. Aside from the perpetual surprise of how well we got along, there were never many other surprises—until one very interesting day.

On the last Monday before spring break, Faye came to my office to visit. When she arrived, I was editing a research report with a red felt-tip pen, which I often held in my right hand while I was reading. I had a habit of putting the top end of the pen in my mouth and twisting and sucking on the cap as I read, something Faye hadn't seen me do. Not realizing it, I began sucking on the end of the pen while she talked to me. Faye suddenly stopped mid-sentence; her smile faded, and her eyes fixated on my pen. She blushed. As she stared, she bit her lower lip with her top row of teeth, holding them there. My smile also faded.

Once I realized what was happening, all I could say was, "Oh my." After a few moments, I bit my lower lip too. We were both speechless. The more I played with my pen, the more flustered Faye became. She began fidgeting in her chair, and her breathing got loud enough that I could hear. Soon, her mouth opened, and her jaw dropped, and her eyes followed the pen wherever my hand moved it. After several minutes of this erotic playfulness, I laid the pen down on my desk, breaking Faye's trance.

The smiles returned to our faces and I asked, "Were you teasing me, Faye?"

"What do you mean?" she responded.

"I mean, staring at my pen, biting your lip, looking sexy and irresistible. You were teasing me, right?"

She answered, "No, I wasn't teasing you at all. Were you teasing me with your pen?"

"No, I wasn't teasing you either," I replied. We continued to stare at each other for a few moments longer, both wondering what just happened between us. Then she giggled and got up to leave for her next class.

Once again, Faye reached over and touched the back of my hand with her index finger and said, "I'll see you tomorrow." After she left, I reflected on what occurred. My thoughts bounced from my actions to hers— what those actions may have meant to each of us, whether we crossed a line, and questioning if it was harmless fun or something deeper. I found myself unable to resist the temptation Faye presented to me. Perhaps that made me a weak person, or even a contemptuous one. But rationalization won out in my reasoning, and I felt I owed it to myself to see where this wonderful connection might lead.

Early the next morning, Faye appeared at my office door. Unannounced, she danced into the room. Since she hadn't done that before, it precipitated a round of laughter from me. Faye sparkled. She wore a very short, thin summer dress, and her hair was not yet dry from her morning shower. I could tell she was happier than usual and less reserved. But I was sure she was wondering how I'd greet her after our "pen" adventure the previous day.

Then she said, "I can't stay long, but I wanted to say good morning before going to class."
"Good morning, Faye. It's lovely seeing you so early." Faye scurried over to me, touched my hand with her finger again, and said, "I have to go now, but can we meet for lunch today?"

"Sure!" I replied as I smiled.

"Great, I'll be back at 11:30 a.m.!"

"Perfect," I answered.

When Faye returned, she wanted to eat at Taco Bell on W. University Avenue, about a mile away and farther from my office than our previous lunches. During our walk through campus on our way to the restaurant on a beautiful spring morning, I again accused Faye of teasing me with her lip-biting behavior. She smiled and denied it once more.

As we walked back after lunch, I commented on how it would have been fun if we drove to Taco Bell in my convertible. Then I implied she'd probably be too nervous to go for a ride with me in my car, but I might be nervous too. Thinking I was joking, Faye didn't respond. Instead, she just looked at me and giggled.

Later that afternoon, I received an email from Faye.

*****

Date: Tue, 6 Mar 2007 13:36:29 (EST)
From: Laura McDonald
To: Phillip Demarco
Subject: Teasing

Hi, Dr. Demarco,

Why do you think I would try to tease you? I would never do such a terrible thing to my favorite professor.

Dr. Demarco, you're amused that I get nervous when I'm around you, aren't you? (Perhaps one of these days I won't, but I doubt it.) To answer your question about the convertible, the only way you'll ever know if I'd be too nervous to take a ride with you would be for you to invite me and find out. And just because I might be nervous doesn't mean I wouldn't go.

Faye

*****

I couldn't quite tell whether Faye was teasing me or being flirtatious. The next morning, she came by for a quick visit, dancing into my office again and wearing a huge smile. We could only chat for a few minutes, but before she left, I asked her again why she still gets nervous around me.

She answered, "I'm not sure why, but I'll try to explain later." Then she added, "Well, are you going to ask me to go for a convertible ride with you or not?"

"I'm thinking about it, but I'm not good with rejection," I replied. She giggled, said goodbye, and walked out.

Faye sent me another message after she finished her classes the next day.

*****

Date: Wed, 7 Mar 2007 15:48:01 (EST)
From: Laura McDonald
To: Phillip Demarco
Subject: Nervous

Dr. Demarco,

Well, I'm nervous around you because of the way you always look at me. When you do, it's like you're thinking something and I'm not sure what. Then again, maybe you aren't, so are you or are you not? If you are, what *are* you thinking? There may be some other reasons for my nervousness too, but those shall stay untold for now.

And I doubt you'd be nervous having me in your convertible. Unlike me, you don't seem nervous when we're together. Why would you be nervous with me in that situation anyhow? Do you think I'd do something to make you nervous? Also, about you not being good with rejection. Well, have I ever rejected you? Just remember, I surprised you when I agreed to have lunch with you, so you never know, I might surprise you again!

Faye

*****

Faye was very curious about my thoughts and if I'd ask her to take a convertible ride with me. In answering her message, I tried to be welcoming of her curiosity but still somewhat evasive. Our mutual "flirtation" continued in a series of messages.

*****

Date: Wed, 7 Mar 2007 19:42:11 (EST)
From: Phillip Demarco
To: Laura McDonald
Subject: Thinking

Faye,

Yes, I am thinking about something when I look at you. Perhaps many things! But I won't tell you what I'm thinking until I know the *other* reasons for your nervousness.

I do get nervous around you, but I try not to show it. I doubt I could hide it if we were taking a ride alone together though. And no, I'm sure you wouldn't do anything to cause me to be nervous, but I might.

So, did I surprise you the first time I asked you to lunch?

PD

                    *****

Date: Thu, 8 Mar 2007 17:04:14 (EST)
From: Laura McDonald
To: Phillip Demarco
Subject: Clue

Dr. Demarco,

Now why won't you tell me what I want to know about what you're thinking? All I'm asking is for you to answer one simple question! And besides, you must already have an idea what other things might make me nervous, don't you? But if you do, you wouldn't say so because you'd rather I told them to you myself. So let's make a deal. I'll give you a clue about my other reasons, and you can give me a hint about what you're thinking, okay? (And I want a good hint!) For your clue, think about this: I'm always coming to visit you when I have no reason to. And we've had lunch together three times now. (Keep in mind, if any other guy, professor or student, were to ask me to lunch, I wouldn't go.) Why would I do these things? Well, I'm not saying anything else! Tomorrow I expect to have a very good hint since I just told you what you want to know.

Yes, you surprised me when you asked me to go to lunch because I wasn't expecting it. (So why did you ask me?) My fiancé would get very upset with me if he knew I've been having lunch with you. And he wouldn't like it very much if he read the messages we've exchanged either.

I have another question I would like to have answered. What would make you nervous if I was in your convertible? If it weren't me, what *would* it be? I'm very curious to know. Since you won't tell me now, when will you?

Remember, I want a *good* hint, and *please* answer my question!

I'll be back later. It could be sooner rather than later if you don't send me that hint!

Faye

*****

Faye's level of curiosity about me appeared to be increasing, but so was mine about her .

*****

Date: Thu, 8 Mar 2007 20:13:21 (EST)
From: Phillip Demarco
To: Laura McDonald
Subject: Reasons

Faye,

Okay, here's your hint about what I've been thinking. When I look at you, I see someone very special whom I would like to do much more with than have lunch. There, that's all I'm telling you.

To answer your questions, you might come to visit me even though you don't have a reason to because you like me a lot and I may have given you the impression that I like you a lot too. But I'm still not aware of all the reasons you get nervous when you're around me, so it's your turn to tell me more. Also, I asked you to go to lunch with me because I wanted to spend time with you outside of school. But the more time I spend with you, the more time I *want* to spend with you. And even though I shouldn't be saying that, it's true.

I think I would get nervous if we were alone in my car because I'd want to do what I envision doing whenever I see you. (I'll finish that thought later.) But I'm afraid it might not be a good idea if I did. It could ruin the wonderful friendship we have, and I don't want that to happen.

PD

*****

Date: Fri, 9 Mar 2007 11:41:36 (EST)
From: Laura McDonald
To: Phillip Demarco
Subject: Your imagination

Dr. Demarco,

So you still won't tell me! Your hint was good, but I want to know what you're thinking! I imagine you already know what my untold reasons might be. But I'll give you one *last* clue: girls don't like it when they can't have something they want. I shouldn't have told you that, but it's not as though you didn't have a good idea. So, now I've said too much. (I hope my fiancé never finds out about our conversations because if he does, I'll be in *big* trouble!)

If we were alone together, I don't think you'd do anything to cause me to be nervous. Besides, I know you wouldn't do the one thing, other than staring at me, that would make me nervous. That's because I'm your student, you know I'm engaged, and most of all, you might not even want to do it. (You can guess what that one thing is, right? If not, use your imagination because I won't tell you.)

So what do you think about me getting married in the fall? You didn't seem too thrilled about it when I told you, so I'm curious to know why.

Faye

*****

Date: Fri, 9 Mar 2007 11:45:41 (EST)
From: Laura McDonald
To: Phillip Demarco
Subject: Nervous

Dr. Demarco,

It's me again! I forgot to ask you a question. So why are you nervous around me? You said you'd finish that thought some other time, and now would be a great time for you to do that.

Faye

*****

Date: Fri, 9 Mar 2007 13:47:07 (EST)
From: Phillip Demarco
To: Laura McDonald
Subject: Hesitant

Faye,

Hmmm. Can you please elaborate on your clue from two messages ago, about girls not liking it when they can't have something they want? Well, I'm very hesitant to tell you my thoughts about you getting married. I think if I was truthful, my answer may make our relationship more personal, and I don't know if that would be a good thing or not.

Okay, to finish my thought, my nervousness around you is because I like you very much, which you knew already.

PD

*****

Date: Fri, 9 Mar 2007 22:37:41 (EST)
From: Laura McDonald
To: Phillip Demarco
Subject: You'd know way too much

Dr. Demarco,

So you want me to elaborate on my last clue?

Well, I meant to imply there's something I want and can't have. I still won't tell you what it might be because then you'd know way too much. So for now, you must wonder what it could be. You know if you'd just tell me what you're thinking, I would be more than happy to tell you my reasons! But I know you won't, so I suppose neither of us will ever know what the other is thinking.

Why would our relationship become more personal if you answer my question about me getting married? Do you consider us to have a typical professor/student relationship? I think we moved beyond that the first time we had lunch together. Now we're sending each other these messages that aren't exactly of an academic nature.

Thanks for explaining your nervousness! I'm sure you already know I like you very much too!

Well, it's late, and I still have homework to do before leaving for Alex's tomorrow. So that's all for now, but I'll see you after spring break. Have a great vacation!

Faye

*****

I found Faye's messages to be delightful! Her bubbly personality and energy were apparent to me in every sentence. It became clear we were curious about what we thought about each other. On the surface, Faye gave me the impression she might like to have a deeper relationship with me. But I had to ask myself why she'd be interested in such a thing. I realized I needed to be very careful because misreading her intentions could be problematic, and it was still possible I could get fired for my behavior. So I decided the best thing for me to do would be to allow Faye to lead our relationship in whatever direction she wanted it to go. But it appeared we were at somewhat of a crossroads, even though I had no idea how we got there.

CHAPTER 3

The Beautiful Princess

Most years, Sophia and I headed to a beach for spring break, often somewhere a few hours' drive from Gainesville. For our 2007 destination, we selected Sanibel Island, a beautiful and serene location on the Gulf Coast of Florida near Fort Myers. While it's more crowded there during spring break than at other times of the year, Sanibel Island didn't draw crowds as large as Daytona Beach, Panama City, or Miami Beach. Even at such a popular time, we could still find secluded beaches. Sanibel's pure-white sand contained many pieces of shells, which created a slight crunch underfoot as we strolled along the beach each morning and evening. Plenty of relaxation and good restaurants added to the experience for us both. There were also several places to explore, including the Sanibel Lighthouse and Captiva Island. The most difficult decision we had to make each day was where we should go to happy hour or have dinner. Our vacation was fun and relaxing, but even during such an enjoyable time with Sophia, I looked forward to returning to Gainesville. I knew the rest of the spring semester would fly by, and summer would arrive soon.

Our first week back at school was a hectic one. Because of our busy schedules, connecting with Faye became difficult. When she stopped by to visit, I'd either be out of the office or on my way to a meeting, and she'd often be unavailable when I had free time. We couldn't connect until Friday. When we did, we talked about our days away and the busy weeks we were having. Later, we exchanged light-hearted messages.

*****

Date: Fri, 23 Mar 2007 15:52:06 (EDT)
From: Laura McDonald
To: Phillip Demarco
Subject: Spring Break

Dear Dr. Demarco,

It was great to see you this morning too, but it was too short of a time for me! I'm glad you had a good break.

When we talked, you forgot to mention if you took any rides in your convertible or not? You did, didn't you? And without me!

Faye

*****

Date: Fri, 23 Mar 2007 16:23:50 (EDT)
From: Phillip Demarco
To: Laura McDonald
Subject: Convertible rides

Faye,

Yes, I took some convertible rides over the break. It's too bad you weren't with me. Perhaps we should plan one, which would be a perfect excuse for you to visit me as much as possible and for us to talk a lot more before school's out. But I wouldn't want you to tire of me.

PD

*****

When Faye came by on Monday morning, she looked beautiful and happy as she made another dancing entrance into my office. Even though such entrances had become common practice for her, I continued to laugh at each one.

"Good morning, Faye. You're here early today," I said.

"Well, I couldn't wait because I didn't like not seeing you much last week at all."

We talked about our weekends, the upcoming week, and events going on around campus. But in all too short of a time, she needed to run off to class.

Faye touched the back of my hand again and smiled as she walked out. Our playful messaging resumed soon after she left.

*****

Date: Mon, 26 Mar 2007 16:16:07 (EDT)
From: Laura McDonald
To: Phillip Demarco
Subject: Terrific idea

Dr. Demarco,

So you think we should do a lot of talking? That's a terrific idea! And I'm sure we can find more interesting topics to talk about than school, don't you agree? And your convertible would be the perfect place to hold our discussions. I also think we need to begin these talks soon. Here's a warning though.

I didn't forget about my question you refuse to answer. You know I'll keep asking until you tell me!

You shouldn't worry about me tiring of you; I won't! I mean, how could that happen when I enjoy being around (and looking at) you so much?

Faye

*****

Date: Mon, 26 Mar 2007 17:33:49 (EDT)
From: Phillip Demarco
To: Laura McDonald
Subject: Questions

Faye,

I agree we can discuss many more interesting topics than school. Okay, when we're talking in my convertible, I'll answer all your questions, as long as you answer mine.

And I like to look at you too!

PD

*****

The next day, I received a rather remarkable message, which shocked me since I didn't expect Faye to say anything like this to me, ever.

*****

Date: Tue, 27 Mar 2007 17:56:25 (EDT)
From: Laura McDonald
To: Phillip Demarco
Subject: What I want...

Dr. Demarco,

I'm sorry I couldn't come by this morning; I had too much homework to do.

When are we going to take a convertible ride and have our talk? I hope it will be sometime soon, but since it's your car, I must wait until you ask me.

So you still won't tell me what I wish to know! I understand why you won't tell me first, but either way, we both will eventually, so what difference does it make who goes first? If it doesn't matter, I suppose I could, right? I want to, but I don't know how you'll react. And besides, I'm engaged, so I shouldn't have anything to say anyhow. But I'll go ahead. I know you won't, and I have to know what you're thinking.

Okay, remember when I gave you the hint "girls don't like it when they can't have what they want"? Well, the answer to your question about what I want is this: I want *you*!

Ever since the first day I came to your office hours, I have been *very* attracted to you. I mean, just being around you drives me *crazy*! I get nervous because I know I can't have you, but I'm still not able to stay away from you. I have never had this problem in my life. In four years, I haven't liked or thought about anyone but my fiancé, and now I have a thing for you. This isn't very good; I'd be in *big* trouble if Alex found out I want someone other than him.

Well, I've said *far* too much, so I'll stop. I hope the things I said don't make you uncomfortable. I know you will answer *all* my questions soon, right? And I'm not joking either!

Faye

*****

I wasn't sure how to react to Faye's message. I suspected we may have had crushes on each other, but how she felt surprised me. It was even more surprising that she told me so. I had also developed feelings for Faye, and I was happy to learn they weren't one-sided. I wanted to answer her message right away, and being more at ease about my feelings now, I could be honest with her about them. But I still needed to be careful in how I approached the situation. I didn't want it to look like I was pursuing her, or worse, harassing her.

*****

Date: Tue, 27 Mar 2007 21:02:34 (EDT)
From: Phillip Demarco
To: Laura McDonald
Subject: How?

Faye,

Thank you for being open about your feelings in your last message. It was wonderful to hear how you feel about me, and no, none of what you said bothered me at all. I'm sure you know by now I feel much the same way about you. I love being around you, and you're always on my mind.

I hope this doesn't make you uncomfortable either. If our relationship weren't a professor/student one, I would have told you first. I know how difficult it must have been for you to express your feelings.

Now, I have a question about your message. *How* do you want me? We need to discuss such an important matter as soon as we can. And I'm very glad you weren't joking.

PD

*****

I was eager to hear her response to my message. My wait was short as I received an email from Faye early the next morning.

*****

Date: Wed, 28 Mar 2007 10:40:31 (EDT)
From: Laura McDonald
To: Phillip Demarco
Subject: Uncomfortable

Hi Dr. Demarco,

I'm glad what I told you didn't bother you. I was afraid to say those things because I wasn't sure if you would like it or not. And no, you've never made me uncomfortable. If you did, I wouldn't come to visit you all the time.

I'm not sure how to answer your question about *how* I want you. We're already friends, so I know it's more than that. I've had thoughts about us doing certain things together most friends wouldn't do (if you know what I mean). But I don't see how we could be more than friends given the situation we're in, do you? I don't think it's just a small crush though. If it were only a crush, I would have gotten over it after I finished dynamics class, but I didn't!

Does me being younger bother you? I never even think about you as being an older man. I realize you are, but it doesn't make any difference to me. All I know is there's something about you, besides the way you look, that drives me crazy. And you're right; we should discuss this soon. I have a class until 6:00 p.m. tomorrow, and you said you have meetings on Friday. So, we'll only have today or in the evening to get together. Alex will be up here all of next week and maybe longer, so I'll stop by your office after class later to see if we can find a time to meet and have our talk.

Faye

*****

When Faye came by later, I asked, "Are you able to meet tonight? Perhaps we could take our convertible ride and go somewhere to talk."

"Yes I am, and I can't wait!" she answered.

So, we planned on meeting at her car on campus at 6:00 p.m. Before she left, Faye touched my hand once more. It was not a gentle touch this time but a harder one, lasting longer than normal.

"I'll see you soon," she said, smiling as she walked out of my office. I wondered what the evening ahead held for us.

After dinner at home, I pulled my convertible out of the garage, lowered the top, and drove back to campus. My car, a navy blue 2001 BMW 325Ci, had a light gray leather interior and a black canvas top. The gearshift and a wide console separated the front bucket seats. This wasn't my everyday vehicle, but more of a toy I only used on weekends. Since Faye loved sports cars, I imagined she'd like it very much.

Mid-spring in Gainesville brought warm days with cool nights, and this evening was a perfect night for a drive. When I arrived at her parking lot, Faye was waiting. I saw her smile grow wide as I drove up. She climbed out of her car and into mine.

The first thing she said was, "I *love* your car!"

"I knew you would. I'm glad you're finally getting to ride in it."

As she buckled herself in, I said, "I thought we could ride awhile before our talk, if it's okay with you," I continued.

"Sure, that'll be fun," she answered.

During the drive through campus, Faye's long blonde hair blew in the wind. As she tried to control it, I reached behind my seat for an old ball cap for her to wear. She straightened her hair and slipped on the cap.

I turned south on Route 441 and drove fifteen minutes more to Micanopy, Florida, a small hamlet and the primary filming location for the 1991 movie *Doc Hollywood*. I knew Faye had seen it, so I surprised her by pointing out some buildings she recognized from the film. We parked and walked along what appeared to be the only street in Micanopy, a two-lane road with little traffic. We visited several antique stores shown in the movie in the fictitious town of Grady, South Carolina. One served as the old hospital, another portrayed a garage, while a third acted as a theater during the annual Grady Squash Festival, which depicted Grady as the squash capital of the south.

Micanopy is a beautiful small Southern town, with live oak trees guarding Main Street, dripping with plenty of Spanish moss. After stopping for ice cream at one of only two cafés in town, we started our short trip back to Gainesville. Faye enjoyed our visit to Micanopy before our discussion. During our drive, we both became quiet, each of us distracted by how our conversation would unfold.

I looped around the southern part of Gainesville on SW Williston Road and headed to Sweetwater Wetlands Park. The park wasn't far from Faye's apartment and offered many hiking trails and quiet areas where we could talk in private. We pulled into a gravel lot across from the park entrance. A single car was sitting unattended at the other end near the cul-de-sac. Once we parked, we stayed in the car to talk there. We looked at each other and smiled, knowing the time for our discussion had arrived.

I reached my hands out to Faye, with my palms facing upward. Faye responded by placing both of her hands into mine, with her palms facing downward. I squeezed them tight. It was the first time I ever touched Faye, aside from the times when she touched the back of my hand with her fingertip. She squeezed my hands in return, and her smile deepened.

I started our conversation by saying, "Well, it appears we like each other a lot, doesn't it?"

"Yes, it does," Faye answered.

"So what should we do about it?"

In typical Faye fashion, she replied, "I don't know. What about you?"

"Well, Faye, I'm crazy about you," I said to her. "I think about you all the time and find everything about you attractive—not only your beauty but also your incredible mind, your wonderful sense of humor, your immense love of life, and how you treat me. I can't ever seem to get enough of you. I've never felt this way about anyone, not even my wife. The relationship we have is amazing and I think we ought to explore it to find out where it might lead." Faye, wide-eyed, listened intently and hung on every word I spoke.

"And to answer your earlier question, no, I don't like the thought of you getting married at all," I said. "I'm afraid after you do, we'll never see each other again, which would make me very sad."

Faye looked deep into my eyes. "Honest? That's how you feel about *me*?"

"Yes, it is!"

Faye answered, "Well, I feel the same way about you." After a few moments, her smile vanished, and once again, she bit her lower lip. Not knowing how she'd respond, I asked, "Would it be all right if I kissed you?"

Faye replied only "Please do" as she leaned toward me.

Our first kiss was long, soft, and very sensual. I put my right arm around her back as she placed her hand behind my head. We tried to get closer, but the center console of the car interfered. Our passionate kisses soon turned into quicker pecks, each of us nibbling at each other. I took my left hand and touched Faye's face, tracing a line with my fingertips over her forehead, across her eyelids, down her cheeks, to her soft lips. As I did, Faye made a low humming sound, like a cat's purring, and kissed my fingers.

Not knowing how she'd respond, I asked, "Would it be all right if I kissed you?"

Faye replied only "Please do" as she leaned toward me.

Our first kiss was long, soft, and very sensual. I put my right arm around her back as she placed her hand behind my head. We tried to get closer, but the center console of the car interfered. Our passionate kisses soon turned into quicker pecks, each of us nibbling at each other. I took my left hand and touched Faye's face, tracing a line with my fingertips over her forehead, across her eyelids, down her cheeks, to her soft lips. As I did, Faye made a low humming sound, like a cat's purring, and kissed my fingers.

We spent an hour at the park, and we both wanted our night to last longer. But it wasn't the time or place for anything more romantic than a wonderful first encounter. After we both regained our composure, Faye looked at me with a serious face and said, "I think we should explore our feelings, too, although I can't promise it will go anywhere if we do. I'm engaged, and you're still married, so I'm not sure what can happen. I know we shouldn't be doing this, but I can't help it. So I'd like to if you still do."

I faced a pivotal moment in my life. I found myself with an exquisite young woman who wanted to explore the romantic possibilities before us, with the caution of an uncertain future. I thought for a few precious seconds while a million thoughts raced through my mind. My decision wasn't difficult. Even if I ended up heartbroken, our time together would be worth it to me.

I smiled, kissed Faye again, and replied, "Yes, I still do, no matter what happens."

Faye beamed and responded, "Good, me too."

Then I said, "But I have an important question to ask. Do you see me as a father figure?"

Faye looked startled at my inquiry before she giggled and answered, "*No*, I promise you I do *not* see you as a father figure!"

"Great, I'm glad to hear it," I replied, and Faye giggled again.

Then she kissed me one last time before we left the park. During the drive back to campus, we held hands with our fingers intertwined, and she rubbed my lower right arm with her right hand as I drove. Our discussion turned to how busy Faye would be with her schoolwork for the rest of the semester. She had term papers, projects, and exams, plus she'd still be seeing Alex, so finding time to spend together would be a challenge. Our talk reminded me of a relevant old joke I knew she'd enjoy, which I told her while driving. It was about an engineer who found a talking frog, and the frog said if the engineer kissed it, it would turn into a beautiful princess and do anything he wanted. He kept the frog but never kissed it because, being an engineer, he was too busy to have a girlfriend, but he thought it was cool to have a talking frog. When I finished telling her the joke, Faye burst out laughing, and her hand covered her mouth as she continued laughing. When we arrived back on campus, I pulled my car up next to hers. I said to her, "I like the frog joke because, like the engineer, I feel like I found a beautiful princess in you." Faye blushed as her eyes and her smile grew large. Then I joked, "Would it be okay if I called you the beautiful princess from now on?"

Faye giggled at my question and answered, "Yes."

I took her hand and kissed it. She bit her lower lip again and said, "I want to see you again as soon as possible." We both smiled and kissed once more before saying good night.

CHAPTER 4

Something I Didn't Expect

The next day, I reflected on the events of the previous evening. I thought about how lucky I was to have found Faye and how I couldn't wait until she came to visit me again since we had our talk. Not long after I arrived at work, she popped in to say good morning before her first class.

I chuckled and greeted her, "Good morning, BP. That's short for 'beautiful princess,' in case you were wondering. I'm glad you came early today. I was hoping you would."

Faye giggled and continued, "I also wanted to say I couldn't sleep at *all* last night. Perhaps I'll tell you why later."

"I hope that's a good thing, and I hope I didn't say too much to you," I replied.

Faye laughed. "Have a great day, Dr. Demarco. I know I will." I soon received a message from her.

*****

Date: Thu, 29 Mar 2007 11:31:42 (EDT)
From: Laura McDonald
To: Phillip Demarco
Subject: Couldn't sleep

Hi, Dr. Demarco,

I had a wonderful time last night. Can you meet me again before Alex gets here this weekend? If not, I'll see you again after he leaves.

I couldn't sleep because I woke up at 2:30 a.m., thinking about you. Isn't that terrible? I was excited about what happened since I've wanted that for a long time.

Last night, I was thinking of everything I'd like to do with you, and none of those include talking. I know you understand what I'm saying, so I won't go into any more detail. No, you didn't say too much to me either. I enjoyed hearing you tell me those things. And just because I didn't say them back to you doesn't mean I don't feel the same way because I do. I just get embarrassed talking about them. Well, I have to run now. I might come by and see you again this afternoon since you told me you like it when I wear shorts.

Faye

*****

Faye's comment about her wearing shorts came from our conversation the previous day. I told her how I liked it when she wore them because they showed off her beautiful legs. I offered my comments in teasing, which Faye always accepted in the fun way I intended them. She possessed the rare ability to laugh at herself, which was one of her most endearing qualities. Faye laughed whether I joked about her clothes, her eating habits, or the funny things she'd say. She also laughed at her occasional "blonde" moment when she did something illogical. Faye didn't have those moments often, but when she did, I couldn't let them pass without calling her on it. Sometimes, I'd even tell her blonde jokes to make her laugh. But she teased me when I did or said stupid things too, which occurred much more often than when she did them.

Back to Faye's wardrobe, she wore either shorts or a light sundress on warmer days and jeans in cooler weather. With shorts or jeans, she usually wore a lightweight cotton pullover top or a button-down blouse. On cooler days, she'd wear a crew neck sweater or oversized turtleneck. She never looked sloppy like some coeds when they come to class wearing a T-shirt and nylon athletic shorts. Besides the way she dressed, Faye also stood out from other female students with how she looked. She was a natural beauty and didn't need to wear makeup or lipstick. Her hair, which was full and thick and contained several shades of blonde strands throughout, always looked fresh and clean.

Although we couldn't see each other again that day since Faye had a lot of schoolwork, we still emailed a lot. The messages we sent drew us closer, much faster than would have occurred otherwise.

*****

Date: Thu, 29 Mar 2007 15:11:43 (EDT)
From: Phillip Demarco
To: Laura McDonald
Subject: Same thoughts

BP,

I'm very glad you enjoyed last night. I also wish we could get together again before Alex arrives. If he doesn't come until later this weekend, perhaps we can meet on Saturday.

The thoughts that kept you awake last night weren't terrible at all. I had many of those same ones myself. Please tell me what you're thinking about us. I'm very curious. Although the next time we're alone, we might not want to talk as much.

Also, I don't believe it's appropriate for you to call me Dr. Demarco any longer. I'd prefer it if you called me Phillip, Okay? (But not in front of other people.)

Phillip

*****

Date: Thu, 29 Mar 2007 16:02:14 (EDT)
From: Laura McDonald
To: Phillip Demarco
Subject: Touching my face

Okay, Phillip!

It's strange calling you Phillip instead of Dr. Demarco. I'll try not to call you by your name in public.

I'm still not sure what time Alex will get here. I wish you weren't busy tomorrow since I'll be free all day. Alex might even stay longer than two weeks because he doesn't work again until April 23, so he could be down here for a while. I'll see you at school, but it won't be the same as being alone with you.

You were driving me crazy when you were touching my face last night. I loved it! I haven't forgotten about you saying you gave good backrubs either. Would you give me a back rub sometime when we're not in a car?

I'll try not to get too embarrassed to talk about my thoughts, but it may take a while since I'm not used to those kinds of conversations. I was less nervous last night than I've ever been with you, which seems like it should be the other way around, doesn't it? Although rather than talking about it,

I'd enjoy us showing each other what we're thinking instead. You wouldn't be interested in that now, would you?

Faye

*****

Date: Thu, 29 Mar 2007 16:57:19 (EDT)
From: Phillip Demarco
To: Laura McDonald
Subject: Back rub

BP,

No, seeing each other in school won't be the same as us being alone somewhere. I'd be happy to give you a back rub. I'm sure we'd both enjoy the experience very much. You didn't seem very nervous last night. Our first kiss may have helped with your nervousness and mine.

Phillip

*****

Date: Fri, 30 Mar 2007 10:32:46 (EDT)
From: Laura McDonald
To: Phillip Demarco
Subject: Intriguing

Phillip,

Alex will get here tomorrow around 2:00 p.m. So I could meet earlier if you can too.

It's good you can't touch my face at school. I might not know how to control myself, and I'd have to leave your office and persuade you to go with me.

Showing each other what we're thinking sounds very intriguing. I think we could find ourselves in some very interesting situations if we did, don't you? There's a good possibility you'd enjoy me showing you the things I've thought about doing with/to you too. Well, at least I'd have fun doing those things, so you might also find the experience pleasurable.

Faye

*****

Date: Fri, 30 Mar 2007 11:28:41 (EDT)
From: Phillip Demarco
To: Laura McDonald
Subject: Excited

BP,

Great! Let's plan to meet tomorrow morning. How about 11:00 a.m. at the lot where you park?

Phillip

*****

Date: Fri, 30 Mar 2007 12:11:07 (EDT)
From: Laura McDonald
To: Phillip Demarco
Subject: I'll be there

Phillip,

11:00 a.m. will be perfect. I can't wait!

Faye

*****

Eleven o'clock on Saturday morning didn't arrive soon enough. When I drove to meet Faye, she was already waiting. She climbed into my car, and I said, "Good morning, BP. How are you?"

Without even saying hello first, Faye responded, "I'm great because I just found out Alex can't come until tomorrow now, so I have as much time today as you want." Sophia had gone to Jacksonville and wouldn't be back until late in the evening, so Faye and I had the whole day to spend together.

It was a gorgeous day. I was with a beautiful girl, and we were in a convertible. I asked Faye if she'd enjoy a drive over to St. Augustine, about seventy-five minutes from Gainesville. She'd never been there, so down went the top, on went the ball cap, and we headed east. We took all secondary roads to the coast.

During our drive, Faye held my hand or touched my arm as it rested on her left leg. She wore a pair of blue-and-white checked shorts and a white cotton pullover tucked into her shorts and pulled down off her shoulders. She looked irresistible!

When we arrived in St. Augustine, we parked in Old City, the historic part of town. Before leaving the car, Faye leaned over and kissed me, the first of what would be many kisses that day.

As we meandered through Old City on St. George Street, we passed little shops, restaurants, and bars. We found a quaint eatery, the Columbia Restaurant, where we had a traditional Spanish lunch of tapas and empanadas. Afterward, we walked a few blocks to Castillo de San Marcos, a seventeenth century Spanish fortress, complete with drawbridges, overlooking the Matanzas River.

After we finished exploring Old City, we drove fifteen minutes out to the beach and walked through the sand holding hands. After taking off our shoes, we splashed through the water's edge, stopping many times for a quick kiss or a peck on the cheek. Faye didn't know it, but since I brought my camera, I snapped some photos of her when, at one point, she walked ahead of me. I'm sure others looked at us because Faye was young enough to be my daughter. But it didn't matter to us. We were off in our own world, not caring what anyone else thought. We were just happy being together. During our walk, we stopped at a little upstairs beach bar for a cold beer for me and a Dr Pepper for Faye, before leaving St. Augustine and driving home. Once again, we took secondary roads.

We didn't want our day to be over when we got back to Gainesville. My first thought was to return to Sweetwater Park or visit another one nearby. After my suggestion, Faye smiled and, without looking at me, asked if I'd rather come to her apartment instead since her roommate was out for the evening. I couldn't refuse such an enticing offer. She lived in Bivens Cove, off SW Thirteenth Street, a few miles from campus. Faye drove her car while I followed in mine.

Faye shared an apartment with another student named Bailee. It was a furnished, two-bedroom, second-floor unit, on the back side of the complex past the tennis courts. Bivens Cove was an older development in a secluded, wooded area. Most of the residents were students, and Faye enjoyed living there. Her apartment was at the top of a set of wooden stairs on the outside of the building. Upon entering, the living room was nearest to the door on the left, with a small kitchen and dining room to the right. A narrow hallway led from the front door to a bedroom and hall bathroom, also on the left. Faye's bedroom was the farthest back on the right and had its own bathroom. The walls were white, and all the rooms had thick light-brown carpeting. The living room had a dark-brown sectional sofa and a small flat-screen television on a stand in the corner. There was a matching love seat next to the sofa facing the TV. Once we were inside, Faye got us some drinks before we settled onto the sofa.

We looked at each other, embraced, and kissed, something we'd been longing for the entire day. We snuggled for the very first time. Our kisses were long and short, passionate and playful, alluring and sensual. We discovered we could draw each other in with our passion. I'm sure we both felt like teenagers again, a distant memory for me, but a more recent one for Faye.

We loved being close, but neither of us wanted to go farther that night. Instead, we were enjoying the small steps and sharing a tender, intimate, loving experience and didn't want to rush it. But we could tell how much we cared for each other already.

Our evening at Faye's apartment passed much too quickly, and I needed to leave. I felt very jealous of Alex coming the next day to spend two weeks with Faye. I didn't like the idea at all, but Faye didn't appreciate me leaving to go home to Sophia either.

I filled the rest of my weekend with thoughts of Faye and our time together on Saturday. When Monday came, she was waiting at my door when I arrived to say good morning before her first class. She smiled the entire time. As I looked at her, it was difficult for me to process the fun and tenderness we shared two days before. When Faye left, she blew me a kiss and scooted off. Afterward, we exchanged messages addressing some of the topics we discussed on Saturday.

*****

Date: Mon, 2 Apr 2007 09:14:22 (EDT)
From: Laura McDonald
To: Phillip Demarco
Subject: What I'm thinking

Hello, Phillip,

How is your day today? Mine is wonderful, so I hope yours is too. You looked very handsome this morning, as usual!

I needed to tell you I had a *great* weekend because of Saturday. And no, I haven't changed my mind about things either (have you?). My seeing Alex again will not change how I feel about you because I've felt this way a long time. I also want you to know I'm not seeing you because I miss Alex. Him not being here doesn't affect how I feel about you. I realize I don't tell you when we're together, but I enjoy being around you, talking to you, and looking at you. (I like the other things we do besides those I've mentioned too, but you already know that don't you?) Well, I better stop writing about what I'm thinking; it wouldn't be normal for me to let you know *all* my thoughts. Once again, thank you for taking me to St. Augustine. I had a *fabulous* time!

Faye

*****

Date: Mon, 2 Apr 2007 14:39:16 (EDT)
From: Phillip Demarco
To: Laura McDonald
Subject: Feelings

Hello BP,

I'm very glad your feelings about me won't change. Sometimes, I find it all amazing though. I feel so very lucky to have you in my life.

I miss you! I miss holding you, kissing you, and touching you!

Phillip

*****

Soon after I sent my message, Faye peeped through my office doorway and entered the room dancing. "I hope it's okay, I'm back again," she said, smiling and giggling.

"Yes, it's perfect!" I said. We talked for a long while that afternoon. She told me Alex arrived on Sunday, and between spending time with him and doing schoolwork, she didn't have much free time. From the comments she made about our fun Saturday, I could tell Faye was in a playful mood, so I thought I would tease her a little. I picked-up my red felt-tip pen again to see how she'd react this time. Her eyes followed the pen wherever I moved it. When I put the end in my mouth, she stopped talking and bit her lower lip. She became transfixed on my pen again. Even after I started laughing and she knew I was purposely teasing her, she couldn't stop staring at whatever I did, with a very serious look on her face. I pushed back in my chair, placed my feet up on my desk, and crossed my legs. Faye's face became flushed; she quit biting her lip, and her jaw dropped. Her wanton expression was very sexy. I began getting "aroused" so I had to stop. My office door was wide open. If anyone had walked past and seen us, I'm sure they would have been very suspicious about what was going on between Faye and me.

Then I blurted out something idiotic. And I didn't know why. "Faye, I know you're engaged to Alex, but are you in love with him?" I asked.

She looked at me surprised, even shocked, and said, "Yes." Then her eyes teared up. I had never seen her cry before.

I knew what I said was wrong. "Faye, I'm so sorry. I had no right to ask you such a question. I apologize." As she cried more, she put both her hands up near the sides of her face, palms down, and began waving her hands up and down to create a breeze to help dry the tears. I felt awful and apologized again.

All she said was, "It's okay, and you didn't say anything wrong." But I knew I had.

After she regained her composure, we returned to joking and teasing, and everything went back to normal. Once more, she reached over to touch the back of my hand with her finger when she got up to leave.

"Wait a minute," I said and walked over, closed my office door, and then added, "I need a hug before you go." Faye threw herself into my arms. We held each other close for a few moments. She looked up as we both smiled, and I kissed her lips. My gesture was a spontaneous one, comforting us both after my stupid comment earlier. I opened the door a crack to check if anyone was outside, and when I didn't see anybody, Faye left.

I couldn't get Faye out of my thoughts. I now realized I was falling in love with her, and I knew nothing I did could keep it from happening. Over the next few days, we exchanged some lovely and tantalizing messages.

*****

Date: Tue, 3 Apr 2007 09:54:40 (EDT)
From: Laura McDonald
To: Phillip Demarco
Subject: Busy hands

I can't believe what you did to me yesterday! You were driving me crazy with that pen again! I was thinking about how wonderful it would be if I could sit on your lap and kiss you. My hands were also very busy in this scenario, but I'll let you guess what they were doing. I won't be able to concentrate during my next class since my mind will be on you and your pen! You are so mean to me! Although, I can't say I didn't enjoy watching you because I did. I'm not sure how, but you know the way to get me excited. How do you know this, anyhow? Everything you do drives me insane. I began having my terrible little thoughts when you put your feet up on your desk. Isn't that ridiculous? Well, I have to change topics now, seeing as I'm getting all flustered.

Also, I'm sorry I cried. The only reason I started crying was because I know you didn't like my answer to your question about me loving Alex. It upset me since I would never want to hurt you, and I figured I did when I said yes. So it wasn't your fault. And don't assume you're meddling in my personal life either. You *are* a part of my life now, so you have every right to ask me those questions. Now don't think I started seeing you because I thought you wouldn't be a threat to my and Alex's relationship. That's not the case at all. I know our relationship could threaten Alex and me. If I had only been looking to mess around, I would have found someone without all the complications. But that's not what I wanted. I realize there's something special between us. I know we have great chemistry. If we didn't, I wouldn't think about you so much. Well, I need to go now (I spent too much time thinking about your pen rubbing against your lips). And I *loved* it when you closed your office door to kiss me goodbye. Thank you!

Faye

*****

Date: Tue, 3 Apr 2007 10:03:56 (EDT)
From: Laura McDonald
To: Phillip Demarco
 Subject: Missing contact

Hi, Phillip,

Also, I want you to know you made my day yesterday when you said you missed touching and holding me. I've missed it too. You don't know how badly I wanted to kiss you, so I'm glad you closed the door and kissed me before I left! (I always seem to have those thoughts around you; why is that?) Well, I'm not telling you anything else until you write me back. And I'm glad your office door doesn't have any windows!

Faye

*****

Date: Wed, 4 Apr 2007 10:21:08 (EDT)
From: Phillip Demarco
To: Laura McDonald
Subject: Chemistry

BP,

I wish we didn't have to wait so long to see each other. I suppose we both have similar thoughts, probably because of the incredible chemistry between us. It's only natural we want to be together as much as possible. We always seem to enjoy it no matter what we're doing, which is why you're not supposed to be with anybody else except me!

Phillip

*****

Date: Thu, 5 Apr 2007 14:46:13 (EDT)
From: Laura McDonald
To: Phillip Demarco
Subject: The chemistry is magical

Hi, Phillip,

I went to your office a few minutes ago, but you weren't there. This upset me very much! I came to ask if you were busy tonight because Alex had to return to work this morning for some emergency, although I'll be seeing him again this weekend. I have to come back to the lab around 6:00 p.m., so if you get this message and you're interested in meeting, email me (if you still want to see me).

Okay, I have to admit, we must have great chemistry. Otherwise, I wouldn't have the thoughts I'm always having. I recognize it since I can't seem to keep my hands off you when we're together. It's almost magical!

I have some questions for you. Why does it bother you if I'm with someone else, and what did you mean when you said, "You're not *supposed* to be with anyone else?" If my being with Alex bothers you, why didn't you tell me when I asked you? Well, I am not fond of the fact you live with somebody either, so I guess I understand why it might bother you, too. (You still have to answer my question though.)

You don't seem to understand why I want you (I know it doesn't help since I never tell you why, right?) Why would

I *not* want you? I find you to be *great* looking, you are *very* intelligent, and you have a *fantastic* personality. Not to mention, I have a great time whenever I'm with you. Then there's something drawing me to you, even though I'm not sure what it is. Well, I'll stop writing for now. I hope to hear from you later!

Faye

*****

Date: Thu, 5 Apr 2007 15:12:41 (EDT)
From: Phillip Demarco
To: Laura McDonald
Subject: Awaiting your arrival

BP,

This is amazing! I already needed to stay late tonight for a student group meeting, which should be over by 7:00 p.m. Stop in after you're done in the lab.

Phillip

*****

A short while after I got back from my meeting, Faye arrived at my door. She walked over to my desk and reached over to touch the back of my hand with her finger again. She said, "I couldn't wait to touch you!"

After a few minutes, it became obvious neither of us wanted to use our unexpected opportunity to only talk. I said to Faye, "Would it be all right with you if I closed the door?"

She looked at me, bit her lower lip, and said yes. When I did, I also flipped off the overhead light in the room. Faye giggled and asked, "Now why did you turn off the light, too?"

"Because I don't want to talk tonight," I said. "How about if you come over here and sit on my lap instead?" Faye smiled and did as I asked. She put her arms around me, leaned her head in, and we kissed and kissed and kissed. We were both very passionate and hungry for each other.

After several minutes, I said, "Let's try this." We both stood up, and I turned around and sat on the edge of my desk. Faye stepped toward me, and I pulled her close, and we kissed again. This position was much better because I could now feel Faye's entire body pressing against mine. Between kisses, I touched her face with my fingertips. She closed her eyes, moaning as I traced over her features once again. When I touched her lips, she sucked my fingers into her mouth. Then I kissed her cheeks, her forehead, and her eyelids before I moved back to her delicious lips. When I did, I felt her legs move apart to straddle my right leg to get closer. The more we kissed, the harder she pressed against me. We were both very excited. I hadn't seen Faye so turned on before. We both felt the heat between us generated by our passion for each other. At one point, she turned her head to the right so I could kiss her left ear, letting the tip of my tongue move over its ridges. Faye moaned louder and forced her body against me even harder. She was wearing a short summer dress, with material so thin it seemed to be nonexistent.

The darkness of my office, lit only by a single dim and distant light in the courtyard below, made for a very romantic setting. We both became lost in our passion. My arms were now around Faye's back, and I moved them lower, below her waist, and pulled her even closer to me. She dropped her hands to each of my legs, and I became very aroused. I knew Faye could feel my erection. As I caressed her, I felt the outline of her tiny thong beneath her dress's thin material. She moaned more when I did. I moved my hands to her front and upward to touch her breasts and her protruding nipples. She responded by kissing me harder, and I felt her hands on my legs. Soon, she moved her hands to my upper thighs, close to my erect penis. It was my turn to moan as Faye turned her caresses into more forceful ones. We continued to explore each other's bodies but didn't remove any clothing. I know if we'd been somewhere more comfortable than my office, we would have made love. This time, we both wanted our glorious, loving encounter to go further, as we couldn't get enough of each other. But before long, it was time to end our evening. We had difficulty separating our lips and our bodies.

"We're learning how to excite each other very well," I said, and we both laughed at my comment.

"Yes, we are," Faye replied.

Before she left, we gave each other one more long, passionate kiss, followed by her whispering in my ear, "I love being with you!"

Faye wrote to me the next morning.

*****

Date: Fri, 6 Apr 2007 11:33:19 (EDT)
From: Laura McDonald
To: Phillip Demarco
Subject: Drawn to you

Hello, Phillip,

I had a *wonderful* time with you last night! You're a quick learner and great at exciting me. Nobody has ever excited me like you do, not even Alex. He doesn't have the same effect on me. It might be because it's not new with him anymore, but I wasn't like this with him when we first met either. It's strange to me; is it for you? I mean, who would have thought we'd have such incredible chemistry? Something drew me to you! Did you also feel an attraction when I had you for dynamics? (You know, I had to work very hard to find questions to ask you, so I could come to your office.) It's too bad we didn't start this sooner; we could have had much more fun together.

I'm interested in exploring this phenomenon between us even more now. In fact, we should explore *a lot*! I can only imagine how much fun we'll have if we have the chance to be alone again. I might find many interesting ways of teasing you (I have to get you back for the way you always tease me). You wouldn't mind, would you? So what if I walked in (and you were sitting in your chair) wearing one of my short, lowcut dresses, sat on your desk, took my shoes off, and started rubbing my feet up and down your legs? I'm sure it would not affect you at all, would it? Well, I want *details* of what would happen if I did that!

Faye

*****

Date: Fri, 6 Apr 2007 13:45:11 (EDT)
From: Phillip Demarco
To: Laura McDonald
Subject: Rubbing my legs

Hello, BP,

Last night was amazing! Yes, it's also strange for me. I've never been so attracted to anyone before like I am to you. And yes, our chemistry is amazing!

I must tell you, I found you *very* attractive the first day I saw you in my class. We should have started this sooner, for sure. It would be incredible if we could explore *a lot* together! I know we'll have plenty of fun the next time we are alone. I have a question for you, though. Do you think it's possible for a person to love two people at the same time? I think it is, but I'm curious about your thoughts.

Well, if you wore a low-cut dress and started rubbing my legs with your feet, what would I do? Hmmm… I'd be very excited and might have to take out my red pen and suck on the end for a while. Perhaps I'd also have to close the door.

Have a nice weekend, BP! I hope you won't be too busy to think about me!

Phillip

*****

My relationship with Faye was developing into something I didn't expect. She was a godsend when I needed one, and I enjoyed everything about her. I felt very fortunate that she came into my life, but I didn't understand yet what brought her to me.

CHAPTER 5

An Absurd Thing to Have Done

I had many erotic thoughts of Faye over the weekend. It had been a long time since I was with a woman as sexually expressive as her. It was beyond exciting, and I knew I didn't have the power to resist Faye's seductive spell. I found her irresistible, regardless of the price I might have to pay. And we were relentless in pursuing each other as our email messages showed.

*****

Date: Mon, 9 Apr 2007 09:54:16 (EDT)
From: Laura McDonald
To: Phillip Demarco
Subject: Creative ways

Hello, again!

You are terrible! I said I wanted *details* and all you tell me is *that*? You're just teasing me, aren't you? Now I won't be able to think about anything else!

Oh, and you need to fix your door so it closes by itself! But if you do, we might get in trouble since I can't seem to keep my hands off you, although I must pay you back for all your teasing. I'm sure I could come up with some creative ways. If you feel it's appropriate, you can too (which would be fine with me).

And no, I wasn't too busy to not think about you! I thought about you a lot. How could I forget about you and your pen? You're always on my mind. Wouldn't you love to know the thoughts I have about you? Well, I could tell them to you, but I'd rather show you!

I never answered your question about being able to love two people at once. I agree, it's possible. Although I don't know if being in love with two people at once is, but that doesn't mean it can't happen, does it?

Faye

*****

Not long after I read Faye's message, she appeared at my office. I was happy to see her after what seemed like a longer weekend than usual. Our relationship was getting stronger, and we were becoming closer. She didn't appear nervous around me anymore, and we enjoyed our time together, no matter what we did. We still talked a lot, but we also teased each other a lot. Whenever she visited, I had thoughts of closing the door to have some privacy. But it wasn't always possible—or smart—with students, colleagues, and staff members nearby, although we both thought about what might happen if I did. Discussing it became part of our regular teasing, along with doing more sexual explorations, which I told her I thought was a great idea.

After our playful discussion, I said to her, "BP, I find your emails to be delightful. Would it be okay with you if I saved them all for a book someday?"

She giggled and responded, "Yes, it's fine. Just don't use my real name in your book," and we both laughed at her comment.

"Don't worry, I won't," I answered.

Once again, Faye had to rush off to class. *Damn classes*, I thought. I could tell she wanted me to kiss her goodbye. Since the door was open, I made a kissing gesture with my lips instead, which brought another huge smile to her face.

Before she left, I said to her, "I'm free on Wednesday night, in case you might be too and want to do something." She smiled and walked off.

Faye and I exchanged more playful messages over the next few days.

*****

Date: Mon, 9 Apr 2007 14:07:38 (EDT)
From: Laura McDonald
To: Phillip Demarco
Subject: Explorations

Hello, Phillip!

I enjoyed seeing you this morning. But I wished you could have held me again! Yes, I can be free on Wednesday. It's been a very long time since we've been alone together.

I wasn't teasing you when I said I was wearing something small under my dress today. I don't think it would have been a good idea to take all my clothes off so you could see, though. But next time we're together, perhaps I'll show you what small things I'm wearing. I mean, I can't have you thinking I was only teasing, now can I?

So you want to do more exploring? I like that idea, and Wednesday would be a perfect time for it! What should we explore first? I could suggest several things, but I'd like to know what your priority would be.

It was difficult leaving your office this morning for three reasons: (1) I missed seeing you last weekend, (2) you were doing a wonderful job of teasing me, and (3) I can't look at you from the computer lab!

Phillip, it's very difficult being close to you without being in your lap! If I had my way, I'd always sit on your lap when I visit your office!

Well, I have a class in one minute (I'll be late as usual, but writing you is more important!) Spend all the time you want thinking about me in (or out of) my dress!

Faye

*****

Date: Mon, 9 Apr 2007 15:24:19 (EDT)
From: Phillip Demarco
To: Laura McDonald
Subject: Your little dress

Hi, BP,

I'm not sure what our top priority in our explorations should be, but *any* exploring with you would be delightful! Maybe we should start by spending a lot of time kissing and touching each other. Then we could take our time and learn more about each other's bodies, although it might be necessary to remove some clothing to do so.

I'm looking forward to thinking more about your little dress... lying at your feet.

Phillip

*****

Date: Mon, 9 Apr 2007 17:54:51 (EDT)
From: Laura McDonald
To: Phillip Demarco
Subject: Pleasing each other

Phillip,

You are doing a good job of making me lose my concentration! After reading your last message, I won't be able to concentrate on any of my classes tomorrow! You're great at getting me excited (and I love it)! If we were in your office, I'd be sitting on your lap again (and I don't think we'd be talking either)!

Well, what should take priority in our exploration is pleasing each other (but I won't go into much detail here. I'd rather show you). I want to know how to satisfy *all* your desires! Then we should explore the wonderful benefits that come with taking our relationship to the next level. I need to quit thinking about all this exploring; I have homework to do!

Yes, my dress being at my feet while you're holding me sounds terrific. But don't expect me to be the only one whose clothes are on the floor. I expect you to be naked too (and it will be my pleasure to undress you!) But we need to get busy with these explorations. I can't take much more of this teasing, so we should start our explorations when we see each other on Wednesday!

I forgot to tell you what happened on Friday. Someone was trying to send me a sign or something. When I was leaving my apartment complex, three blue BMW convertibles drove right past me before I pulled out of the parking lot! It was very unusual. There aren't very many cars like yours in Gainesville, and what is the likelihood three of them would all pass Bivens Cove within ten seconds of one another? Don't you find that strange?

Faye

*****

Date: Mon, 9 Apr 2007 20:33:59 (EDT)
From: Phillip Demarco
To: Laura McDonald
Subject: Exciting possibilities

BP,

Your story about those BMWs was funny. It must have been a sign you should have stayed here with me last weekend instead of going to Georgia.

I *love* your list of exploration priorities! I can't wait until Wednesday to get started. And there's no teasing allowed, like when you told me about what you were wearing under your dress. Next time, you need to show me instead of telling me!

Phillip

*****

Date: Tue, 10 Apr 2007 10:08:24 (EDT)
From: Laura McDonald
To: Phillip Demarco
Subject: Wearing something

Hello!

I'm coming to your office around 1:00 p.m. You should fix your door because I'm wearing something tiny today!

Faye

*****

When Faye arrived, I met her as she entered, and without saying a word, I closed the door and locked it behind her. I

grabbed her hand and pulled her toward me. I cupped her face
in both of my hands and kissed her. She dropped her backpack
to the floor and returned my kisses with open-mouthed ones
of her own, accompanied by soft moans of pleasure. When I
put my arms around her, she moved closer and I leaned back
against the wall. As we kissed, Faye pressed forward against me
and ground her body into mine. She threw her head back and
shut her eyes as my kisses moved to her neck and down to the
top of her chest.

Faye was wearing very short shorts and a halter top
showing her bare midriff. I wanted to reach my hands under
her halter, but I resisted.

I didn't want Faye's kisses to stop, although she couldn't
stay long and needed to get to class soon.

Before she left, she looked at me and said, "Whew!"

I asked, "What are you thinking, BP?" But Faye didn't
answer; she only smiled and walked out. After her class, she
sent me a message with her answer to my question.

*****

Date: Tue, 10 Apr 2007 14:40:21 (EDT)
From: Laura McDonald
To: Phillip Demarco
Subject: An education

Hello!

Well, my visit to your office was very educational for
me. How about you? It amazed me you shut your door
right away! I kept thinking about the areas of your body I
have yet to explore. I hope we'll get to some of those areas
tomorrow.

The next time I visit you, I promise to wear a very
little dress. I didn't lie today when I told you I'd be
wearing something tiny. I did, but you couldn't see it. I think

I think you would have liked what it was, well, if you like red.

Faye

*****

I knew Faye wrote her last message from the student computer lab downstairs, so I thought I'd have a little fun. I walked down, entered the room from the back door, and sat a row behind her, so I could look at her without her knowing. I stayed for about twenty minutes, pretending to work on a computer, but watching her instead. After I left, I sent her a message and disclosed my "spying" activity.

*****

Date: Tue, 10 Apr 2007 15:16:42 (EDT)
From: Phillip Demarco
To: Laura McDonald
Subject: Your legs

BP,

Here's something you don't know. For the last twenty minutes, I've been sitting behind you, staring at your beautiful legs!
    I have a question for you. How would you feel about coming over to my house tomorrow? My wife won't be home until after 11:00 p.m. I live out in the country, so nobody will see you, and it will be safe. We can be alone and continue our explorations. If you're comfortable coming over, I'll give you directions.

Phillip

*****

Date: Tue, 10 Apr 2007 15:56:08 (EDT)
From: Laura McDonald
To: Phillip Demarco
Subject: My business

Hi!

You are *terrible*! I was sitting here studying, minding my business, and you were behind me looking at my legs. I can't believe you did such a thing! I would never look at your legs! Would you like to know why? Well, it's because I'd be staring at something else above your legs, that's why!

Yes, I can come to your house tomorrow if you're sure your wife won't show up. I'm ready for our exploring to begin. I had a hard time in class this morning. It would be much more exciting if I was in your office (with the door closed).

Faye

*****

The first thing the next morning, Faye came to pick up the directions to my house, but she couldn't stay. She wanted to get her schoolwork done so it wouldn't interfere with our 'exploring' time later. We planned for her to come over at 7:00 p.m., but I received another message from her soon after she left my office.

*****

Date: Wed, 11 Apr 2007 08:31:26 (EDT)
From: Laura McDonald
To: Phillip Demarco
Subject: Staring?

Phillip,

I'm sure you would love to know what I am staring at above your legs, wouldn't you? Instead of telling you, I'll let you wonder.

I can't wait to see you later. I'll be there right at 7:00 p.m.!

You can think about this until tonight. Remember when you said how beautiful my legs were? Well, imagine how they'll feel when they're wrapped around you!

Faye

*****

I lived in a very secluded area east of campus, off Lakeshore Drive near Newnans Lake. Our house was large for two people, with four bedrooms, three bathrooms, and over 3,500 square feet. An architect friend designed it as a two-story A-frame-style cottage. It had high ceilings and many windows, giving plenty of light, and since we built it at the top of a small ridge, we added a basement to have a game room and a wine cellar. The front door was on the ground level, and it opened to a large den extending through the house to a wall of tall windows in the back facing a patio and swimming pool. A small pool house sat to the right, and Newnans Lake was visible in the distance. The kitchen and dining room were to the left of the den, with three bedrooms and two bathrooms off to the right. The master suite occupied the entire second floor, which also had a wall of windows overlooking the deck and pool. The entire house had beige walls and white oak hardwood flooring. A long driveway from the main road led to a detached three-car garage. I thought the house was beautiful and comfortable, and Sophia and I both loved living there.

When Faye arrived, I gave her a big hug and a sensuous kiss. Then I showed her the house, the patio, and the pool, holding her hand while I did. We were both excited and nervous. Then I walked Faye downstairs to the game room, which was more of a TV room with two recliners and a large soft sofa positioned in front of a sixty-inch flat screen TV. A computer desk and printer occupied one corner. It was a room I used to work and relax. We found our way to the sofa and became entangled in each other's arms. It didn't take long to begin our explorations.

We got lost in our kisses. Soon, we turned to lie down and we could feel the length of our bodies pressing against each other.

I began touching Faye's breasts, and she responded by saying, "That's nice!" She was wearing shorts and a blouse I began to unbutton. After undoing the first button,

I asked Faye if it was okay if I continued, and she answered with a soft yes! When I loosened the last button, she sat up and removed her blouse, revealing the prettiest pink bra, like those seen in Victoria's Secret ads. But I didn't admire it for very long as I reached behind her to undo the fastener. It slid off her shoulders, exposing Faye's beautiful, large breasts. I couldn't resist moving my kisses down her neck to explore her hardening nipples. Faye became more excited. She threw her head back and moaned. I moved my hand down between her legs, which she opened to allow me access.

When I touched her through her shorts, Faye surprised me when she said, "You might find something down there you don't expect."

I thought for a moment, laughed, and asked, "What? Are you really a guy?"

She giggled and answered, "No, silly. Something's just missing down there." Curious about what Faye meant, I unbuttoned her shorts and slid my hand down inside her bra-matching pink panties. I soon learned Faye was referring to her shaved vagina.

I looked up at her and said, "Mmm... I *love* it, BP," which extracted yet another giggle from this beautiful young woman. Now our passion built even further as I continued to kiss Faye's breasts while I explored inside her panties with my fingers. After a few moments, Faye reached down to feel my hard erection and began exploring me. She unbuckled my belt, unsnapped my jeans, pulled down my zipper, and slid her hand inside my boxer briefs. Now her actions caused me to moan. Next, we removed the rest of each other's clothing.

Once we did, I stopped to admire her beautiful and very sexy body, comparable to any magazine centerfold. "BP, your body is gorgeous!" I said.

And Faye, knowing it was, responded, "Thank you!"

We spent the evening exploring each other and making love in the most tender, caring way possible. It turned out to be an incredible night for both of us!

The time flew by, and before we knew it, Faye needed to leave. I wished she could have stayed all night so I could have woken up with her in the morning, something I hoped would happen someday. After getting dressed and walking to the door, we both stared at each other for a moment and smiled. I said, "Now remember, this won't affect your grade in my class." Faye laughed and said, "Well, I'm not *in* your class anymore," which caused us both to laugh. I walked her to her car, kissed her goodbye, and watched her drive away. I went to bed before Sophia got home, although I didn't sleep much at all.

Faye emailed me early the next day to discuss our evening together.

*****

Date: Thu, 12 Apr 2007 08:55:15 (EDT)
From: Laura McDonald
To: Phillip Demarco
Subject   Lying next to you

Phillip,

I had a *great* time last night and I hope you did too! It was wonderful to lie down next to you, touch you, and talk (?) to you. My favorite part of the evening was right before I left when we were gazing at each other. I loved being able to look up and see your handsome face and your beautiful blue eyes! I was thinking about how much I enjoy spending time with you and how special you always make me feel with the things you say to me! I hope we have another opportunity to explore again soon.

I think we should talk more about our relationship next time. I realize I never say much, but I enjoy talking to you a lot. Someday, I may be comfortable telling you everything, but it'll take me a while. Also, I care more about you each time we see each other. It might not be a good thing, though. It keeps getting harder for me to deal with the fact I can't have you. And yes, our relationship is still a threat to Alex and me. We even argued over him coming here this week. He asked to come yesterday, and I wouldn't let him because I wanted to go to your house instead. Isn't that terrible? Well, I've told you way too much, so I'll stop now before I say anything more.

I need to run, so I guess I won't see you until Monday since Alex will be here when I finish classes tomorrow. I want to tell you again what a wonderful time I had with you last night!

Faye

*****

I knew I'd think about Faye the entire weekend, and I now accepted the fact I had fallen in love with her, even though I realized it was an absurd thing to have done!

CHAPTER 6

Before You Know It, We'll Be the Same Age

It was a long weekend for me, with constant thoughts of Faye and wondering how everything happened. Even with my anxiety, I was glad we made love, although I struggled with my infidelity. I could make excuses for my behavior, but I found myself unable to turn down the opportunity to be with Faye. She was always on my mind, and I couldn't get enough of her. It made me happy she felt the same way.

I hoped to see Faye early Monday morning. She didn't disappoint me as she stopped by after her first class. I couldn't hug her when she came in because my door was open, and other students were nearby. Her visit may have been to reassure herself about the events of Wednesday night, but her demeanor also reassured me us making love wasn't a mistake. I think we were both pleased that our relationship had moved to a higher level. Our communication did too, with each of us being more forthcoming in our conversations, both in person and in our emails. We discussed our feelings for each other, including the notion that we should talk more about them. We spent an hour talking about our relationship, which was a very different type of conversation for Faye. We continued the conversation in a series of messages. Then it turned playful.

*****

Date: Mon, 16 Apr 2007 11:07:00 (EDT)
From: Laura McDonald
To: Phillip Demarco
Subject: Thinking

Phillip,

I enjoyed seeing you this morning. I wish you wouldn't have resisted the temptation to close the door and give me a big hug (you could have kissed me too). Over the weekend, I thought about how wonderful it would be to have you hold me again. Thank you for telling me you thought about me. It means a lot because you're *always* on my mind, even when I'm with Alex. If you don't tell me those things, I might assume you don't like me, so I need to know this information!

Why are you so puzzled? Is it because I still haven't told you why I want you? I would inform you of the exact reasons if I knew them. All I know is you are a *wonderful* man and I enjoy being with you. Like you said yourself, we have great chemistry, so that must be what draws me to you. Just remember, I want you to be more than a playmate. (It worries me you might think I'm only using you for sex. I hope not because that's not it.)

I also think we should talk more! If we do, the more I'll tell you what you want to know. But I've said *much* more than I ever have with other guys. I have *never* told a guy I liked him first before, so I have said a lot! But I'd rather listen to you talk than talk myself. I enjoy hearing what you have to say, so you can tell me anything.

I wish I could have you as my own, but I know it's not possible. Even if I weren't with Alex, there's no way I could have you because you're already married to someone else. I realize (and understand) this. So I don't think you could ever be mine, do you?

Faye

*****

Date: Mon, 16 Apr 2007 16:40:37 (EDT)
From: Laura McDonald
To: Phillip Demarco
Subject: Pursuing me

Phillip,

I forgot to tell you I missed seeing you over the weekend. Sorry to hear you didn't have a very good one. If we could have seen each other, I'm sure it would have been better. In case you can't tell, it bothers me when you aren't happy. And if you were mine, your happiness would be my top priority. I'd do anything to make sure you were happy.

So if I weren't with Alex, you would pursue me like crazy? How would you go about doing that? It wouldn't take much to win me over considering the way I already feel about you. We could have a fantastic and long-lasting relationship, couldn't we? Wouldn't it be great if we could see each other all the time without worrying who's around and who will find out? Last Wednesday, I didn't want to leave your house because I wanted to spend the entire night with you and wake up next to you in the morning. Isn't that terrible of me?

Don't worry, Phillip, you haven't scared me off either! You always feel you've told me too much, but you never have and could never scare me away. But you can tell me whatever you want because I love hearing what you have to say. And just so you know, our relationship is not one-sided because I feel the same way you do. I know I never tell you this, but I promise you my feelings will not change.

Faye

*****

Date: Mon, 16 Apr 2007 17:21:53 (EDT)
From: Phillip Demarco
To: Laura McDonald
Subject: Kissing something

Hello, BP,

So you'd want to keep me happy? Hmmm... I like that idea very much. Yes, I'm sure we could have a long and wonderful relationship. I've never felt this way about anyone before, so I know it would be terrific if we were together. You're very special to me. And if you were here now, I'd unbutton your clothing and start kissing something.

Phillip

*****

Date: Tue, 17 Apr 2007 08:25:13 (EDT)
From: Laura McDonald
To: Phillip Demarco
Subject: Kiss what?

Hello, Phillip!

So you wanted to unbutton my clothing and kiss something? What did you want to kiss? I wish you had! I guess you can show me the next time we're alone.

Faye

*****

Date: Tue, 17 Apr 2007 09:39:35 (EDT)
From: Phillip Demarco
To: Laura McDonald
Subject: Terrible of me

Good morning BP,

I wanted to and still want to kiss…everything. I woke up thinking, if you were next to me, I'd wake you up with hundreds of kisses all over your body. Am I being terrible? Come visit me if you have time later.

Phillip

*****

Date: Tue, 17 Apr 2007 10:05:49 (EDT)
From: Laura McDonald
To: Phillip Demarco
Subject: Hundreds?

Hello, Phillip!

   The thought of you waking me up with hundreds of kisses is wonderful. After I read your words, I got a huge smile on my face! No, it's not terrible that you're interested in doing those things. I'm glad that you are. And yes, *your* happiness would be my priority. I mean, how could I be happy myself knowing you weren't?

   I'm sorry this message is so short, but I have some homework to finish before I come see you around 2:30 or 3:00 p.m., okay? Perhaps we can get back to our experiments. I'll touch (or kiss) your body in *many* places. Then we'll record your response(s)!

Faye

                    *****

   Faye came to my office at 3:00 p.m. Since there was a seminar scheduled, my department was quiet. I skipped it because I didn't want to miss my "BP time" for a dull lecture. When she arrived, I locked the door once again, which surprised her but made her happy. She threw her arms around me and kissed me passionately. What a greeting! I knew it would be a fun afternoon. After our hug and kiss, I reached over and turned off the overhead lights so it appeared I wasn't there. Faye giggled, grabbed my hand, and led me over to my desk. I sat on the edge, and she stepped closer to kiss me again. My hands soon slid up under the short summer dress she was wearing. Her kisses became hotter, and she tilted her head back. My lips moved to her neck, ears, and then again to her forehead, eyelids, and cheeks. She closed her eyes and moaned as my lips glided over her.

"I love it when you kiss me that way and when you touch me like you do," she whispered. Then she spun around to face away from me and leaned back into me, and my erection pressed against her. As I kissed the side of her neck, she grabbed my hands and moved them under the front of her dress and guided them up between her legs. Then she turned her head sideways to kiss my lips. I rubbed my hand over the outside of her panties and found them to be already moist. After I pushed the thin fabric aside, my fingers slid inside her as she continued to grind against my hard penis.

We were both lost in each other's passion, when I said to Faye, "Is this one experiment you wanted to do?"

Faye's only response was a giggle and a soft yes. It was all I could do to keep from unbuttoning her dress and letting it fall to the floor, as I often fantasized. Somehow, I resisted.

We spent two hours exploring each other, kissing, touching, and making each other feel wonderful. I know we both would have liked to remove our clothing had we been elsewhere. We continued to hold each other and kiss until someone suddenly began pounding on my office door with a fist.

Then we heard, "Phillip, are you in there?" I recognized the voice to be that of my department chair, Robert. Several more knocks followed, then another, "Phillip?" Faye and I looked at each other, both surprised at being disturbed since I had turned off the light.

I put my finger to my lips and whispered, "Shhh." After Robert departed, we both breathed a sigh of relief. His interruption brought us back to reality, and it was time for Faye to leave. After a final kiss goodbye, I opened the door and checked the hallway for others before Faye slipped out.

Prior to walking out, she said to me, "I love being with you." It was another lovely afternoon. Every minute we spent together, regardless of what we did, reaffirmed my opinion about Faye being a captivating young woman.

Early that evening, we wrote to each other and exchanged messages over the next several days. The messages tell a clearer story of how our relationship was progressing to a place neither of us ever expected.

*****

Date: Tue, 17 Apr 2007 18:40:33 (EDT)
From: Phillip Demarco
To: Laura McDonald
Subject: My response

BP,

It was wonderful seeing you this afternoon. I enjoyed the experiment you performed on me, and you seemed to like my response. But you may not have viewed it in its entirety. I love spending time with you no matter what we're doing. I still can't believe what's happening between us. I'm very lucky to have you in my life. And it would appear we might be "falling" for each other. I hope that idea doesn't scare you.

Phillip

*****

Date: Tue, 17 Apr 2007 19:42:57 (EDT)
From   Laura McDonald
To: Phillip Demarco
Subject: Experiments

Hello, Phillip!

I may have missed a response you had during my experiment. You need to tell me what it was because if you don't, my results won't be accurate! I guess I must repeat the experiment so I can record your complete response! I'll add a kissing stimulus to my next test, and we'll see how well you can concentrate. But you're the professor, so you should also be conducting these experiments. And since I'm so interested in them, I'll allow you to do some tests on me too! (I think you already began testing me, but you may not have recorded *all* my responses either!) You looked *very* good today, but you do *every day*! When we were in your office, I was dying to unbutton your shirt and kiss your chest! I thought I'd share that with you.

Well, I've got to go home to eat something and finish my homework. I'll write again later if I get my work done and respond to what you said in your last message, okay?

Faye

*****

Date: Tue, 17 Apr 2007 21:54:44 (EDT)
From   Laura McDonald
To: Phillip Demarco
Subject: Fate

Hello, my dear professor!

I finished my homework, so now I can answer you. It was a very exciting afternoon today, don't you think? We must continue those experiments later.

I can't believe you thought I forgot about the first time I came to your office! How could I ever forget? I remember it well. I came to ask some questions about class, and you were working at your desk. When I knocked on your door, you looked up and said, "Hello, Ms. McDonald!" You seemed *very* surprised I would come to your office hours. It was the day my little (?) attraction to you began. Now if I had never come to ask questions, none of this would have happened. It's a good thing I did because I'm having a *wonderful* time! And I know fate played some part in our meeting because, as you know, you got to teach my dynamics class at the last minute. But we could have gotten together anyhow if we met some other way because there's just something about you (and I'm still not sure what) that drives me *crazy*!

So you believe we're falling for each other? I guess we show all the signs, don't we? There's a definite possibility we share more than a great friendship. If we were only friends, we wouldn't have a problem being in the same room together without being able to touch each other, right? Why do you still insist I'll change my mind about our situation? I'm not planning to, but even if I was, I couldn't do it. My feelings for you are *way* too strong to ignore them. So, to answer your question, no, I couldn't forget about you, ever, because I liked you a lot before any of this happened!

Well, I need to go to bed now. It's too bad you can't be here with me because you might enjoy seeing what I sleep in if you like silk. I hope you dream about me tonight. I know I'll dream about you.

Faye

*****

Date: Wed, 18 Apr 2007 8:53:21 (EDT)
From: Phillip Demarco
To: Laura McDonald
Subject: Punishment

BP,

The messages you sent me last night were terrific. It seems you've been "teasing" me a lot with the things you tell me. That's very mean of you. I think some "punishment" may be in order for your terrible behavior, don't you agree?

I *love* silk! The thought of *you* in silk is very, very erotic. And yes, I think extra punishment is appropriate for telling me that right before I *tried* to go to sleep last night. You're so bad! I miss you!

Phillip

*****

Date: Wed, 18 Apr 2007 10:09:05 (EDT)
From: Laura McDonald
To: Phillip Demarco
Subject: Magnets

Phillip,

So you plan to punish me for teasing you so much? Well, you *should*! I'm willing to do *anything* to make up for my terrible behavior! You should give me extra experiments to conduct for my punishment (as long as you'll be assisting me).

We were like magnets in the hallway and in your office today. I have a difficult time keeping away from you. I always want to touch and kiss you and do other things to you. I wish we had been in the elevator alone so I could have kissed you! I was looking forward to the possibility of that all day. Now what were you trying to do to me when you stood so close to me? You might get me in a lot of trouble by doing that because I had to work very hard to keep myself from touching your, well, let's just say, something instead of staring at it! I still don't know if I'm driving up to see Alex this weekend. If I go, I'll be coming back early to study, so we could meet somewhere if you'd like? If I don't go, maybe we can do something on Saturday. I should know by tomorrow whether I'm staying here.

Faye

*****

Date: Thu, 19 Apr 2007 10:35:17 (EDT)
From: Phillip Demarco
To: Laura McDonald
Subject: Flustered

BP,

If you're around this weekend, I'll make sure I can spend some time with you. I can't miss out on such a great opportunity. So let me know when you find out.

Why did you look so flustered when I came into the computer lab yesterday afternoon? I wasn't teasing you; I had to load some software on the computers, although I hoped you'd be in there. I didn't think you'd mind. It's difficult being around you when other people are nearby, though. We're like magnets attracted to each other! It was driving me crazy that I couldn't touch you. But I must be careful in front of others, which has become very difficult. I'm sure you can understand why.

Phillip

*****

Date: Thu, 19 Apr 2007 13:14:10 (EDT)
From: Laura McDonald
To: Phillip Demarco
Subject: Overwhelming

Phillip

I'm very excited about the possibility of seeing each other this weekend. We'll have a *wonderful* time!

I thought you had forgotten about me because you didn't come to the computer lab when I was in there earlier. I was *very* upset about this! And you didn't bother me when you came in yesterday, I enjoyed your little visit; I wish we had been alone in there so I could have touched your hand or another part of you! The chemistry we have is overwhelming, isn't it? I've never felt such intense magnetism either. I find it very exciting. What do *you* think all of this means? I know you mean so much to me, and I like/want you more every time I see you. I have also realized I care for you not only as a wonderful friend but also much, much more. I shouldn't say anything else until you give me your opinion about what's going on between us!

Faye

*****

Date: Thu, 19 Apr 2007 16:02:55 (EDT)
From: Phillip Demarco
To: Laura McDonald
Subject: Crazy thing

BP,

Well, the more we're together, the stronger our feelings seem to get. This is amazing since I'm a professor, and you're a student, *and* I'm so much older than you (but I won't be for much longer since you're catching up to me in age... I'll explain how later). Does that thought scare you? I think it might because it scares me a little. *But*, I like you too much to worry about it.

I'm excited we'll get to see each other this weekend. We can make plans tomorrow.

Phillip

*****

Early the next morning, Faye came to my office to ask what I meant when I said I wouldn't be older than her for much longer. I replied, "Yes, you're catching up to me in age." She looked puzzled and responded, "Whaaaat?" So I explained.

"Well, when you were twelve, you were one-third my age. When you turn twenty-four, you'll be half my age, then when you're forty-eight, you'll be two-thirds my age. And before you know it, we'll be the same age."

In one of Faye's "blonde" moments, she said, "Oh, I never thought of it that way." I laughed, but she didn't, still not catching on to my twisted math logic.

*****

Date: Fri, 20 Apr 2007 11:30:02 (EDT)
From: Laura McDonald
To: Phillip Demarco
Subject: Frightened

Phillip,

I'm not frightened by where our relationship is heading, and I'm not sure why. It may be because I don't know how much you've fallen for me. But I will worry about it someday because I know the more I'm with you, the more I want to be with you. We have a wonderful relationship (even with all the complications)! Imagine how great it would be if we didn't have all those minor (?) issues.

Okay, I'll stop by in a minute to make sure we're still meeting tomorrow. If you're not there, I'll meet you at 2:00 p.m. at our usual place. So I'll see you in a minute or tomorrow!

Faye

*****

CHAPTER 7

Just Don't Use My Real Name

On Friday evening, Sophia informed me she was attending a seminar in Orlando all day and all evening on Saturday. I viewed this as an opportunity to spend even more time with Faye than we planned. We were becoming more relaxed, more intimate, and more loving with each other, and I looked forward to spending another full day with her. I called her to tell her the good news, and she was happy to hear it.

To start our day together, we drove out to Paynes Prairie Preserve State Park a little south of town and close to Micanopy, where I took Faye on our first drive. This surprised her as she'd never been there, and I hadn't told her why we were going. I chose Paynes Prairie because it was very scenic, with beautiful shrubs and trees, walking paths, and gazebos sprinkled throughout the park. As we turned into the entrance off Highway 441, we passed under a shady canopy formed by tree branches on both sides of the entrance. We drove through the guard gate to a small parking area a short distance down the road. I thought it would be a great location to photograph Faye in the woods, although I didn't mention it to her beforehand. When I described my plan, she blushed a bit and balked at being photographed, but she soon changed her mind after we arrived and I took out my camera. Faye looked beautiful in her denim shorts and a turquoise pullover top, with white sneakers. She was very photogenic, and the sun's rays shining through the tall trees made her blonde hair glisten and her green eyes sparkle. She posed for me: in a gazebo, leaning against trees, peeking out from behind them, and glancing back over her shoulder at me. Her various poses were inquisitive, flirtatious, and alluring—I even snapped one of her with her hands positioned on her hips, trying to look annoyed—all while smiling, giggling, and laughing. When I asked Faye to pose in whatever way she wanted, she pretended to pull up the front of her shirt before breaking into a laugh and stopping. In every picture, Faye appeared sexy and irresistible to me.

After our "photoshoot", we drove over to the nearby Lake Wauburg and found a bench near the water where we sat and talked, and talked, and talked. We discussed our feelings for each other and I mentioned we should try to spend an entire night together soon, even though it might be hard to arrange. Time flew by, and I don't even remember many other topics we discussed. In between talking, we held hands, hugged, and kissed, sometimes with passion and sometimes just playful pecks, more befitting of being somewhere in public, even though no one else was around.

Later, we thought about getting some dinner. Faye suggested we go back to her apartment and order out since Bailee planned to be gone most of the evening. I liked her idea, so off we went to retrieve her car on the way. Soon after arriving, we both forgot about food, and Faye took my hand and led me to her bedroom where we kissed and tumbled onto the bed. We couldn't get enough of each other, and both seemed more desperate to make love than to tease each other with continued discussions of experiments and human responses. As we lay there groping each other, the front door opened, and Bailee came home early. Faye and I looked at each other in amazement, as the situation was very much like when Robert surprised us at my office a few days earlier. Our shock of almost being "caught in the act" twice in one week soon turned into quiet laughter and whispering jokes to each other.

We wondered how I would escape the apartment without Bailee seeing Faye was with someone other than Alex. With our romantic encounter ruined, we both sat up and straightened our clothing to wait for an opportunity for me to leave. After about thirty minutes, I snuck out when Bailee went to take a shower. Faye gave me a quick kiss goodbye and one last giggle as I walked out the door. Bailee never knew I was there, and Faye didn't need to explain. It was just too bad we couldn't finish what we started.

My thoughts focused on Faye throughout the weekend, which had now become my typical activity. It thrilled me at how our relationship had developed, and I was excited about what might come next. Faye told me on Saturday she planned to attend summer school, so I would get to spend even more time with her in the months ahead and before her pending marriage. Then we exchanged a few interesting messages.

*****

Date: Mon, 23 Apr 2007 10:19:13 (EDT)
From: Laura McDonald
To: Phillip Demarco
Subject: Entire night

Phillip,

Good morning! I hope you're doing wonderful like I am. Do you want to know why I'm wonderful? Well, I'll tell you. It's because I keep thinking about you and the *great* Saturday we had together, which puts me in a terrific mood. I always have a great time when I'm with you, and I thought about you the rest of the weekend.

Your description of how you feel about me drove me crazy on Saturday. I can't wait to try all those things we talked about. And you think we could spend a whole night together? How would we arrange such a thing? It would be wonderful to wake up next to you. (But who says we'd ever get to sleep?)

I thought I might have been falling for you in the last few weeks, but now I know I have. If that wasn't the case, I could think about something besides you, and I can't. I hope you've fallen for me too because if not, this relationship is one-sided. Well, have you fallen for me or not?

Faye

*****

Date: Mon, 23 Apr 2007 1:21:43 (EDT)
From: Phillip Demarco
To: Laura McDonald
Subject: Questions

BP,

I only have a minute, but I wanted to answer your questions before I head to a meeting. The answers are *yes*, I'm sure of it. And *yes*, it will be possible for us to spend an entire night together sometime.

PD

*****

Date: Tue, 24 Apr 2007 9:40:50 (EDT)
From: Laura McDonald
To: Phillip Demarco
Subject: More experiments

Phillip,

I am *very* disappointed I missed seeing you yesterday! I came by your office at about 4:15 p.m. to check if you were around, but you weren't there.

I'm glad you think we can spend a night together, even though I'm not sure how I could get away, since I have a *very* curious roommate. What would we do if we spent a whole night together? You may see us watching TV or something, right? Well, I don't! I think we should experiment more instead because I still need to find out how you react to the mouth stimulus situation!

I have some good news. Alex might have to go to Texas in two weeks for work, so we'll be able to spend another weekend playing together! Isn't that exciting?

Are you telling me the truth about falling for me? You'd better be because I've also fallen for you. It wasn't too difficult to tell you. I could have told you on Saturday, but I didn't know if it was a good idea. I don't like to say too much because I'm afraid after I do, you'll change your mind about what you want to happen between us, and I'll end up getting hurt. I've been hurt before and didn't like it! I'm counting on you not to change your mind about us because I enjoy spending time with you *so much*!

Okay, after I finish my homework, I'll be on my way to visit you. I hope you'll be there!

Faye

*****

Since the semester was nearing an end, I was happy to see Faye after our Saturday adventure. We were entering a period when we'd both be very busy, followed by the break from school, so we wouldn't have many opportunities to be together until summer arrived. We talked for an hour. I kept my office door open because students and faculty were everywhere in the hallway. Having no privacy didn't seem to matter much as we both enjoyed each other even when we weren't being intimate. We spent most of the hour smiling, laughing, and flirting. Before we knew it, Faye needed to leave. She touched her finger to the back of my hand again and said, "I love touching you any way I can."

Our long talks and the time we spent together brought us closer. Faye's messages were now becoming more direct and warmer as she continued to shed her inhibitions.

*****

Date: Tue, 24 Apr 2007 15:50:31 (EDT)
From: Laura McDonald
To: Phillip Demarco
Subject: Worried

Phillip,

I enjoyed seeing you this morning! I feel closer to you now since we've fallen for each other, too. (But what does that mean to you?) Have I gotten *any* better at telling you these things? Do you still think I haven't said enough? I know you wouldn't hurt me like I wouldn't hurt you. But I worry about saying too much. The more I tell you, the closer we'll get, which means I'll keep liking you more and more. Now I *am* worried about falling for you because I'm afraid I'll move beyond just liking you. And I'm not sure if it would be a good thing considering all the complications we have. What's your opinion?

I'll work on a plan so we can spend the night together. There could be a time when my roommate's out of town and Alex won't be here, but it might be on a weekend, so I don't know if you could manage it. I imagine you'd want to conduct more experiments, wouldn't you? But after all our experimenting, I'd need a shower. And right in the middle of it, I'll remember I forgot a towel. Then you must bring me one *before* I could get out of the shower (I'm sure you wouldn't want me to get cold). While you're in the bathroom with me, I might realize I need some help to rinse all the soap off my body. Since you'll be the only person there, you must help me. You wouldn't mind, would you?

I can't wait to kiss and hug you again. I wanted to in your office, but once again, it wasn't possible. I want to do it *every* time I visit you. That's why when I get up to leave, I always come to stand next to you. Well, I'll see you tomorrow, even though I'd love to sit on your lap right now!

Faye

*****

After reading about Faye's shower scenario, I wrote her back with a few suggestions for additions to the scene she described. She liked what I proposed.

*****

Date: Wed, 25 Apr 2007 13:24:22 (EDT)
From: Laura McDonald
To: Phillip Demarco
Subject: Experiments in the shower

Phillip,

I enjoyed your additions to my shower idea. How could we make drying off erotic? (I'll let you put your descriptive talents to work on this question, so tell me *everything* you imagine happening!) You know, it could get *very* slippery with all the soap, so I'll keep my arms around you the whole time. I wouldn't want either of us to fall. Perhaps I can conduct more experiments while we're in the shower. This is necessary to see how you also react to the mouth stimulus under running water.

So you need clarification about what I mean when I say I've fallen for you? Well, I mean I care about you very, very much, and I love spending time with you. I guess I'll leave my explanation at that because I don't think I should tell you anymore. It would be great to move beyond just liking each other. But I don't know how well that would work out. If it weren't for you being married, I'd definitely want it to happen. I think we get along great, and we could have a fantastic relationship if we moved past where we are now, don't you? If not for all the complications, we might have a future together, if you're interested in having a future with me.

I hope I get to see you tomorrow night. Let me know if you can go, anytime is fine with me!

Faye

*****

Date: Wed, 25 Apr 2007 18:42:00 (EDT)
From: Laura McDonald
To: Phillip Demarco
Subject: Devouring me

Phillip,

It's too bad I couldn't come to your office today, wasn't it? I was all prepared to sit on your desk in my short skirt and "everything"! I guess I'll save that for another time. So you think about me when you're lying in bed? Well, I think about you too. I love the thought of falling asleep in your arms after a night of explorations and waking up with you, giving me hundreds of kisses.

The mere thought of you devouring me time after time makes me want to sigh! Now how would you go about doing that anyhow? I can think of several ways I'd enjoy devouring you! Are you sure you won't tire of me after that? I know I never will! I have those "thoughts" about you every time I hear your voice! This is strange to me because I seldom think about Alex the same way. But with you, those things always come to mind. I can't figure out why. Perhaps somebody's trying to give me another sign or something. What do you think?

Why would you like me to call to tell you I want and need you? You already know I do, don't you? You should because it's the truth. You make me happy. And knowing I can call and talk to you is wonderful! I can't imagine what it would be like if I could never see you again (which I hope I never have to find out!) I enjoy *all* the time we spend together. I always have fun with you, and the best part is looking into your wonderful eyes!

Well, I've got an exciting meeting to attend. But I'll meet you later as we planned.

Faye

*****

Date: Thu, 26 Apr 2007 19:27:10 (EDT)
From: Laura McDonald
To: Phillip Demarco
Subject: Mesmerized

Phillip,

I had a *great* time last night—as usual—and I'm happy you could get away. I didn't want to let you leave me; in case you couldn't tell. It's always difficult to say goodbye. The reason it's so hard for me is because I'm *crazy* about you! I've known that for a long time.

Why were the hugs your favorite part of last night? I realize it's a stupid question since I was there, and I know how wonderful they felt. I thought about you *a lot* afterward, and about how much I enjoyed it. What I liked best was gazing into your enchanting blue eyes! I'm always too mesmerized to say anything when I look into your eyes.

I'll miss you this weekend. Do you think it's a sign of something? It must be. Why else would I miss you when we were together only a few hours ago?

Faye

*****

Since final exams began the following week, Faye could only stop by for brief visits. The end of the semester was also a busy time for me with exams, meetings, and handling student crises, which always appeared. The most common crisis occurred when students realized they were going to receive a bad grade in my class. A few of them always came to ask how they could improve their grades. Years earlier, I learned how to respond in the best possible way.

I'd say, "Well, when you repeat my class next year, work harder from the beginning, and don't wait until the end of the semester to become concerned about your grade." My answer was never the one they hoped to receive.

I knew Faye would visit again before going to Tennessee for semester break. Her twenty-second birthday was on Friday, so on my drive to work, I stopped to buy her a card and some chocolate truffles at Thornebrook Chocolates on NW Forty-Third Street. Faye liked chocolates but hadn't had truffles before. When I gave them to her later, I surprised her, and she loved me remembering her birthday. Faye beamed, not only because it was her birthday but also for another reason I didn't know.

As we chatted, she looked at me as her smile widened until she laughed. "What's so funny?" I asked.

"Would you help me with my course schedule for the summer term? I need more interdisciplinary elective hours."

"Sure, I'll be happy to help Faye."

Then she said, "Well, would it be all right if I took your structures class?"

Surprised, I stared at her and smiled, while holding back a laugh. After a long pause, I said, "Why are you interested in taking another mechanical engineering class?" I expected Faye to tell me she somehow developed an interest in structures, or that she thought the course might be fun.

Instead, she looked straight at me and answered, "Because you're teaching it, Phillip, that's why."

Laughing, I said, "There may be better reasons to take such a class."

"Well, you teaching it is a good enough reason for me," she responded.

"Okay, but you know our relationship won't affect your grade in my class, don't you?"

She laughed and replied, "I know that silly!"

Before she left, I said, "Faye, I've told you this before, but I plan to write a book about us someday."

Faye giggled and answered, "Okay, just don't use my real name when you do."

"Well, we'll see," I said.

She giggled and peeked out into the hallway to see if anyone was nearby. When there wasn't, she gave me a quick kiss goodbye and said, "I'll see you when I get back after the break. I'll miss you.

CHAPTER 8

Other Secrets

A wonderful summer was ahead for us. Having Faye as a student in class again, along with the fact we'd both have more free time, gave me thoughts of elevating our relationship even higher. Summer academic terms are much more relaxed than regular semesters. Enrollment is lower, and most of the faculty members are doing something different from the normal school year. Professors may take jobs in government labs or industry, and others may travel. Most, however, work on their research on-campus, but on a more irregular schedule. My assignment for the summer included teaching one class and working part-time on a small research project, which translated to a one-half time appointment. Since Sophia worked full-time and often longer, I'd have plenty of opportunities to spend time with Faye.

I returned to campus a few days early to get a head start on my project and prepare for my course. It was a productive period because the building was quiet with the students gone. As a result, I got a good jump on my research, so I knew the summer would be a relaxing one. I didn't hear from Faye while she was in Nashville, which wasn't unusual, so I was eager to see her when she returned to Gainesville.

When the first day of classes arrived for the summer semester of 2007, I was more excited than usual to walk into my classroom. Faye sat in the front row instead of the back of the room like she did when she took my dynamics class. As I walked to the podium, I caught her eye. Her smile was wide, and she looked happier than normal.

The class was small, with only twelve students. All of them were mechanical engineering majors, except Faye. With so few enrollees, I envisioned teaching it in a less formal manner with more interaction and student engagement, which was seldom possible with a larger number of students. After completing my typical first class day activities and chatting with the students as a group, they reinforced my notion the summer would be a good one. When we finished for the morning, Faye walked down the hall with me, and we chatted before her next class. After she left, I sent her a message to tell her how much I missed her over the break and that I couldn't wait to be "alone" with her again. I soon received her response.

*****

Date: Mon, 14 May 2007 11:59:25 (EDT)
From: Laura McDonald
To: Phillip Demarco
Subject: So mean

Phillip,

You are SO mean to me! I just finished reading your message and now I have to sit in class. How can I ever concentrate? I may have a huge smile on my face the entire time. I'll answer your letter after class and I WILL come to visit you later. I might have to close the door too!

Faye

*****

When Faye arrived at my office, she leaned back and turned her head both ways as she entered to check if any 'intruders' were nearby. When she didn't see any, she closed the door and locked it behind her. As soon as she did, Faye rushed across the room and threw her arms around me. We kissed, and she pushed me against my desk. I pulled her as close to me as I could. She looked beautiful, felt wonderful, and her kisses tasted delicious! We spent thirty minutes reconnecting. I asked Faye how Alex was doing, and she started crying again. I wasn't sure why, and she didn't tell me. Once again, I apologized for saying something wrong, even though I didn't know what it was. I was only trying to be gracious.

On Wednesday morning, Faye walked into my office before class and said, "Good morning! I have something for you." She handed me an envelope containing a letter she'd written to me, then she smiled and left. But I couldn't read it until after class. Faye wrote her letter with a red pen, the kind I used to tease her. I knew she did it to tease me in return.

*****

Phillip,

You may wonder where your email message is, right? Well, I went home to eat dinner last night and my internet was down, which is why you don't have one. I figured I'd write you a letter instead and give it to you before class! (How do you like the red ink? Do you have any idea what pen I used?) I had fun again today, and you were driving me crazy when you kept kissing my face! I wish you'd do that every time. And I'll be waiting for you to show me how you'll devour me! Your description was good, but a demonstration would be better. So could you whisper that you want me and need me in my ear while you're devouring me? I love to hear you whisper those kinds of things to me because I enjoy hearing them and your voice is *so* sexy it drives me insane! I almost called your office answering machine tonight to leave a voice mail, but I didn't want my roommate to hear me. I thought about you a lot after our conversation. I apologize for crying again. But you were more upset the last time I cried. Why was that? Is it because you enjoy the fact that I'm confused about my relationship with Alex? This whole situation is *very* confusing to me. You are the first person I've wanted since him. I've met many guys in the last four years, but I didn't like *any* of them until you. I can't stay away from you. I always have this problem with you, and I'm not sure why! Well, it's 11:25 p.m., and I have to take a shower. It's too bad you're not here to join me. I wish you could be here to give me more goodnight kisses! And you could pick several other places on my body aside from my lips to kiss since I typically wear something tiny (or perhaps nothing at all) to bed!

Faye

*****

Now I understood why Faye was snickering in class before I began my lecture. Having received such a tantalizing letter, I felt I needed to respond right away. I tried to be as interesting in my response to her, and she answered my message soon thereafter.

*****

Date: Wed, 16 May 2007 09:54:46 (EDT)
From: Laura McDonald
To: Phillip Demarco
Subject: Making you happy

Phillip,

I enjoyed your last little message! I'm glad I continue to brighten your days because, as you know, I want to make you happy. I'll see you this afternoon!

Faye

*****

Date: Thu, 17 May 2007 09:06:43 (EDT)
From   Laura McDonald
To: Phillip Demarco
Subject: Sneaking out

Phillip,

Yesterday was great! It didn't bother me too much that I had to sneak out of your office, but maybe someday I won't need to. I'll talk to you tonight at 7:00 p.m., okay?

Faye

*****

Our relationship escalated to us spending as much time together as we could. We began talking on the phone in the evenings often and going to lunch with her became a regular occurrence. While it was still difficult to arrange being alone, time together in my office, in the park, and on afternoon convertible rides became common. Sometimes, I'd bring her more chocolate truffles or little trinkets to let her know I was thinking about her. Even though Faye continued to spend most of her weekends with Alex, our affection for each other grew, and we looked for every opportunity to spend time together.

Likewise, Faye also began bringing me small gifts when she went home to Nashville or to visit Alex. She gave me things like beer and shot glasses, candy, and souvenirs from the Music City or Tennessee or boiled peanuts or succulent peaches from Georgia. I always appreciated her thoughtfulness, but it made me feel even better knowing I was on her mind during her trips.

*****

Date: Fri, 18 May 2007 12:20:22 (EDT)
From: Laura McDonald
To: Phillip Demarco
Subject: Whatever you say

Phillip,

Thank you for the lovely letter and my little guardian angel. I will keep it with me at *all* times because I need *you* with me at all times! Yes, I am much more comfortable around you now. I'm not even nervous anymore. Amazing, isn't it? I have a lot of things, one in particular, to tell you, but I'll wait a while longer before I do. I had fun with you last night, as usual. I'm disappointed I can't do something with you this weekend. Maybe I can next weekend. You looked *very* handsome today. I would have loved to put my hands all over you! I'll miss you, but I'm sure I'll think about your beautiful eyes, your smile, and your touch the whole time! (Don't you love the way I constantly change topics?) I'm sorry this message is short, I promise to make it up to you next week, okay? If you need cheering up on Monday from not seeing me, I'll be happy to do anything to help you return to your normal self. I'm lonesome for you already!

Faye

*****

Date: Mon, 21 May 2007 09:52:01 (EDT)
From: Laura McDonald
To: Phillip Demarco
Subject: Very educational

Phillip,

So you thought about me a lot last weekend? Well, what were you thinking? I thought about you also, as usual. You might not care to hear this, but I'll tell you anyway because it's something you may be interested in knowing. Every time Alex kisses me, I pretend it's *you*! I'm sure you don't enjoy hearing about him kissing me, but I figured you would enjoy the fact that I'm thinking about you when he does! I always wish I were kissing you. I know you'll tell me it's another sign, won't you? I never used to do that, and now it happens *all* the time!

I hope we can get together this weekend, and that we can spend more than a few hours with each other, which never seems to be long enough when I'm with you. I'm still looking forward to spending an entire night with you, too. If I didn't have a roommate, I would have already come up with a plan. Oh, well. I guess we'll have an opportunity someday.

You look handsome in your green shirt today! But you'd look better with it laying on the floor and my hands or lips (whichever you prefer) on your chest! Then again, you'd be even *more* desirable without those khaki pants! Why don't you come to work wearing nothing at all? I think it would be very educational for me!

Faye

*****

One of my playful activities with Faye was to give her pet names, besides Beautiful Princess or BP. I'd often make up new names when she visited, most of which I devised on the spot to describe something about her looks or engaging personality. I called her things like Dancing Queen (from the 1976 song by the group ABBA), Blondie, or Sunshine. But the pet name that surprised her most was when I referred to her one day as Moonbeam.

When I called Faye "Moonbeam," her jaw dropped. Then she said, "Where did you get that name?" When I didn't answer, she said, "You'll never believe this, but my parents almost named me Moonbeam when I was born! You are amazing!"

I replied, "Really? Your parents almost named you Moonbeam McDonald?"

"I know, right?" she said.

"Did they used to be hippies?" I asked.

"Well, they were a little hippie-ish, yes," she answered.

"Shocker. I like Laura Faye much better," I replied.

"So do I," she responded.

But Beautiful Princess was by far my favorite name for her!

Faye was also great at giving nicknames to other people she didn't know, but only in private conversations. She'd make up nicknames using adjectives based on their personal characteristics. For example, she'd refer to different people as "bad dresser tall guy" or "short girl with dirty hair" or "loud-talking skinny guy" or "muscle guy with old shoes," etc. The names were always funny, and the recipients of her humor were never aware of how she perceived them.

Over the next several days, we exchanged a series of messages that were very revealing of what we thought of each other.

*****

Date: Tue, 22 May 2007 09:10:35 (EDT)
From: Laura McDonald
To: Phillip Demarco
Subject: Another sign

Phillip,

I need to say, you're wonderful, just *wonderful*! I love how you can always put a big smile on my face! Your pet names for me are getting better every day.

Our time in your office yesterday afternoon was fantastic! I'm glad you closed your door because I needed a giant hug and a kiss. Now I still don't know what you're referring to when you said, "Don't do that when Allen is in the elevator." I mean, I didn't do very much, well, except for grabbing you somewhere. It's your fault I did because if you didn't look so good, I could keep my hands off you! I'm looking forward to Thursday; it will be great to be out in public with you again. How exciting!

Why are you glad I think about you when I'm kissing Alex? I'm not sure what it means, but it could be another sign. It shows I don't just have a crush on you, but I've known that for a long while now. If the same thing happens to you, it must mean you're more than just infatuated with me, right?

Well, I'll see you at lunch! I'll also come by later this afternoon because lunch won't be enough time with you. Plus, I have some questions about our homework for class.

Perhaps I can put my hand on your cute little knee (or something else) while I'm there!

Faye

*****

Date: Tue, 22 May 2007 10:45:15 (EDT)
From: Phillip Demarco
To: Laura McDonald
Subject: It IS a sign

BP,

Yes, I am much more than infatuated with you! And there's no doubt that you thinking about me when you're kissing Alex is another sign. I think it's a sign you'll end up with me instead of him! Have I ever told you I think of you when I kiss Sophia, too?
I'll see you in a few minutes!

PD

*****

Date: Tue, 22 May 2007 16:10:57 (EDT)
From: Laura McDonald
To: Phillip Demarco
Subject: Delectable

Phillip,

Hello, handsome! Lunch was wonderful with you today, as it always is! I'm about to head home now to finish my homework and eat more of those delectable cookies I baked last night! I guess you can call me Betty Crocker now, too.

So, why do you think I'll end up with you instead of Alex? Would you want me to be with you? I mean, if I did, you'd never get rid of me. How would you handle being stuck with me forever?

You looked terrific today, as always! I wanted to sit on your lap so you could describe all those experiments you need to conduct on me. I guess you can tell me about them on Thursday (and I won't forget either)!

Well, I'll come by tomorrow! And I'll be wearing something tiny, very sexy, and *very* easy to remove (with your hands *or* teeth, although I'd prefer your teeth)!

Faye

*****

Date: Wed, 23 May 2007 09:43:06 (EDT)
From: Laura McDonald
To: Phillip Demarco
Subject: Concentration

Phillip,

I didn't mention it at lunch yesterday, but I enjoyed reading how you think I'll end up with you instead of Alex. If you have thought about that happening, you must want it to happen, right? I like it when you ponder those things because I ponder them a lot! I always think how wonderful it would be to hold you and kiss you *every* day! And wouldn't it be great to spend all our nights together and wake up in each other's arms? And, Phillip, I have a secret, but I can't tell you what it is yet. I know you won't believe me, but it's true. Maybe I'll tell you someday soon.

Why would you think I'm tired of writing to you? One of my favorite parts of the day is getting to read your wonderful messages and write you back! You know, I was thinking how happy you make me! My dream about becoming more than just your student came true. I'm glad it did because I enjoy all our talks, stares, hugs, etc., and the time we spend together. Every day, I wake up, and I get all excited and anxious about seeing you. You're always on my mind. I am *crazy* about you, and I've fallen very hard for you! You are *terrific*! Well, I'm off to class. I can't wait until tomorrow night!

Faye

*****

Date: Wed, 23 May 2007 15:08:19 (EDT)
From: Phillip Demarco
To: Laura McDonald
Subject: Choices

My dearest Faye,

Your message was wonderful. Thank you! You always seem to know how to brighten my day. How do you know this, anyhow? You make me feel great. Seeing you in the morning or speaking with you or getting a message from you makes me happy too! I hope you're *never* able to concentrate on anything but me! I'd enjoy it more if you only focused on me! I'm not having a great semester in the concentration department either and I'm sure you know why.

To answer your question, *yes*! I *would* want you to end up with me! I contemplate it a lot too and how wonderful it would be if we were together always, and the thought of spending *every* night with you is, well, overwhelming! I'm very glad you've also considered these possibilities. Do you want it to happen too? I hope so.

So you have something to tell me? I'm sure I'd enjoy hearing it *every* day! And I *love* when you talk about choosing me and us being together always. It's important to me to hear those things from you to help me understand what this relationship means to you. There may be something I want to say to you, too. Perhaps we could tell each other this important information at the same time! I'd rather we told each other sooner instead of later, wouldn't you?

I know we'll have fun tomorrow night! You drove *me* crazy this morning telling me about your see-through whatever-it-was you were wearing! I've had some wild fantasies over it already, and you say *I'm* mean to *you*! It's *you* who's mean to *me*!

Well, I just hung up the phone from talking to you. I love when you call me. In fact, I love *everything* you do, sweet princess!

Phillip

*****

Date: Thu, 24 May 2007 02:33:56 (EDT)
From: Laura McDonald
To: Phillip Demarco
Subject: Sooner not later

Phillip,

Now what are you going to tell *me*? And when should we tell each other these things? I think I'd also prefer to do it sooner rather than later. I'm so happy we found each other too. You always make me feel wonderful! I'll finish this letter tomorrow, okay? I can't wait until tonight!

Faye

*****

Faye and I went to dinner at the Olive Garden on Clark Butler Boulevard in southwest Gainesville. The Olive

Garden was Faye's favorite restaurant, and it was at an out-of-the-way location where we didn't need to worry about being seen together. We sat at a small table against the left wall in the bar area behind the entrance and had a fun conversation about many things while we ate. When we finished eating, we didn't have much time, and Faye's roommate was home, so we couldn't go to her apartment. Instead, we drove out to Gum Root Park near Newnans Lake on NE Twenty-Seventh Avenue., close to my house. We found a quiet and deserted lot where we parked, talked, held hands, and kissed. I felt the passion in Faye's kisses more than ever, and I was sure she could feel mine. We touched each other, expressing our mutual desires before we melted into each other's arms.

Faye looked at me and said, "Okay, I'm ready to tell you my secret. Do you want to hear it?"

"Yes I do, BP. I've been waiting."

Then she sat up straight, appeared to be a little nervous, and said, "Well, Phillip, I love you, and I have for a long time. I couldn't wait any longer to say it. I hope you wanted to hear it."

"Faye, I'm glad you told me because I love you, too. I'm sure of it!"

We smiled at each other, and Faye said, "You do? You love me too? I'm *so* glad you told me, Phillip! It's amazing to hear!"

We both felt relieved and happy, and we kissed and kissed again, and our kisses became more meaningful than ever.

Soon, we had to call it an evening, so I drove Faye back to her car and followed her until she parked in front of her building, walked up the stairs, and went inside, so I knew she was safe. It took a tremendous amount of restraint on my part to not follow her into her apartment. After class the next morning, she wrote me.

*****

Date: Fri, 25 May 2007 09:23:01 (EDT)
From: Laura McDonald
To: Phillip Demarco
Subject: Your eyes

Phillip,

I had a *great* time with you last night! Thank you for dinner. It was wonderful! When can we meet this weekend? I hope it's for more than a few hours because I need more time to gaze into your beautiful eyes!

I'm very glad I told you my secret because I enjoyed hearing yours too! Please tell me you love me anytime. In fact, I wouldn't mind hearing it right now!

I wish I could see you tonight, but I know I can't. How sad! Bailee won't be home tomorrow, so you could come over to my apartment if you can get away. I hope you can!

Faye

*****

Date: Fri, 25 May 2007 12:50:11 (EDT)
From: Laura McDonald
To: Phillip Demarco
Subject: The Laws of Faye

Hello, handsome!

Well, the letter you sent was wonderful! I loved *every* word! So you'd do anything to win me away from Alex? What would you do? I think you've already been trying very hard. Well, if you have, you've been doing a superb job! All I ever do is think about how wonderful I feel when we're together. I'm so glad you have the same feelings for me as

I do for you. All I could think about in class this morning was how much I wanted to touch you, kiss you, and tell you I love you!

I wish we could do something again before next week because even though we were together last night, I already miss you. This is a fantastic relationship we have, isn't it? I didn't expect any of this to happen. I figured you'd be tired of me by now, but I was wrong. As I have told you many times before, I will never tire of you. I would be content if we could spend all our free time together. I am so glad we told each other our secrets because it has made our wonderful relationship even better. What other secrets does your heart hold? You know you can tell me anything, anytime, don't you? (*hint, hint*). I love hearing you tell me how you feel about me! So, from now on, the laws of Faye require you to inform me of *everything*; otherwise, I will punish you! Well, I must go now, but I'll stop by your office before I leave so I can gaze into your beautiful blue eyes! I'll be there in a few minutes, or later. Faye

*****

The next Thursday, Sophia needed to go to New York for work and would return on Monday. She asked me to join her, but I declined. I made the excuse my class schedule wouldn't allow me to be gone on both Friday and Monday. But I told her that so I could stay in Gainesville alone. Since Faye wasn't leaving either, we'd have more time together. And we spent every hour possible with each other over the weekend! We ate out, watched movies, took drives, went rollerblading, and made love—sweet and tender love, and very passionate love. And although we still couldn't spend an entire night together for fear of her roommate finding out, we did everything else we wanted.

Faye enjoyed rollerblading and went often, but I'd never been, and she wanted me to try it. She had trained as an ice-skater and dancer and was excellent at "blading." She found a great place to rollerblade: an industrial park with a small lake encircled with a concrete sidewalk. The lake also had a dock and a gazebo near the parking lot. Since we'd planned to meet there on Saturday at 11:00 a.m., I stopped at the gazebo before picking her up and laid a pink rose on the wooden bench where I planned for us to go first. When Faye found it after we arrived, a teardrop rolled down her face from each eye before giving me a big hug and kiss. As the crying began, so did her classic hand waving to help dry her tears. I never liked to see Faye cry, even when she cried because of something good. I loved surprising her with a rose.

*****

Date: Mon, 28 May 2007 11:19:58 (EDT)
From: Laura McDonald
To: Phillip Demarco
Subject: Your rose

Phillip,

I'm about to go rollerblading since you have a lunch meeting. I'm sorry you can't come with me again! I loved *every* minute of last weekend! And you are very charming. I didn't know what to say when you put the rose in the gazebo for me. Your gesture made me feel so special! Thank you! I can't believe we spent so much time together over the weekend, can you?

You'd better think about me while you're in your meeting! Thank you again for the wonderful three days we had together. I enjoyed everything we did.

Faye

*****

Date: Thu, 31 May 2007 18:03:20 (EDT)
From: Laura McDonald
To: Phillip Demarco
Subject: Whispers

Phillip,

    I'm glad I surprised you again today! And you could have seen me twice. I got out of my lab at 4:00 p.m. and walked by your office and guess what? You weren't there! I was very disappointed! I'm sorry I never sent you an "I don't have time to write, but I love you" message. Since we won't see each other tonight, you could always call me to discuss experiments or something else educational. It would help me deal with not seeing you. But if you call and use the same voice as when you whisper in my ear, I might attack you! You'd never want me to take advantage of you, right?
    Well, I've got a headache, so I'll close now. It must be from missing you or something. I *love you*!!!!!!!

Faye

*****

    Soon after class on Friday morning, I received another lovely and romantic message.

*****

Date: Fri, 1 Jun 2007 11:01:40 (EDT)
From: Laura McDonald
To: Phillip Demarco
Subject: Most of all

Phillip,

    I just wanted to say…………*I want you*! *I need you*! *I miss you*!

But most of all, *I love you*!!!!!!!!!!!

Faye

*****

We desired to spend even more time together during the weeks ahead. So, we thought we'd find a place where we could both park in the morning and we'd get to walk to our cars together each afternoon. We found the First Lutheran Church on NW Fifth Avenue, which offered free parking for us both, so Faye and I could have twenty more minutes together each day while walking to our cars.

CHAPTER 9

I Wanted to Surprise You

Over the next few weeks, the written playfulness between Faye and me not only continued, but also intensified. Her messages were always entertaining, and they brought us closer. As a result, our relationship became more open, more fun, and much more sexual! We'd only known each other for ten months, but it felt like much longer because of our mutual openness.

*****

Date: Fri, 1 Jun 2007 16:21:15 (EDT)
From: Laura McDonald
To: Phillip Demarco
Subject: Attacking me

Phillip,

I see you enjoyed my little message. I wish we could have seen each other more this week. I'm having withdrawal pains because I haven't had your wonderful hands all over my face enough. I guess we'll make up for it next week, and I'll remember everything you said this morning, especially that you love me. You may wonder why I don't always say, "I love you too" after you say it to me. Well, I'm too busy purring, that's why. Hearing you say it makes me feel incredible! I'm too focused on what you said to answer. (Does that make any sense? If not, I'll explain it later). I hope you have a good weekend, even though we won't be together. I hate it that your wife ignores you. It even annoys me when she does. I never would. There might be times when I'd rather not talk because I'd want your delightful mouth to be doing things other than talking, if you know what I mean! You may attack me whenever you wish. Now I've started thinking about doing certain things with you, and I can't quit. This is terrible! If you're anywhere near me, I want to touch you and kiss you. It's a good thing we're always in your office or out in public because if we weren't, I'd be *all over you*! Well, I must stop thinking about this. Have fun playing golf if it doesn't rain. I'll miss you this weekend! Remember, I love you!

Faye

*****

I didn't enjoy weekends not seeing Faye. Sophia and I weren't having much fun anymore, and they often seemed to drag. Faye was on my mind no matter what I was doing: working on my car, doing yard work, shopping, grading exams, and even when I was with Sophia. The thought of Faye distracted me constantly, and I was sure Sophia knew my thoughts were elsewhere. Maybe that was why she ignored me so often, or there may have been other reasons. Sophia and I had now been married for fifteen years, which was almost as long as Faye had been alive. I felt guilty about my relationship with Faye, but I always rationalized I couldn't let her go, regardless of the inevitable consequences ahead for me. She made me feel young again and being with her was exciting! There was no doubt we loved each other. But I still didn't understand her being in love with me. Perhaps someday I would.

I looked forward to Mondays because I knew I'd see Faye in class. Sometimes, it was difficult to teach and stay focused with Faye seated in the front row, smiling and looking irresistible. She often followed me to my office after class when she had time. But she always found time to write.

*****

Date: Mon, 4 Jun 2007 09:25:06 (EDT)
From: Laura McDonald
To: Phillip Demarco
Subject: New swimsuit

Phillip,

Don't people realize they're not supposed to come to your office at 9:00 a.m.? I just walked by, and someone was in there, meaning I won't see you anymore this morning! I'm very upset about this. The *nerve* of some people!

So you enjoyed the voice mail I left on your answering machine last night? Why didn't you return my call? If you got my message ten minutes after I left it, I wasn't asleep yet! Can you call me tonight instead?

I bought a new swimsuit yesterday. I think you'll like it even though I don't know when you'll see it. Then again, you'd enjoy removing my swimsuit more than looking at it, wouldn't you?

I won't have much free time after today because I have three projects due, and I must also study for the exam in your class. It will be a miserable week!

Well, I'll walk by your office later to see if you're alone. I hope so!

Faye

*****

Date: Mon, 4 Jun 2007 20:15:01 (EDT)
From: Laura McDonald
To: Phillip Demarco
Subject: Hang up

Phillip,

I was too busy with schoolwork to write you back earlier. I'm sorry. I finished working on one of my many projects, and now I'm about to study for your test. Sounds exciting, doesn't it?

It was great to see you this afternoon. After this weekend, I needed a giant hug from you, so thank you! I still wish you had called last night so I could have heard your wonderful voice! Remember, you can call whenever you want. If my roommate answers, just hang up or something. I'd love to talk to you tonight, so please call, if possible. I know this message is *another* short one, but I have to study.

Faye

*****

Date: Wed, 6 Jun 2007 19:26:29 (EDT)
From: Laura McDonald
To: Phillip Demarco
Subject: Enough of you

Phillip,

I've had a *very* long day. I'm in severe need of having your arms wrapped around me. I'd love to talk to you since I didn't get my "Faye hour" with you today. So if you have the chance, *please* call me!

Are you sure you'd do *anything* for me? I love the thought of that. Do you want to know why I can't wait long before seeing you again? Well, I'll tell you. It's because I *always* have a wonderful time when I'm with you. I love talking (?) to you; you make me feel incredible (do I make you feel the same way?), and *I love you*! I could *never* get enough of you. I would be content if I could stare at you all day long!

I hope you can call tonight, but if not, I'll see you tomorrow since I must come by and tell you happy birthday! (You may have thought I forgot all about it? Well, I didn't!) I miss you!

Faye

*****

After class that next morning, Faye and I walked to my office together. While she didn't have time to stay, she handed me a birthday card! Faye also sent me a message later in the morning. Our playfulness continued, and these messages opened new areas for our teasing.

*****

Date: Thu, 7 Jun 2007 11:26:07 (EDT)
From: Laura McDonald
To: Phillip Demarco
Subject: Celebration

Phillip,

Thank you *so* much for calling me last night. Your whispers are *very* exciting and the things you said to me were *very* sexy! I would have taken my panties off if you had been there. It wouldn't be any fun if I took them off when I was alone. I'm sure you left all your clothes on too, now didn't you? Sorry I didn't whisper back to you, but as you know, I was too busy purring. You were driving me *crazy*! I don't know why, but you're the only person who does that just by whispering to me.

It's too bad we couldn't spend today together since it's your birthday, and I know a very personal way we could celebrate. We can't celebrate the same at the gazebo. I suppose I'll give you this other gift the next time we're alone, okay?

Don't forget, I'm upset with you for giving us such a hard test yesterday. I'm glad you said you'll make up for it! I liked your idea about how you will too. You seemed surprised when I told you I liked it. Why was that? I would go anywhere you wanted if it meant we could have some time to be alone. You know, you are *wonderful*! I love everything about you, except that you're married! You always know how to make me smile. All you have to do is sit there and let me stare at you to put a smile on my face. I saw you an hour ago, and I miss you already! I'm very jealous of your wife getting to go out to eat with tonight on your birthday. I wish it were me instead. Well, have fun tonight (just remember to think about me)!

Well, I've got to get lunch before my lab! Oh, is our homework due tomorrow or on Monday? *Happy birthday*!!!!!!!!!!!!!!!!!!!!!

Love, Faye

*****

Date: Thu, 7 Jun 2007 1:42:37 (EDT)
From: Phillip Demarco
To: Laura McDonald
Subject: Jealous

BP,

I loved calling you and whispering to you! I may have even removed some of my clothing last night during our conversation. You should have been there.

Faye, I'm glad you're jealous of my wife. But remember, I'm envious of Alex too!

I might leave early today since I can't walk to the parking lot with you because of your late lab. I'm not sure where we will have dinner. How about if I call you later?

Phillip

*****

Date: Thu, 7 Jun 2007 16:26:39 (EDT)
From: Laura McDonald
To: Phillip Demarco
Subject: Missing clothing

Phillip,

So, you removed some clothing last night while we were talking? Just what did you remove? My guess is you took off your shirt or something boring, right? I have a question for you: what were you planning on telling me to do if I removed my panties? Here's another question: what were *you* doing after taking off whatever clothing you claim to have removed? I'm sure you weren't doing anything since you took nothing off, were you? Yes, call me later because I'm dying to know the answers to these burning questions! If you call me, I'll do anything you wish. I'll even take off all my clothes if that's what you want!

I would have come by your office after I got out of my lab early at 3:45 p.m., but I figured you already left. Now I know why you made the homework due on Monday instead of Friday! You were just trying to keep me busy so I wouldn't have time to do anything else on the weekend. That's so sneaky of you.

Why are you glad I'm jealous of your wife? You should know I'm always a little jealous because you spend so much time at home with her. I would rather have you with me instead. I assume you feel the same way about Alex, though, so I guess we're even. Well, I'm going home now, so I'll talk to you later.

Remember to call me at 1-900-PURRING tonight. I would love to hear your seductive little whispers again! Have fun at dinner! (I hope they sing to you in the restaurant!) Happy birthday again!

Faye

*****

Date: Fri, 8 Jun 2007 09:40:00 (EDT)
From: Laura McDonald
To: Phillip Demarco
Subject: Payback!

Phillip,

So you enjoyed our phone conversation last night? I found it to be very stimulating. But I *will* get even with you for all your teasing. When you asked me why I was smiling this morning, I was thinking of ways to pay you back. And I already know the method I'll use. Tying your hands together would be a perfect way. Then I can tease you and do whatever I want, and you can't stop me! I could kiss your entire body while letting my fingers explore. And I'll do some of those oral experiments I described on the phone. I'll start by... well; I guess you'll find out some other time!

Are we going to have lunch at the park someday? That'll be fun! If I was alone with you there, I might not let you go back to work! I can't believe you said you took off your socks when we talked on Wednesday night. That's not what I expected to hear. Perhaps you'll take off more next time. I even took my shirt off last night!

Faye

*****

In the afternoon, we went rollerblading during the two hours Faye had free before Alex arrived for the weekend. It seemed our rollerblading dates had evolved into a short time skating, but mostly talking in the gazebo, feeding the ducks, and kissing when nobody else was nearby. Still, we both wished we could find more time to be alone together instead of always being in public.

On Monday, I received more amusing messages from Faye.

*****

Date: Mon, 11 Jun 2007 09:43:42 (EDT)
From: Laura McDonald
To: Phillip Demarco
Subject: More passion

Phillip,

Hola, como estas? Creo que estes muy bien esta tarde! Quiero que tu sepas que you te quiero, te necesito, y la mas imporatante, te amo!

I could continue to write in Spanish, but it wouldn't be much fun for you to receive a letter you couldn't read. Try to figure out what it says. But here's some advice. It might be a mistake if you ask someone to translate it for you!

This weekend, I confirmed you and I have far more passion than Alex and me, even though I've known that for a while. I thought about you the whole time we were apart. Well, I'm out of time, so I'll meet you at 4:45 p.m., okay? I can't wait to have you run your fingers through my haa-ir!

Your passionate princess

*****

Faye studied Spanish for several years in school and was fluent in the language. I wasn't, which she knew, so she wrote those first sentences to tease me. But the University of Florida has a large and wonderful library system. So off I went to find some Spanish books to help me translate her message, and in less than one hour, I did.

Faye's message translated as, "Hello, how are you? I think you're very well this afternoon! You need to know I want you, I need you, and the most important thing, I love you!" Now Faye had me purring!

The "haa-ir" reference was about the way she pronounced the word hair. She didn't have much of a Southern drawl in her speech except for certain words. And "hair" was the one she pronounced with the deepest drawl of all, using two syllables, which I teased her about every time she said the word. But Faye was always wonderful at laughing at herself, which was another reason I found her to be so delightful!

*****

Date: Mon, 11 Jun 2007 22:56:09 (EDT)
From: Laura McDonald
To: Phillip Demarco
Subject: Matching clothing

Phillip,

I had a very good time in your office this afternoon. It's frustrating we can't spend more time together away from campus. I hope we can soon though. You looked incredible today in your green shirt. (You know it would match my green bra and panties! Maybe someday, we should see how well they do. But we'd need to take them off to see.) I wish you could have called me tonight because I would have loved talking to you.

Are you sure you won't lose interest in me? I hope not, because I'll *never* lose interest in you! How could I when you make me purr so much? I know I still don't always tell you what I'm thinking as much as you'd like. Sometimes, I'm only focused on wanting to tear off your clothing. But the rest of the time, I *am* having other thoughts. They're always very good thoughts about you and how much I enjoy seeing you and how much I love you! I also think about the wonderful life we could have together. Now you have some idea about what I'm always thinking!

Okay, I'm finished rambling. I've been missing you ever since I left your office, can't you tell?

Faye

*****

Date: Wed, 13 Jun 2007 10:50:23 (EDT)
From: Laura McDonald
To: Phillip Demarco
Subject: Making me purr

Phillip,

So my low-cut shirt got your attention this morning in class? I was trying to, so I'm glad I did. I'm very upset we couldn't close your office door so I could sit in your lap today.

Last fall, it worried me I wouldn't see you anymore. Now I see you almost every day. I'm *so* glad all this happened! We'd have a great time if we were always together, wouldn't we? Just thinking about that makes me purr!

Now remember, you are to call me tonight if you can! I need to hear your wonderful whispers! All I ever do anymore is think about you! You are *terrific*!

And one more thing, *Pour le dejeuner en lundi, tu n'as pas besoin d'acheter la nouriture parce que la seul chose que je veux a manger est tu!*

Faye

*****

Yes this time, Faye was teasing me in French. Now I needed another trip to the library to decipher her French message. This one took longer, but I translated it as "For lunch on Monday, you don't need to buy the food because the only thing I want to eat is you!" Yes, Faye had overcome her inhibitions, and I *loved* it! But now it was my turn to tease her back, so I needed to visit the foreign language section of Smathers Libraries again the next morning so I could write something to her in Italian!

*****

Date: Thu, 14 Jun 2007 11:41:15 (EDT)
From: Phillip Demarco
To: Laura McDonald
Subject   Language of love

Faye,

I have a question for you: does it make you uncomfortable when I talk about us being together always? The reason I'm asking is because sometimes, I feel you'd rather not discuss it when I bring it up. I guess I don't always know what you're thinking, so that's why I ask. But I never want to make you uncomfortable.

And yes, the shirt you wore yesterday was very sexy, and I had a difficult time concentrating in class because of it. So it's your fault my lecture was so bad.

I'm glad I make you happy! You do the same for me, and I don't tell you that enough. And here's something else I don't say often enough: *Il tuo nome è una melodia per le mie orecchie e il solo pensiero di si illumina la mia giornata immensamente! E io vi amo molto!*

Did I ever tell you I'm saving all your wonderful emails for a book someday?

Phillip

*****

Date: Fri, 15 Jun 2007 18:31:09 (EDT)
From: Laura McDonald
To   Phillip Demarco
Subject   Melody to your ears

Phillip,

Yes, you told me about saving my emails many times already. That's fine, but when you put them in a book, don't you dare use my real name!

And no, it doesn't make me uncomfortable when you talk about us being together. Sometimes, you ask questions I know you won't appreciate the answers to, like when I tell you I would miss Alex if we were together. That's why I try not to bring it up. But don't think you can't ask me those things because you think it might bother me because it won't.

Now what did you write to me in Italian? Here's my guess (without using a dictionary). It says something about my name is a melody to your ears. Am I anywhere near the correct translation? I thought I'd try, at least. I'll see you on Sunday, and I'll miss you until then!

Faye

*****

Faye's translation was correct for the first part of my Italian message, although she didn't get the most important part. The complete translation is this: "Your name is a melody to my ears, and the mere thought of you brightens my day immensely! And I love you very much!"

A friend of mine had a boat he kept at Lochloosa Harbor near Hawthorne, Florida, a little southeast of Gainesville, off Highway 301, which he'd let me borrow from time to time. Since he planned to be out of town for the upcoming weekend, I asked to use it so I could take Faye out on the water on Sunday afternoon. I gave her directions, and she met me at the dock at 2:00 p.m. It was a beautiful but hot day, and it was nice to cool off with the breeze on the boat. We explored a lot of the lake, although there were many boats out. After about an hour, we stopped at a small, deserted island in a secluded location. It was a perfect place to take a dip in the shallow water and relax with Faye. We parked under some shady trees, shut off the engine, threw out the anchor, and jumped in the lake. After we climbed back into the boat and dried off, I folded down the seat so we could enjoy each other the way we both wanted. Faye was jaw-dropping gorgeous in her tiny and tight bikini. It didn't take long for us to lie down next to each other and start kissing and groping each other. Soon, her bikini bottoms found their way to the deck of the boat, and we were free to make love. Except, during our tantalizing foreplay, another boat pulled up to the island about fifty yards away. Faye and I looked at each other, first panicking, then chuckling at the situation. Since neither of us was an exhibitionist, we thought it would be best if we got dressed and drove off before anyone saw us there naked. After returning to the dock and laughing and joking most of the way about what happened, we had another good story to tell. And it was one more episode of our playtime being interrupted.

As the summer progressed, we took advantage of every opportunity to be together—having lunch, walking to our cars in the afternoon, rollerblading in the early evening, and meeting at night and on weekends whenever we could. We also spent many hours in my office, and I saw her in class. But it was difficult to arrange time alone. Although when we did, it was worth the wait. Faye would often ask how I got my other work done, since I spent so much time with her. I laughed and told her she was my top priority. The next day Faye wrote to tell me she enjoyed the boat ride. Then during the week, we spent some time alone in my office, which she discussed in later messages.

*****

Date: Mon, 18 Jun 2007 10:25:39 (EDT)
From: Laura McDonald
To: Phillip Demarco
Subject: My mouth

Phillip,

I had a marvelous time at the lake with you yesterday. Thank you for inviting me! I think I'll call you "Skipper" from now on, or at least when we're in a boat. All that "sitting" in the boat drove me crazy! I can't believe our activities got interrupted *again*! I still want to spend a night together soon.

Faye

*****

Date: Tue, 19 Jun 2007 11:44:27 (EDT)
From: Laura McDonald
To: Phillip Demarco
Subject: Your lips

Phillip,

Well, I was expecting a message from you this morning, and I didn't receive one! I'm very disappointed with this!

You are terrible! I looked up, and there you were, staring at me from behind a pole in the computer lab, and you were playing with your lips! Why do you always insist on teasing me? I never tease you that way! Why do you keep looking at me? I came to the lab to write you a message, and if it makes no sense, it's your fault because you're distracting me! I love the shirt you're wearing today. It's too bad I can't take it off you right now!

Now back to my letter. I missed you last night! I'm sorry I was *so* late getting to your office yesterday. I'll make it up to you in some special way, okay?

I wish I could see you, but I know you're busy. I'm heading home after I finish this, and I won't be coming back until tomorrow. I hope we can talk later!

Faye

*****

Date: Thu, 21 Jun 2007 13:24:01 (EDT)
From: Laura McDonald
To: Phillip Demarco
Subject: Saved kisses

Hello, handsome!

I had a *wonderful* time yesterday. And thank you for calling last night. You surprised me! You should have driven over to my apartment instead of calling. All I could think about today was yesterday afternoon. You excite me so much! You only need to touch me, or whisper in my ear to get me excited. I loved doing all those experiments on you. Did you enjoy them too?

I wish you weren't going to a conference next week. You better have plenty of kisses saved up for me when you get back. I'll be waiting to receive them. You'll be on my mind the entire time you're gone.

Yesterday, when you kept asking me what I was thinking, and I gave my usual answer of "nothing", my thoughts were about how much I love you! It's far more than you realize, and I just want you to know that! Well, I'll quit writing now so I can come and gaze into your beautiful eyes before I leave. Besides, I have some wonderful news to tell you. So I'll talk to you in a minute!

Faye

*****

Just as I finished reading Faye's message, she arrived at my door and danced into my office.

I asked, "Faye, what's up? You look very excited."

Faye answered, "Well, that's because I am. I have some fabulous news!"

"What news is that?" I responded.

"I'm moving out of Bivens Cove. I found a little house to rent, and I'll live there all alone until Alex and I get married. Isn't that great?" she responded.

"It's better than great, Faye. It's amazing!" I said.

I didn't want to hear about Faye marrying Alex, but it thrilled me to know we would now have more opportunities to be alone together.

Faye added, "And the best part is, it's close to campus and only a short walk from where we park!"

All I could say was, "Wow! Why didn't you tell me you were thinking of moving?"

"I wanted to surprise you," she answered.

"Well, you sure did!" I replied.

CHAPTER 10

Smacked Back to Reality

Faye rented a small, two-bedroom, furnished house just north of W. University Avenue, close to the lot where we began parking our cars earlier in the summer. It was about a twenty-minute walk from my office, and Faye would no longer need to drive to school. The best part was she'd live alone until Alex moved to Gainesville after they got married and he separated from the military. We both had visions of spending many hours at her new place in the weeks and months ahead. Neither of us could wait!

The first thing I needed to do after I got back from my conference was to load some software on the machines in the computer lab. Faye was in the lab working, although I didn't know it. I received this message from her when I got back to my office.

*****

Date: Thu, 28 Jun 2007 10:24:01 (EDT)
From: Laura McDonald
To: Phillip Demarco
Subject: Where?

Phillip,

I'm so glad you're back from your conference. I missed you! You don't know it, but I'm in the computer lab right now staring at you! I'll only be here for a little longer because I've got to go to my new house to finish my move-in sheet and have lunch before you come over at 1:00 p.m. I thought it would be a good idea to give you my address; it's a little white house at 1918 NW Second Avenue. I'll be there on time too, so don't be late!

Faye

*****

Faye's house was a single-story, wooden-frame home with a tiny porch in front. The door opened into the living room, which had a fireplace in the far left corner, and the kitchen was on the right. A hallway on the left led from the living room to two bedrooms and a bathroom. The walls were white, and the carpeting was gray throughout the 1,200 square-foot house.

We hadn't been alone together in quite a while, which was obvious when I arrived. Within seconds after I knocked on the front door, Faye opened it, smiled, grabbed my arm, and yanked me inside, slamming the door behind me. She pushed me back against the wall and kissed me harder than ever. As we began tearing the clothes off each other, we stumbled down the hallway into her bedroom and fell onto her bed. Our kisses were wet and frantic, as it had been over a month since we made love. It felt wonderful to kiss her, touch her, hold her, and undress her again. We spent the entire afternoon playing, teasing, and loving, with no interruptions, no roommate, and no need to be anywhere else. We explored each other in ways we often talked about, and we performed some of those experiments we joked about, too. I learned more about Faye's likes and dislikes and what sexual things excited her, and she learned the same about me. It was a glorious afternoon of us expressing our love for each other. When it was time for me to go home, we were both exhausted. Still, we hated saying goodbye, which took a long time. The first time I attempted to leave after I dressed, we kissed and couldn't resist falling back onto the bed to make love once more before I could get out the door. It would have been easy for me to stay all night.

*****

Date: Fri, 29 Jun 2007 13:08:25 (EDT)
From: Laura McDonald
To: Phillip Demarco
Subject: Certain body parts

Phillip,

I had a *wonderful* time yesterday! But next time, I might not let you leave at all! What would you think about that? I wish Alex wasn't coming this weekend so we could see each other more, but I guess I won't get my hands on you again until next week.

You looked great in class this morning. I'll bet you can figure out what I was thinking about when you were writing on the board, can't you? All I'm saying is, it was very hard for me to concentrate and not stare at certain body parts of yours I reacquainted myself with yesterday!

Faye

*****

We continued to meet at her place every chance we had, often in the afternoons before I went home for the day. The next week, we met three days in a row before I left on a business trip to Washington, DC, on Thursday. I would be away an entire week, so it would be a long time until I'd see Faye again. I wanted her to come to DC with me, but she couldn't arrange it with her classes, her schoolwork, and Alex. I knew I would miss her terribly. During my trip, I received several messages from her. I could tell she missed me, too.

*****

Date: Fri, 13 Jul 2007 13:12:40 (EDT)
From: Laura McDonald
To: Phillip Demarco
Subject: Tantalizing voice

My dear professor,

I miss you *more* than I thought I would! All I did yesterday was think about you. I have gotten so used to spending time with you I've now gone into "Phillip withdrawal"! I hope you're having a great time even though I'd rather have you here with me. I'm waiting to touch your wonderful face and body. I hope you are missing me too, and that I get to hear your tantalizing voice on Sunday when you call; just talking to you will drive me crazy!

Faye

*****

Date: Wed, 18 Jul 2007 13:09:35 (EDT)
From: Laura McDonald
To: Phillip Demarco
Subject: Missing you BAD!

Hello, handsome,

I wish you would hurry and come home!

Faye

*****

After arriving at the Gainesville Regional Airport on my return from Washington, DC, I drove straight to Faye's house, even though I didn't have much time. Faye was happy I stopped to see her before going home. She was passionate, playful, and loving, which always made me want her even more.

*****

Date: Mon, 23 Jul 2007 13:21:06 (EDT)
From: Laura McDonald
To: Phillip Demarco
Subject: Very disappointed

Phillip,

Well, I came to your office, and you weren't there! I was very disappointed! I wish I could have seen you more last week, but with your trip and all my schoolwork and Alex being here on the weekend, it made it very hard. This week, I'll have more time, so perhaps we can get together a lot. I might go rollerblading, but I'm not sure what time yet, so if I go, I'll call and leave a message so you can come and see me (if you have time). Well, I am about to starve to death, so I must eat lunch. I'll talk to you later or tomorrow (I hope)!

Faye

*****

Date: Tue, 24 Jul 2007 11:11:39 (EDT)
From: Laura McDonald
To: Phillip Demarco
Subject: Come to my house

Phillip,

I wondered if you'd be interested in meeting me sometime today. So are you? If you are, just let me know what time you can come over, okay? As you may have guessed, I didn't rollerblade yesterday because of the rain, which was very disappointing! I hope you're able to come over later; I need to see you bad!

Faye

*****

Date: Tue, 24 Jul 2007 12:33:51 (EDT)
From: Phillip Demarco
To: Laura McDonald
Subject: YES!

BP,

I miss you too, and I would *love* to meet you today! I'll be there at 3:00 p.m.!

PD

*****

We spent a lot of time together the rest of the week: in my office, at her house, rollerblading, and in class. But once again, I had to leave on the following Monday evening for yet another conference, this time in Denver, and I wouldn't get to see her at all for another entire week. I used to enjoy attending conferences and out-of-town meetings, but now those trips became miserable for me when Faye and I were apart. I thought how wonderful it would be if she could go with me. Perhaps she could someday.

*****

Date: Fri, 27 Jul 2007 13:58:26 (EDT)
From: Laura McDonald
To: Phillip Demarco
Subject: Interrupted

Phillip,

I had a great time in your office, even though we got interrupted! I'll miss you this weekend when Alex is here and next week when you're gone (again)! I'll stop by on Monday so I can gaze into your beautiful eyes once more before you leave for your trip! *I love you*!

Faye

*****

Faye came by for a short time before I had to head to the airport. Each time, it became harder saying goodbye, and it was even more difficult when I knew I wouldn't see her for a week. When I returned, it would be the week of final exams, so we wouldn't have class either. I wrote her after I arrived at my hotel in Denver.

*****

Date: Mon, 30 Jul 2007 22:43:15 (EDT)
From: Phillip Demarco
To: Laura McDonald
Subject: Delete this message

BP,

Well, I just got settled in my hotel room, and I thought about you the entire trip. I can't ever seem to get you off my mind. I wish you were here with me right now! In fact, it would be wonderful if you were with me all the time wherever I was! I want to be lying next to you, holding you, kissing you, and making love to you. And I long to kiss your soft lips and leave a trace of kisses across your face, your ears, and your neck. I crave to touch your beautiful body. I want to undress you, first with my eyes and then with my hands, kissing every inch of you as I do, and make love with you in every way we can think of, standing, sitting, on the bed, on the floor, even against the wall, in front of you, and behind you. And I want to taste every inch of you as we do and then wake up with you in the morning and spend every minute of every day together. I don't enjoy being apart from you at all. Good night. I love you.

PD

PS. Delete this message immediately!

*****

Date: Tue, 31 Jul 2007 14:14:34 (EDT)
From: Laura McDonald
To: Phillip Demarco
Subject: NO!

Phillip,

Thank you for your amazing message last night! And *no*, I will not delete it; I'm keeping it forever! I *loved* every word! Maybe you can use it in your book!
I hope you continue to think about me your entire trip!

Faye

*****

Date: Tue, 31 Jul 2007 23:19:51 (EDT)
From: Phillip Demarco
To: Laura McDonald
Subject: Lonesome

BP,

It's very lonesome out here without you! And the conference is very boring. I keep thinking about all the fun we could have if you were with me. And I wish it wasn't so late back in Florida right now so I could call you, but I don't want to wake you. Well, I know this message is short, but I'm tired. So good night, my love!

Phillip

*****

Date: Wed, 1 Aug 2007 13:24:23 (EDT)
From: Laura McDonald
To: Phillip Demarco
Subject: In desperate need

Phillip,

You should be here because I'm in desperate need of some affection! Please call me tonight!

Faye

*****

I called Faye later, and we had a long and marvelous conversation. We missed each other very much. It was a shame we had to be apart, and neither of us liked it at all.

*****

Date: Thu, 2 Aug 2007 12:28:38 (EDT)
From: Laura McDonald
To: Phillip Demarco
Subject: I guess I was wrong

Phillip,

Did you have a good day at the conference? I enjoyed talking to you last night! It's been way too long since I've seen you, but I'll be away this weekend when you return, so I can't see you until Monday. Then after finals next week, I'm going home to Nashville for two whole weeks. So once again, we'll be apart. Here's something that will make you happy though (it was supposed to be a surprise when you got back). I'm taking another one of your wonderful classes next semester! So after the break, I'll get to be with you all the time again, just like in the summer. Isn't that great?

I loved it yesterday when you told me, "I love you very much." I was afraid you wouldn't feel the same way about me after being gone for so long, but I guess I was wrong. I LOVE YOU!

Faye

*****

Faye's news that she would take another one of my classes during the fall semester both surprised and thrilled me. She hadn't told me she was considering doing so. After spending a wonderful summer together, I expected those times would end after Faye got married. I was at a loss to envision what would happen between us. But I'd be content to enjoy Faye in whatever way possible. If all it could be was having her in class for another semester, I could accept it, even though it wouldn't be my first choice. I'd be happy with any time I'd get to spend with her, and each moment would be a gift I would always cherish.

Since there was no class on Monday, I didn't see Faye in the morning. I knew she had a final at noon and was preparing, but she took a short break, though, to send me a message.

*****

Date: Mon, 6 Aug 2007 10:21:20 (EDT)
From: Laura McDonald
To: Phillip Demarco
Subject: Kissing my neck

Hello, Phillip!

How's it going, handsome? Well, I'm fine now since I'm away from the storm in Georgia! It worried me I might get stuck at Alex's place, which would have been terrible! I missed you very much this weekend. I did nothing fun up there because the storm ruined my entire weekend. I should have stayed here with you!

I'll be stopping by after my exam, so I hope you'll be there! It's been way too long since I've seen you! Could you kiss me on my neck while I'm there, please? I'd sure appreciate that! It doesn't matter to me when we go to lunch this week because my only other test is yours tomorrow morning, so after that, I won't have much work. So let me know what days you can go, okay?

Will you have time to meet me at my house this week? We have a lot of catching up to do.

Faye

*****

Date: Mon, 6 Aug 2007 10:29:30 (EDT)
From: Laura McDonald
To   Phillip Demarco
Subject: Kissing my neck... again

Hello again (or not),

I know this will sound stupid, but I just wrote you a message, and I don't know if I sent it. So did I send you one already?

Faye

*****

Faye arrived at my office after her exam around 3:30 p.m. When I met her at the door, she threw herself into my arms as soon as I closed it. It seemed like months since I'd seen her. We could only spend a short while together again because she had to study for my exam at 8:00 a.m. the next morning. I spent some time kissing on her neck as she asked but also touching her breasts, and even reaching under her short skirt to feel her soft, exciting body. Before she left, we agreed to meet at her house after our exam. I couldn't wait! I planned to bring lunch for us, even if we wouldn't take the time to eat it.

*****

Date: Tue, 7 Aug 2007 11:16:57 (EDT)
From: Laura McDonald
To: Phillip Demarco
Subject: You WILL be punished!

Phillip,

I'm sure I did well on your test. That's why I'm writing you while you're still in there waiting for the others to finish. I think I got at least a B!

I would stay here at school and walk home with you, but it might be a better idea if we met there instead, okay? Why did you insist on staring at me during the exam? You know how I get when you look at me. I'm sure everyone was wondering why I kept smiling during the test! I *will* punish you for that and I don't think you'll like it either (but I'll love it)! I'll see you in a few minutes!

Faye

*****

We had a fun afternoon at Faye's house. I arrived with lunch at 1:00 p. m., and I stayed for three hours. Each time I was with her, I loved her more than the time before. Faye ended up getting an A on my final exam, and an A in the class, but our relationship had no effect on her grades. She did well in school because she was very intelligent and worked very hard.

The next day was the end-of-semester student party held at a colleague's home. The annual pool party and cookout had become a regular departmental event in recent years. Since Faye was taking my class, and even though she wasn't a mechanical engineering major, the other students in the class invited her to attend. She'd been around the department enough in the last year that many people recognized her and didn't realize she was majoring in a different curriculum.

Faye and I arrived in our separate cars and tried our best not to spend too much time together, but we still enjoyed interacting with each other in an environment with so many others. Faye was a hit with everyone there since she was friendly and outgoing, and also because she was wearing a tiny bikini. Most of the attention came from male students hoping to connect with her, which Faye didn't encourage. She wasn't shy about telling them she was engaged and showing them her ring. It was a fun afternoon of swimming, volleyball, water polo, eating, and drinking beer, although Faye stuck with Dr Pepper. When the party ended, I hoped to go home with her, but she wouldn't hear of it. She did *not* want to give anyone the impression something was going on between us. As much as I appreciated her discretion, it disappointed me.

*****

Date: Thu, 9 Aug 2007 11:14:04 (EDT)
From: Laura McDonald
To: Phillip Demarco
Subject: Whatever is appropriate

Hello, Phillip!

I had a fantastic time with you yesterday. I hope I didn't make you mad when I wouldn't leave the party at the same time as you, but I didn't want it to get mentioned later that we left together. That's why I made you to leave first. Yes, I can meet you at 3:00 p.m. today. I can't wait! I think you need to punish me for making you leave the party without me, so please take any action you feel is appropriate!

Faye

*****

Friday was the last day of exams for the summer. Faye planned to leave on Saturday to drive back to Nashville for the semester break. Sophia was going to Orlando with some friends for the day, so I hoped to spend more time alone with Faye. When I mentioned the idea to her, she stopped me mid-sentence and said she had changed her plans and was leaving on Friday to spend the weekend with Alex in Georgia before heading to Tennessee. I expressed my disappointment to her, but I wasn't at all tactful in doing so. I wanted to be with her as much as possible, but I forgot how complicated our situation had become. Faye sent me a message in the evening.

*****

Date: Thu, 9 Aug 2007 20:41:40 (EDT)
From: Laura McDonald
To   Phillip Demarco
Subject Tired of me?

Phillip,

After our discussion this afternoon, I get the impression you're tired of seeing me. Am I correct? It appears I'm a disappointment to you. I can't give you any more time right now. You know I'm still in love with Alex and can't leave him. I've tried to spend as much time as possible with you, but it doesn't seem to be enough to keep you satisfied. I wish we could have spent more time together last week also, but we were both very busy. I understand you're tired of me going to see Alex. Don't you think I feel the same way about you going home every day to be with your wife?

I guess what I'm trying to say is, if you can't be happy with the time we spend together, there's no point in seeing each other because I can't give you anything else. It seems I only make trouble for you, and that's not what I want. I've always told you I never wanted to hurt you, and now I have. I only want you to be happy, but I seem to bring you more unhappiness than happiness. Now don't think I don't want to see you anymore because that isn't it. Well, I'll quit rambling. I hope I'll talk to you soon—if you still want to talk to me after reading this letter. Call me if you do, okay?

Faye

*****

Faye's message smacked me back to reality. I was acting like a jackass, and she called me on it. I phoned her and apologized for my inconsiderate behavior. I knew the rules going in, but I had forgotten about them because of my selfishness. I said I was very sorry and was not tired of her at all, and I would never tire of seeing her under any circumstances. I also told her I loved her very much. She was happy to accept my apology and put the matter behind us. Faye was remarkable in that way; she never let things bother her for very long. When an issue got settled, she forgot about it and moved on. It was another attractive quality of her personality, one few people possessed, and I was the lucky recipient of this trait more than I cared to acknowledge. Before we hung up, Faye told me she would stop by my office to say goodbye before she left. She still wrote me again in the evening.

*****

Date: Thu, 9 Aug 2007 20:41:40 (EDT)
From: Laura McDonald
To: Phillip Demarco
Subject: So happy

Phillip,

Thank you for not being mad at me! I was afraid you wouldn't want to talk to me anymore. I'm so happy everything's okay between us. I'll miss you over the break, and I'll think about you the entire time. I love you!

Faye

*****

Faye came to my office early the next morning before leaving Gainesville. Once again, she danced through the doorway, beaming and looking beautiful. I grinned at her and asked if I should close the door, to which she answered, "You'd better!" After I did, we held each other close and kissed goodbye for a few moments. We were both sad at the prospect of not seeing each other for two weeks, but also happy because our relationship was back on track and as strong as ever. It had been a marvelous summer getting to know each other better and loving each other more than we envisioned. Before she walked out, she touched the back of my hand with her fingertip once more. I smiled and gave her a final air-kiss, to which she grinned and mouthed an inaudible "I love you" before walking out.

I sat in my office for a few minutes alone and reflected on the wonderful summer we shared. I thought how grateful I was Faye was a part of my life, regardless of the circumstances.

CHAPTER 11

One More Thing I Didn't Mention

The break from school at the end of the summer was good for me because Sophia always took off from work too, and we'd plan a getaway to refresh ourselves before the busyness of the fall began again. This year, we decided on a car trip to Key West, Florida, a town we had never visited. It was a very scenic eight-hour drive from Gainesville, some of which was along the Atlantic Coast, leading to a gorgeous excursion on US 1 through the Florida Keys. The trip through the Keys offered many opportunities to drive on a narrow strip of highway with beautiful blue water on both sides of the road. Our time in Key West was fun, relaxing, and entertaining. We snorkeled and rode jet skis, visited a few famous historical sights, and ate at some fine restaurants. We enjoyed visiting the Ernest Hemingway Home and Museum and the Harry S. Truman Little White House. The outstanding restaurants we found included the A&B Lobster House, the Half Shell Raw Bar, Two Friends Patio Restaurant, and Sloppy Joe's. These establishments had long histories in Key West, which made them even more interesting. Sloppy Joe's, in particular, had a very colorful story behind it. It was one of Hemingway's favorite hangouts and where he spent many evenings after fishing. A marvelous collection of photos of Hemingway mounted on the walls of the restaurant provided the evidence. Another fascinating establishment was Captain Tony's Saloon on Green Street, in the same building that housed Sloppy Joe's before it moved to Duval Street. in 1937. Captain Tony's is a tiny old bar, complete with dollar bills and car license plates tacked to the walls and a wide variety of brassieres hanging from the ceiling. It was a well-known hangout for famous artists, writers, and celebrities and the establishment where Jimmy Buffett got his start in music. Legend has it that Buffet used to perform there for ten dollars and three Budweiser beers. Buffet immortalized the saloon and Captain Tony in his song, "Last Mango in Paris." Captain Tony Tarracino, the saloon's namesake, was an infamous fishing boat captain, a gunrunner, a gambling casino operator, and the onetime mayor of Key West. A highlight of our visit there was to meet and chat with Captain Tony himself, who confirmed some of the notorious stories about both him and the saloon.

After a wonderful vacation, it was back to Gainesville for the start of another academic year, which marked the first anniversary of my meeting Faye. It seemed I had known her for much longer. The new semester would be different after Faye married Alex in November, and I couldn't imagine our relationship would, or could, stay the same. I prepared myself for the inevitable change about to occur, although we never discussed what was ahead for us. I was in love with her and didn't want to focus on the future, even though it presented a huge uncertainty. Plus, there was still three months before she got married over Thanksgiving.

The fall semester of 2007 started in the usual way, except my anticipation of having Faye in class again made it more exciting than normal. I didn't see her until I walked into the classroom on the first day. Once again, she sat in the front row and looked radiant. She followed me back to my office afterward to talk about our breaks and was as warm and as engaging as always. We had one of our typical wonderful conversations.

When she was ready to leave, the ever-present smile slid from her face, and she said to me, "Phillip, you know I'm getting married in a few months. I've been thinking it might be best if we didn't spend as much time together this semester as we did over the summer to make it easier for me after I'm married."

I responded, "Yes, Faye, I understand. I expected our relationship would change because of your upcoming marriage. But I want you to know I still want to see you as much as you're comfortable with, and I'll treasure every minute— no matter how much, or how little time we get to spend together."

With my response, the smile returned to Faye's face, and she said, "Thank you, Phillip. I knew you'd understand." Then she touched the back of my hand with her finger, giggled, and was off to her next class.

As the semester progressed, I saw Faye at school, but she resisted meeting at her house, taking drives, or even rollerblading with me. But we still talked in my office when we could and met for lunch at least once a week. Faye continued to study and do homework in the computer lab in my building, and we ended up seeing each other at school most days, so she didn't email me as often. We just didn't have time alone away from school like we did over the summer. But I was happy to spend any time I could with Faye, whether those times were intimate or platonic. Although, it was difficult for both of us to break the romantic ties we had established, and we were incapable of ending the loving feelings we had for each other. Faye and I just weren't able to stay away from each other. Although we tried, we couldn't help ourselves. We often joked and teased each other about our attraction and past activities, which I suspected she might have secretly wanted to continue. Over the next few weeks, we became even more flirtatious and playful than usual. Then around mid-semester, I received this message from her, confirming my suspicions.

*****

Date: Thu, 18 Oct 2007 14:41:05 (EDT)
From: Laura McDonald
To: Phillip Demarco
Subject: Redoing experiments?

Hello, handsome!

     I'm sure you're surprised to get a message from me, aren't you? Well, I just finished taking a test and walked by your office, and you weren't there! I was very disappointed! I wanted to tell you I've missed being "alone" with you. It's all I seem to think about every time I'm around you. I know I shouldn't say this, but I'd like to redo all the experiments we did together, if you're interested. If you are, maybe we can find some time before November 24, if you want to, I mean. Well, I must go since I've got homework to do. I'll see you tomorrow, my handsome prince!

Faye

*****

     Faye's forward message surprised me but didn't shock me. And I was very pleased she missed being with me. So I wrote her back immediately and accepted her proposition to redo our experiments.

*****

Date: Thu, 18 Oct 2007 15:07:19 (EDT)
From: Phillip Demarco
To: Laura McDonald
Subject: Yes!

Hello, BP,

I would love to redo our experiments!!! Let's talk about when and where. I already know why!

Phillip

*****

After having called Faye BP for so long, she now began referring to me as her "handsome prince," calling me HP for short, a reference going back to the princess/frog joke I told her many months earlier. We had a lot of fun joking about it when she first started, and somehow, both BP and HP ended up sticking as our pet names for each other.

Several days later, Faye was having trouble with one of the homework assignments in my class. She couldn't get a computer program to work and became very frustrated over it. Despite providing her with some small hints, she still couldn't fix the problem. So, I sent her an email to suggest more changes she should try to get her program working. I often gave hints to help students, not only Faye, but she didn't know it. So I thought I'd have a little fun with her by making her think I was giving her special treatment, which wasn't the case at all. I also told her she owed me "big time" for the individual attention she received.

*****

Date: Tue, 30 Oct 2007 22:57:26 (EDT)
From: Laura McDonald
To: Phillip Demarco
Subject: Returning your favor

Hello, HP!

Well, I guess you will do anything for me, won't you? You didn't have to give me such a big hint about my homework! I hate to say it, but even after I made those changes, my program still didn't work! So I got mad and started all over! I named my new one No Clue. At least I calculated an answer with this one, even though it's not the correct answer.

You know you didn't have to give me hints about my homework, don't you? I'd still consider you to be my handsome prince, even if my program never works. (Does that make any sense?)

Please enlighten me, how must I return your huge favor? I'm sure you have something in mind since you said, "You owe me big time!" I guess you can let me know later.

Faye

*****

We discussed when we could get together outside school. I mentioned I had some free time in the evenings over the weekend. With a sheepish smile, Faye asked me if I'd like to come over to her house on Friday night since Alex wasn't arriving for the weekend until Saturday. I was happy to accept her invitation.

When I arrived, she met me at the door with a loving kiss, and we soon found our way to the sofa. We spent several hours making love on the sofa, on the floor, and in her bed. We couldn't get enough of each other after months of being apart. At one point, we talked about her upcoming marriage, and Faye cried again. Perhaps it was because she perceived my sadness, or maybe it was her torn feelings surfacing in front of me. I comforted her, and she was fine a little while later. It was very difficult for me to leave her, but I did so, loving her as much as I ever have.

The next afternoon, I received another uplifting message from her.

*****

Date: Sat, 10 Nov 2007 14:37:02 (EST)
From: Laura McDonald
To: Phillip Demarco
Subject: Crying again

Hello, HP,

Well, I have some good news: Alex is not coming this weekend at all because of work! So if you want to get together again, then call me! I'll leave a voice mail on your answering machine in case you don't receive this message. I hope you get one of them! I'm sorry I started crying again last night, but I couldn't help it. I don't know if you realize it, but I still love you! I know you may not believe it since I'm getting married in two weeks, but it's true! Why else would I always want to see you and make love with you so much?

Faye

*****

Two nights in a row with Faye was more than I had hoped for, since it might have been our last chance to be together. I thought about planning a special night, perhaps dinner at a romantic restaurant, a hike through Sweetwater Wetlands Park, a convertible ride through the moonlight, followed by time alone back at her house. After I received Faye's message, I called her to propose my idea, to which she laughed and said, "Phillip, that sounds beautiful, but no thanks! Just get over here as fast as you can!" And so I did.

I raced to her house. She and I spent the evening not only making love but also adoring each other every way we could. At one point, we closed our eyes, and I traced my fingertips over her entire body, trying to memorize each curve and crevasse and every other inch of her in case it was my last chance to be with her. Then she did the same to me. We loved each other with our touches. And we filled the night with laughter and teasing, as was so common with us. I wished our night wouldn't have ever ended. It was difficult to leave because we both knew what was ahead. As I walked out the door, we were both in tears; I realized I would never get over her, and Faye may have felt the same way about me.

*****

Date: Sun, 11 Nov 2007 23:27:31 (EST)
From: Laura McDonald
To: Phillip Demarco
Subject: I was wrong

Hello, HP!

I wanted you to stay last night and Friday night! I kept thinking about how great it would be if you could spend the night with me. And you were right, as usual; I regret not spending more time with you early in the semester. I guess I thought if I didn't see you as much, it might be easier for me, but I was wrong! I still love you, and that won't change. You need to know, if I weren't with Alex, I would run away with you in a second. You'd only have to ask!

Faye

*****

We only had a few more classes before Thanksgiving break, which was a weeklong holiday from school, and right before Faye's wedding in Tennessee. We had lunch twice that week, and we spent a few hours talking at school, but we couldn't meet to be alone again before she left on Friday for her trip home. As she left my office for the last time as a single woman, I gave her a long, warm hug and told her congratulations on her wedding. I meant what I said, but I did so with a heavy heart. Although I tried to hide it from her, she knew how I felt. What I didn't tell Faye was I wished she wasn't marrying Alex because I was the one she should be with, not him. And we should be the ones planning to build a life together. But I couldn't tell her those things. I wanted Faye to be happy. If she could be happier with Alex, I would respect her decision—if there were ever a need for her to make one.

When Faye returned to school after Thanksgiving, she was a married woman. Now we had another thing in common. In class the first day back, she was grinning nonstop, and I couldn't help but think how happy she looked. After class, she was bubbling with excitement and couldn't wait to tell me about her wedding, which was a small affair with only family and a few friends in attendance. She also showed me some photos. Faye made a beautiful bride, and I was even more envious of Alex now. She had her long hair pinned up to appear shorter than it was—about shoulder-length—and with subtle body waves, which I hadn't seen before. She wore a touch of makeup and soft pink lipstick, which made her look different, but even more stunning than normal. In each photo, Faye was beaming!

We talked for an hour, and I loved seeing Faye so happy. I asked if Alex had moved into her house, to which she looked puzzled by my question. Then she said, "Oh, I guess I didn't tell you. Alex won't be moving here until January, after he separates from the service. He'll start school next semester, so I'll still be living alone until then."

In all the time we spent talking, I couldn't believe the topic never came up before or that she didn't think to mention it to me. I suppose it wouldn't have mattered since she was now married. And we only had two weeks of school left until Christmas break anyhow, so I guess it was irrelevant to our situation. But it still surprised me.

As we finished our conversation, and Faye began walking toward the door to leave, she stopped and walked over to my desk and touched the back of my hand with her fingertip, as she'd done countless times. Then she said, "I missed you!" She smiled, blew me an air-kiss, and left, leaving me surprised, puzzled, and confused. How could this incredible young woman miss me when she was off getting married to someone else? I had no explanation!

Faye and I were both very busy, and the last week of school and final exams were soon over. We had lunch once more and spent several more hours talking in my office. Although we flirted, our conversation was benign and neither of us suggested we meet outside school. So, my confusion cleared up as I rationalized Faye had missed me over Thanksgiving as a friend and no longer as a lover. But on her last afternoon in town before the break, Faye came to my office to say goodbye. As she entered, she closed the door and locked it behind her, which shocked me. She rushed over, threw her arms around me, kissed me, and whispered, "Phillip, I've been thinking about this a lot, and I miss you so much! I want to keep seeing you like we did before I got married. I hope that doesn't make me a horrible person, but I can't help how I feel." "Faye, how could we when Alex will be here with you now?"

"There's one more thing I didn't mention, Phillip, because I didn't think I should, but now I want to tell you. After Alex gets discharged from the military and comes down here for school next semester, he'll still be in the Air Force reserves and will need to spend one weekend each month away on reserve duty. We could see each other during those times, if you still want to, okay?"

Stunned, I looked at Faye and replied, "Yes, BP, I'd love to, if it's what you want!" And just like that, I couldn't wait until the holidays were over and school was back in session!

CHAPTER 12

I Have Bad News for You

The spring semester of 2008 brought many changes. I didn't have Faye as a student in class; she was now married, and Alex was in Gainesville and enrolled in school. He was studying business and had two years of school left after having taken classes at a junior college before entering the military, while Faye was on schedule to graduate in May. Although she was still undecided about her plans after graduation, I was sure she'd have plenty of options. There weren't many local jobs available in her discipline, so I expected she would accept a position somewhere away from Gainesville near a school where Alex could finish his degree.

Faye was taking most of her classes near my building again, and she always studied in the computer lab in my department. She came to visit me for our regular "Faye hours," and we continued to have lunch together often. After one week of classes, Alex had his first weekend of reserve duty. Faye and I spent most of those two days going on drives, hiking, and rollerblading. And we spent time at her house. She was as passionate and as loving as she was before she got married, and it remained difficult to leave her when I had to go. It surprised me that her marriage didn't appear to affect our relationship much at all, other than not having as many opportunities to be alone. We loved each other, and we tried to show it when we were together. But since we were both married now, the prospects of us ever ending up together looked bleak.

Faye's emails were still delightful, even when she felt neglected. She continued to be persistent in sending me messages, and I loved them all.

*****

Date: Tue, 29 Jan 2008 18:32:23 (EST)
From: Laura McDonald
To: Phillip Demarco
Subject: I've been abandoned!

Hello, handsome man!

How's it going? As usual, I'm here in the computer lab working on a project. I figured I'd write to you now since I won't get to see your lovely face tomorrow. My handsome prince has abandoned me! He's too busy for me now! Well, I've got to make a chart or something ridiculous, so I'll talk to you later!

Love ya,

Faye

(PS. I don't know if I sent this the first time, so I'm sending it again, maybe.)

*****

Date: Tue, 29 Jan 2008 09:27:41 (EST)
From: Phillip Demarco
To: Laura McDonald
Subject: Lack of attention

Hello there, BP,

Thanks for sending me your message twice, but I only received it once. I'm sorry to hear you feel like I abandoned you, although nothing could be further from the truth. This job interferes with my life sometimes. To make up for my lack of attention, why don't you visit me on Friday? I know you won't have much time, but I'm free all afternoon, and I promise I'll give you my *complete* attention for as long as you can stay, okay? And I love you too!

PD

*****

Date: Sun, 03 Feb 2008 13:14:55 (EST)
From: Phillip Demarco
To: Laura McDonald
Subject: Always exciting

Hi, BP,

I had a great time with you on Friday! It's always so much fun (and exciting) to be with you. I hope you liked it too, and that I made up for neglecting you.

PD

*****

Date: Sun, 03 Feb 2008 16:48:03 (EST)
From: Laura McDonald
To: Phillip Demarco
Subject: Join me?

Hello, handsome!

Well, I'm in the computer lab again. Care to join me? I wish you would! Ever since I saw you on Friday, I can't get you off my mind. You're great at driving me crazy! I've got to quit thinking about that since I have more work to do. I'll be here until 6:30 or 7:00 p.m. if you'd like to come and visit me. And yes, you sure made up for neglecting me!

Faye

*****

The following Saturday, I had to leave to attend a conference in San Antonio, Texas. It turned out to be terrible timing because it was a weekend Alex would be on reserve duty and Faye would be home alone. Although I was looking forward to the trip, it disappointed me to be losing out on time with Faye. When I arrived at the hotel, I couldn't wait to call and tell her so. I surprised her when I did.

*****

Date: Sun, 10 Feb 2008 01:23:49 (EST)
From: Laura McDonald
To: Phillip Demarco
Subject: Strawberries

Hello, handsome!

How's Texas? I was so surprised to get a phone call from you yesterday; I loved it! I hope you are having an excellent time (even without me being there with you)! It's too bad you aren't here this weekend because, as you know, I'm all alone! I know we could find some exciting things to keep us occupied if you were here. Guess what I bought today? Strawberries! I thought of you when I was buying them, but I suppose I must eat them by myself instead of having you feed them to me like the last time. How sad! Well, I still have homework to finish. Have a great day tomorrow and be careful driving out there. I couldn't handle it if something happened to you!

Love,

Your beautiful princess

*****

Date: Wed, 13 Feb 2008 19:25:02 (EST)
From: Laura McDonald
To: Phillip Demarco
Subject: Running off with you

Hello, handsome…I have to tell you, it's been strange not having "Faye hours" this week! I'm going through terrible withdrawal! The grad students down the hall must think I ran off with you or something! But I'll be back at your office

door on Thursday morning so I can see your handsome face
once again!

Faye

*****

The conference was good, and it was fun to visit San
Antonio—one of my favorite cities. But it was a long time
being away and what seemed like a longer trip home,
with a layover in Atlanta on the way back to Gainesville. I
couldn't wait to see Faye on Thursday morning, and she
didn't disappoint me, as she was waiting at my office door
when I arrived. Even though I felt tired from traveling,
we talked for over an hour, catching up on the time we
missed. I was sure we could have chatted all day had it not
been for our classes and an afternoon meeting I had to
attend. We also squeezed in lunch to be together as much
as possible.

Since it was Valentine's Day, I stopped on my way to work
to buy Faye some chocolate truffles again. I hadn't given her
candy since she got married, but I loved to surprise Faye, and
she was always excited when I did.

*****

Date: Thu, 14 Feb 2008 15:40:48 (EST)
From: Laura McDonald
To: Phillip Demarco
Subject: Chocolates

I would have come back and visited you again today, but
I figured you've already gone home. So, I guess I'll wait until
tomorrow to see you. How disappointing! Anyhow, thank you
again for the truffles. You know how much I love them! It's

too bad you couldn't feed them to me, but maybe you can some other time.

Faye

                              *****

Date: Sun, 17 Feb 2008 23:18:10 (EST)
From: Laura McDonald
To: Phillip Demarco
Subject: Forgetting something

You are so terrible teasing me like you do! I didn't get your message until now, so I couldn't write you back in time to meet you. I enjoyed rollerblading with you on Saturday, even though we were not there for long. It's a good thing you left because who knows what might have happened if you would have stayed longer. You were about to drive me crazy when you kept touching me, and you knew it too, didn't you? You just do those things on purpose (and I love it)!

I know I'm forgetting something, but I can't seem to remember what. It may be about how much I adore you, but I'm not sure!

Love,

BP

                              *****

Date: Sun, 24 Feb 2008 18:28:07 (EST)
From: Laura McDonald
To: Phillip Demarco
Subject: Running away

Hello, handsome!

It was quite a beautiful day today! I wish I could have seen you, but Alex was home! I had fun with you yesterday, as usual! And I agree we'd have a great time if we ran away together. You know, if I weren't with Alex, I would have run off with you long ago. Well, I would have, in case you don't believe it. And yes, I meant it when I told you I still love you. And that will never change!

Love,

BP

*****

Date: Thu, 28 Feb 2008 01:30:20 (EST)
From: Laura McDonald
To: Phillip Demarco
Subject: Lovely time

What are you doing? I am done with my project, and it's only 1:30 a.m. Amazing, isn't it? I had a lovely time in your office yesterday afternoon! Can I see you again today around 1:00 p.m.?

BP

*****

Date: Fri, 29 Feb 2008 13:28:57 (EST)
From: Laura McDonald
To: Phillip Demarco
Subject: Short little sweater

Hello, handsome,

   Where are you? I just came by, and you weren't there! I'm very disappointed! I assume you haven't left for the day because your office light is still on. Well, I need to go home because I have some studying to do. I'm even wearing a short little sweater today, but now I won't get to show it to you! And don't forget to send me your joke!

BP

*****

Date: Fri, 7 Mar 2008 16:37:44 (EST)
From: Laura McDonald
To: Phillip Demarco
Subject: Something in mind

   That joke was terrible! But I enjoy all of your jokes— terrible or not! Oh, and how will you make up for not seeing me today since you were too busy? I'm sure you have something in mind, don't you? Have a fun spring break. I'll miss you!

BP

*****

   Over the week of spring break, I thought a lot about Faye graduating and leaving, something I knew would make me very sad. As I pondered my future without her, I came up with what I viewed as a brilliant idea of how she could stay in Gainesville after she graduated, if she was interested. I planned to discuss it with her when classes resumed.

The Monday following our break, Faye came to my office; she was her usual cheerful self as she danced through the doorway and sat in "her" chair next to my desk. We joked, laughed, and talked about our breaks. Then our discussion turned to her upcoming graduation. When I asked about her plans afterward, she told me she'd try to find a job somewhere near a college, so Alex could finish his degree, since there were very few jobs in her field in Gainesville.

"Have you considered attending graduate school instead?" I asked.

"No, I haven't because I can't afford to stay in school," she answered.

Since Faye hadn't investigated graduate school, she was unaware that she could be eligible for a graduate assistantship, which would pay her tuition, plus a stipend for living expenses. Faye didn't know that most graduate students had assistantships or that it might be an option for her. I surprised her by suggesting the possibility. Then in my normal teasing manner, I asked her if she'd be interested in attending graduate school in the mechanical engineering department.

She looked at me with a very serious face and answered, "Wait, what? How could I do that? Could I do that?"

Then I said, "Well, my research group just received a large grant, and we're looking for some graduate students to hire to help on the project. Having had you in class several times now, I'm sure you could handle the work. And you'd get your tuition paid and receive a salary too!"

Still with a serious face, she shook her head from side-to-side and asked, "Let me get this straight. You could pay me to go to graduate school, and I could get a master's degree?"

"Yes, provided you do well on the Graduate Record Examination [GRE], but your master's would have to be in mechanical engineering instead of electrical. Would you consider that?" I knew her GRE score was only a formality as she had a GPA of over 3.8, and the university would accept her with any score of 1,000 or better on the exam.

Faye asked again, "Wait, so do you mean if I did, I wouldn't have to pay tuition, and I'd still get a salary?"

"Yes, but the salary would be less than you would get from a regular job—only around $1,500 per month."

"Well, if you can pay me and cover my tuition too, then yes, I am definitely interested!"

I smiled and replied, "But there's a catch."

"I knew there'd be some kind of catch! Okay, what is it?"

"Well, you'd have to agree to be my graduate student and work for me for your master's degree."

Faye laughed and said, "Are you serious, that's the catch? That would be *great,* I'd *love* it! I'll absolutely agree to work for you!" Faye was very excited about the opportunity, and so was I.

Then I said, "Okay, go schedule your GRE, and if your scores are acceptable, we'll have a deal!" Faye got up to leave to find out about scheduling the exam.

On her way out, she touched the back of my hand, smiled, and said, "Thank you so much for thinking of me for this. I appreciate it!" After Faye left, I thought how wonderful it would be if she could stay for two more years and be my graduate research assistant. I considered that my hiring Faye might be self-serving because of our relationship, but she was a well-qualified student whom I knew would be successful. Besides, in my best professional opinion, with Faye's academic capabilities, it would be a wise move on her part to get an advanced degree. Regardless, the decision about whom I hired to work on my grant was mine, and mine alone. Since I needed to hire several students anyhow, I wanted Faye to be one of them. While nothing was official until she took the GRE, applied to the graduate school, and the university accepted her for graduate study, I felt good about the chances of her becoming my graduate student and staying in Gainesville.

Within a few days, Faye submitted her application and was scheduled to take a computer-based GRE in two weeks at the Kaplan Testing Center in the Reitz Student Union on campus. She'd receive her unofficial scores when she completed the exam, so we'd both know where she stood right away. Faye bought a GRE review book to help her prepare and began studying. I told her if she received a total verbal plus quantitative score of at least 1,000 (out of 1,600) on the general test of the GRE, she wouldn't have any problem being admitted for graduate study with her high GPA. The next two weeks were a bit of a waiting game for us. I was confident of the outcome, but Faye remained nervous about the exam with so much riding on the results. Since she was busy preparing for the GRE and also taking her regular classes, we didn't see each other much during the time she was studying.

To tease Faye a little, I told her I'd write her an erotic story so she wouldn't forget about me while she studied. We had talked about me writing one someday, but I never did. So I tried. It was my first attempt at writing erotica. The story involved Faye and me spending the night in a penthouse hotel room overlooking Miami Beach, complete with a private hot tub, fresh strawberries, chocolate syrup, massages, an unlimited number of butterfly kisses, and a variety of sex toys. It was a long and detailed description of everything we did, some of which occurred in front of the large windows overlooking the beach with the curtains wide open. When I wrote the story, I found it to be very arousing for me, so I felt certain Faye would also enjoy it.

*****

Date: Thu, 3 Apr 2008 16:37:23 (EDT)
From: Laura McDonald
To: Phillip Demarco
Subject: I ALWAYS will!!!!

Well, hello!

Wow! What a story! It got me very excited reading it; I caught myself biting my finger a few times! You should have let me read it when I came to your office yesterday and you could have seen how easy my shirt unsnaps! How about if you read it to me tomorrow when I see you? What a coincidence Dr Pepper played a role in this escapade. Your erotic writing drives me crazy too! So when will you send me another one? Please, hurry. I'll be waiting.

I couldn't pay attention to what you were saying yesterday because all I was thinking about was how wonderful you looked! So, never think I don't still love/want you because I'm married now! Because you know I always will!

BP

*****

When I saw Faye the next day, I wished her luck on the exam on Saturday. I knew she'd do well, and even though she was prepared, she was nervous about taking it. Then Saturday evening, I received this message from her.

*****

Date: Sat, 5 Apr 2008 20:23:00 (EDT)
From: Laura McDonald
To: Phillip Demarco
Subject: Bad news

Hello.

Well, I have bad news for you! It looks like you'll be stuck with me for the next couple of years! Here are my scores: verbal 650 and quantitative 690. And it would have been higher if I could have finished the darn thing, but I guess 1,340 is good enough. (At least I hope so!) I'd love it if I could go to graduate school here and work with you!

BP

*****

Faye was right; her overall score was high enough for admission. Once the Graduate Admissions Committee received her official scores, they admitted her to the graduate program in the mechanical engineering department. Being Faye's adviser meant I would direct her program of study, and she would work as one of my research assistants on my project. She'd also need to take more classes from me. We were both excited at the prospect of working together, and we both expected it would be great fun.

Our project was getting ready to kick off in mid-May. Before it did, we scheduled an organizational meeting with our research group. The group included one other faculty member, Charles, and four graduate students. Two of them, Michael and Yongsun, were doctoral degree students assigned to Charles. Michael did his undergraduate work at Purdue University in Indiana, while Yongsun was from South Korea and did his undergraduate work there. They were both about to receive their master's degrees in mechanical engineering from the University of Florida. The other two were Faye and Nicole, both new master's degree students assigned to me. Nicole was also just graduating from Florida, but with a degree in physics. Her boyfriend, James, was a doctoral student in the mathematics department.

The research project was a large one, funded over a three-year period and dealt with the structural analysis of space vehicles. It would require a major effort by the entire team to complete in the time allotted. At our first meeting, we discussed the details of the project, the tentative schedule, and made a preliminary assignment of tasks so we'd be ready to "hit the ground running" when it was time to begin work at the start of the summer semester. I could tell it would be a good working group, composed of capable and energetic members with outgoing personalities. I envisioned it would be productive and fun for all of us. But I knew Faye and I would have the most fun.

*****

Date: Wed, 16 Apr 2008 08:31:13 (EDT)
From: Laura McDonald
To: Phillip Demarco
Subject: Your behavior

Hello, handsome!

I'm writing to mention you were being very mean to me yesterday during our meeting! And don't say, "I don't know what you're talking about" because I know you do! And when you bit your lip (as you always do around me) and looked right at me, you knew it would drive me crazy, didn't you? I almost started laughing at you. You're terrible (but I love it)! Will you be around after 2:00 p.m. today? I hope so because I'm planning on visiting you. I came by yesterday at around

4:00 p.m. but you weren't there; I was very disappointed by this! I wanted to see you in your green shirt again!

BP

*****

Date: Fri, 18 Apr 2008 10:40:04 (EDT)
From: Laura McDonald
To: Phillip Demarco
Subject: How aggravating

Hello!

Well, I just came by your office, but there's a line of people at your door waiting to talk to you! How aggravating! I guess I'll just see you tonight as we planned! I can't wait!

Faye

*****

Alex left on Friday afternoon for his reserve duty. It was great to have a night alone with Faye , since it had been quite a while since we had an opportunity. We stayed in at her house, ordered a pizza, and planned to watch an old movie. But after eating, our mutual lust won out, and we spent most of the night playing, frolicking, and making love in her bed. Although I hadn't yet written her another erotic story, I read some of my first one to her in person. Faye was a passionate and enthusiastic lover, but my reading a part of the story had the effect of exciting her to a level I hadn't seen before. It was a night to remember, and as always, it was very difficult to leave her.

As the end of the semester was now upon us, classes were concluding, and students and faculty were all preparing for final exams. Faye was also getting ready for her graduation on Saturday, May 10, the day following the last day of final exams. But amid everything else, there were also employment forms for her to complete and other related issues she needed to address before becoming a university employee and starting graduate school.

On Thursday, she surprised me at my office with her family, who were in town for her graduation. I met her mother and grandmother, and Alex for the first time. Everyone was very nice and appreciative of me hiring Faye, so she and Alex didn't have to move. Her grandmother's given name was Faye, which was where Laura Faye's middle name originated. She was outgoing and funny and called me Professor P the entire time. Her mother, Diane, was shorter than Faye, about five foot three, with shoulder-length brunette hair. She was also very attractive. It was easy to see where Faye got her great looks. Diane told me Faye inherited her height and blonde hair from her father. Alex was quiet and didn't say much. He was short and had thinning dark hair, not someone I would have guessed to be Faye's type. It was great to meet them all, and I'm glad she introduced me to them. Now I could relate better when Faye talked about her family and Alex.

Before they left, I reminded Faye she needed to stop by the departmental office as assignments for graduate student offices were being posted, and she had to pick up her keys.

Later that afternoon, after Faye received her office assignment from the secretary on the second floor, she ran up the stairs and into my office screaming with excitement and smiling to the point of almost laughing. Waving a sheet of paper in the air, she asked me, "Did you have anything to do with this?"

"What are you talking about, Faye? I didn't do a thing!"

"I just got my office assignment!"

"What's wrong? Is there a problem with the office?" I responded.

"No, there's nothing wrong at all! It's room 303, right across the hall from you! Ahhh!" she screamed again.

Room 303 had been a vacant faculty office, and I didn't know they were turning it into a graduate student office. "Faye, I had nothing to do with it, but I think it's *great!*" We both laughed to the point of almost crying. It was common practice for two or three students to share an office due to space limitations. It turned out Faye would share the office with Nicole, whom she already met at our organizational meeting and liked very much.

So, instead of Faye graduating and moving away, she was staying on as my research assistant. She would also take more classes from me and have an office across the hall! What an unbelievable turn of events!

CHAPTER 13

The Unimaginable

After Faye's graduation and a short break, she and Nicole both began their graduate studies in the summer semester of 2008. They settled into the office they shared across the hall from mine, and we started work on the research grant. Faye soon began having fun with our new set of circumstances.

*****

Date: Mon, 12 May 2008 08:42:11 (EDT)
From: Laura McDonald
To: Phillip Demarco
Subject: Guess where I am?

Hello!

I'm right across the hall from my handsome prince!

The beautiful princess

*****

Faye and Nicole's office was identical to mine in size, shape, and color, but it faced the loading dock in the back of the building, not the courtyard in the front, as mine did. It was also rather sparse in terms of furnishings. There were two gray metal desks next to each other and against the wall on the right side of the office, and a small computer table behind each desk against the left wall. There was also a chalkboard on the left wall and two spare chairs for visitors, but there was nothing else in the room.

Faye and Nicole were both taking two classes to begin their master's degree coursework, but I wouldn't have either of them in class again until the following spring semester.

Nicole was a short, fiery redhead with a pixie hairstyle. Since she was outgoing and had a dry sense of humor, she and Faye got along well. Nicole didn't spend as much time in their office as Faye did because Nicole's boyfriend had an office in a nearby building, and she spent much of her time with him. Although, when she was in her office, it was fun because she also did a lot of joking and laughing and was skilled in sarcasm. Nicole also cursed a lot, which made it even more fun. We teased her about "swearing like a drunken sailor," which she admitted. She wasn't aware of the relationship between Faye and me, and we planned to keep it a secret.

As Faye adjusted to her role as a graduate student and my research assistant, it didn't take long for her to become comfortable. She was now a part of the department where she'd spent so much time and was enjoying her new environment. Her research duties mostly involved computer programming—something she was good at and enjoyed. We needed to work together on different aspects of the project, which was even more fun than I expected.

Faye soon became more of a fixture in my office than ever before, and she spent more time in mine than in hers. Besides the many questions she had about her work, she visited me whenever she wasn't busy. But we spent most of our time talking and joking with the door open with other people nearby. We got our work done and enjoyed spending more time together. It didn't take long until we became inseparable. In the morning, Faye would arrive at her office, drop off her backpack, and come straight to my office to start the day with a "Faye hour." We began having lunch several times a week, and she was asking me questions about her work or we were just chatting much of the rest of the day.

The frequency of Faye's emails decreased since I was right across the hall and more accessible. It was now easier for her to come over rather than to email. But Faye didn't quit emailing altogether, especially when I wasn't available or she wanted to tell me something important, like she missed me. But each week, we found times when it was quiet enough in the department to close and lock my door. Faye continued to enjoy sitting on my lap or leaning against me as I sat on the edge of my desk. I still loved holding her close, kissing her with passion, and touching her face and body. On the weekends, when Alex was on reserve duty, we often met at her house to share intimate and loving times. Our attraction to each other grew stronger as time went by. But our relationship was much more than a romantic one. Faye was fast becoming my protégé and a colleague, and even more of a trusted friend.

If I was unavailable—for whatever reason—Faye hated it. Whenever she couldn't find me, I'd get messages expressing her annoyance.

*****

Date: Wed, 9 Jul 2008 15:07:39 (EDT)
From: Laura McDonald
To: Phillip Demarco
Subject: You're missing!

Hello!

Well, I needed a handsome prince, so I came over to your office, but you were missing! Where are you? I'm not happy when you aren't right here beside me! I suppose I'll wait until tomorrow to see you. How sad!

BP

*****

Our research group met twice a week—on Monday and Thursday mornings. These meetings were ones where Charles and I assessed the progress we were making as a group, provided direction for the project, and made individual work assignments to each team member. They were casual and everyone contributed by describing their activities since the previous meeting. I always tried to sit across the table from Faye, so I could tease her with looks, smiles, and glares when nobody else was looking. She knew what I was trying to do with each glance in her direction. Sometimes, it was difficult to keep a straight face, and it was even harder to hide our playfulness from the others. After our meetings concluded, Faye often sent me messages scolding me for my behavior.

*****

Date: Thu, 10 Jul 2008 10:46:34 (EDT)
From: Laura McDonald
To: Phillip Demarco
Subject: YOU ARE JUST TERRIBLE!

You got me all flustered during our meeting with those looks of yours! I knew what you were thinking every time you looked at me! You will get us both in big trouble if you keep it up, so you better stop! (But you know I love it!) See you in a minute because I'm on my way over there right now.

BP

*****

Faye was playful when she came over. My open door didn't stop her from flirting with me and hinting at what could happen if we weren't at school. Our teasing turned to references about the first erotic story I wrote for her, and she said she wanted me to write her another one. I told her I'd consider it, and if I had time, I might. Faye wouldn't let me forget it.

*****

Date: Thu, 10 Jul 2008 14:16:21 (EDT)
From: Laura McDonald
To: Phillip Demarco
Subject: Story

Handsome prince,

   Remember, I'm waiting for one more of your fabulous erotic stories!

Beautiful princess

*****

   Over the weekend, I found time to write her a second one.

*****

Date: Sun, 13 Jul 2008 19:04:53 (EDT)
From: Phillip Demarco
To: Laura McDonald
Subject: Showering together

BP,

   Do you remember when you said you wanted us to take a shower together? Well, here's one about us doing that.

> I arrive at your house as we planned. You open the door, and I kiss you with passion. Without saying a word, I grab your hand and lead you toward the bathroom. After I start the water in the shower, I turn you to face the large mirror. I undress you first, then myself. We study our reflections in the

glass as I stand behind you. My arms reach around your shoulders, and I slide my palms down to your breasts. We watch ourselves as I pinch your hardened nipples. I turn you and lift you onto the counter so I can take a nipple between my lips. Your hands hold my head against your chest as the mirror fogs. After a passionate kiss, I help you down and walk you to the shower. I step inside first, and you follow me under the water, which runs over your head, across your face, and trickles down your nose and off your chin. I lean forward to kiss you through the droplets before they fall to the floor. You move backward so it sprays on both of our faces. With our eyes closed, I push your body against the wall before moving away to reach for the soap. I lather my hands and run my palms over your shoulders, your arms, your breasts, down to the top of your thighs, and around to your back. Then I kneel on the floor and soap your feet and calves before moving up and sliding my soapy hands between your legs. You push your hips toward me as I slide two fingers inside you. My eyes never leave yours as I smile at your reaction to my fingers. I lean closer to you and move my tongue until it locates your hardened clit. You tilt your head back as you feel the sensations my touch arouses in you. I lick from side- to-side and then in circles, teasing you until you can't take it anymore. You try to hold my head between your legs, but I resist and stand-up before you under the spray. I wrap my arms around you, pulling your body into the warm water with me. You take the soap and lather it in your hands. You reach up and rub them over my chest, shoulders, stomach, and down my legs. Now you slide your soapy fingers around my hardness until I'm covered in bubbles. With a firmer grasp, you stroke me as I tease your nipples between my fingertips. I move us both under the stream of water again to wash the soap away, leaving our skin clean and reddened from the heat. Once more, I move your body back to the wall, and this time, I lift you off the ground so you can wrap your legs around my waist as I slide myself deep inside of you. We feel the warmth between us as our desire reaches a feverish pitch. My lips find yours, and my tongue moves to enter the warmth of your mouth. Our kisses are intense as my hips push harder. I'm throbbing within you, and your muscles tighten to hold me there. A low groan escapes me as you feel my movements halt, only for a second, before I begin again, pumping and driving myself into you with reckless abandon. I shudder and fill you with hot sperm. Your orgasm isn't far behind. With your arms tight around my neck and your body on fire, we move under the warm waterfall, with our eyes closed.

Sleep well, my dear! Your HP

*****

I received Faye's response soon after she read it.

*****

Date: Sun, 13 Jul 2008 20:20:04 (EDT)
From: Laura McDonald
To: Phillip Demarco
Subject: When?

Hello there, shower guy!

That was quite a story! It was *well* worth my wait! But now, I won't be able to look at you during our meeting tomorrow.
I'm still up here in my office, all alone, working on this program. It's too bad you aren't here to keep me company. I'll be here until 10:30 or 11:00 p.m. I suppose I'll just have to be lonely since my friendly professor isn't here!
So when do we get to take a shower together?

BP

*****

Besides spending as much time as possible with Faye, I tried to play golf on the weekends. I also played evening softball in the Gainesville Adult League. A close friend invited me to join the UF Hillel team, sponsored by a campus Jewish organization. It was fun, but our team wasn't good. One reason was because it included many faculty members who were a lot older than the players on the other teams in the league—most of whom were students. So, we weren't very competitive.
We played games on Tuesday nights at Westside Park off NW Eighth Avenue, a short drive from campus. There

were two games scheduled each night with a one-hour break between them. It was an established tradition our team would spend the time between games drinking beer in the parking lot. Most of us had a beer-buzz by the time we played the later game. As a result, it was unusual for UF Hillel to win the second game of any night. But we seldom won either game. Except for one strange evening. During the first game, everything went our way—every hit, every close play, and every call—and we won 13—9 over the first-place team in the league. Since we had something to celebrate during the between-game break, we drank even more beer than usual. In the nightcap, we were playing another terrible team, and their best player couldn't attend. We won that game 10-2, despite the extra beer consumption. It was the only time in recent memory UF Hillel won two games in one night, and I couldn't wait to tell Faye about the momentous event.

*****

Date: Tue, 15 Jul 2008 22:46:55 (EDT)
From: Phillip Demarco
To: Laura McDonald
Subject: An amazing night

BP,

I couldn't wait to tell you we won two softball games tonight! Even with extra beer drinking between games to celebrate our win in the first game. I wish you were there to see this amazing event. Now don't you feel bad about all those terrible jokes you made about my softball team?

HP

*****

Date: Tue, 15 Jul 2008 23:51:42 (EDT)
From: Laura McDonald
To: Phillip Demarco
Subject: A miracle!

HP,

Are you telling me the truth or are you just teasing me again? Well, I guess congratulations are in order since your team did the unimaginable! So congratulations! I should have been there to watch your amazing (?) team! I want to hear all about it tomorrow!

BP

*****

The next morning, when Faye came to my office, she was more excited about my team's softball victories the night before than I was. She wanted to know all the details, which I did my best to describe. But I told her more about the good time we had continuing our beer-drinking afterward to celebrate the occasion. It was a fun night. I learned a lot about my teammates, and I heard some funny jokes, which I told Faye the next day.

The following week was a busy one for me with meetings and appointments outside the department. Those commitments kept me away from my office much of the time, except for our research group meeting on Monday morning. I'd forgotten to mention my appointments to Faye, and she wasn't pleased with my absence.

*****

Date: Tue, 22 Jul 2008 13:28:53 (EDT)
From: Laura McDonald
To: Phillip Demarco
Subject: Where are you?

Hello!

I have an important question for you, HP: where are you? I thought you would be here all day and now it's 1:00 p.m. on Tuesday, and you're not here! That's two days in a row without a "Faye hour," and I hate it!

You were terrible at our meeting yesterday! I think Yongsun saw the 'little' wink you gave me. (He may have thought you were winking at him or something!)

Anyway, I'll see you tomorrow, handsome!

BP

*****

Date: Wed, 23 Jul 2008 13:02:44 (EDT)
From: Laura McDonald
To: Phillip Demarco
Subject: Neglecting your duty

Well, once again, my handsome prince is neglecting me. You must spend an entire afternoon with me to make up for these lost hours! I hope you are having a marvelous day wherever you are, while I'm here writing yet another computer program. It's not fair! Perhaps I'll get to see you tomorrow at last. I miss you!

BP

*****

I was sorry Faye felt that I was neglecting her again. It had been a few weeks since we were alone together, and Sophia was at work. Faye was afraid we'd get caught together somehow, and it would ruin everything. After I convinced her we wouldn't, she agreed.

We left school a little before lunch to meet at my house. We drove in separate cars since Faye had been to my house before and couldn't stay long anyhow. I stopped on the way to get some sandwiches, and we ate lunch on the deck by the pool. After eating, we changed into our swimsuits in the pool house. Faye came out wearing her new, tiny, revealing bikini, and we jumped into the water. It only took a few minutes before we became wrapped in each other's arms. Faye put her legs around my waist as we bobbed up and down in the warm water. I bounced over to the shallow end of the pool nearest to the deck, which had three steps leading out of the water about four feet wide with water jets on both sides, like a Jacuzzi. With Faye's legs still wrapped around me, I laid back onto the steps so she could sit on top of me while the jets of warm water massaged us. As we kissed, I untied her bikini top, and it fell behind her, freeing her beautiful breasts. Faye giggled and kissed me harder. After a few more minutes, I loosened her bikini bottoms and pulled them off, and placed them on the side of the pool. Soon, she reached down and slid off my swimming trunks to discover my rock-hard erection waiting for her. She giggled again and went under the water to take me in her mouth. Now I was the one giggling. When she surfaced, we both began laughing for a few moments. When we stopped, I pulled her on top of me again, and we attempted to make love, only to find out water is not the best lubricant. The more we tried, the more frustrated we both became. Then I lifted her out of the water and sat her on the pool's edge. I pushed her legs apart and moved my head between them. I kissed her inner thighs— first one, then the other, moving closer to her vagina with each kiss. I soon reached my goal, and Faye moaned when I did. She enjoyed receiving oral sex and knew what was about to happen.

She threw her head back, closed her eyes and bit her lower lip as she had done many times before to savor the experience. I brought her to the brink of orgasm several times before easing up, only to take her back again. When it seemed she was ready to explode, I helped her have a marvelous orgasm. Once she caught her breath, she slid back into the pool and into my arms as we kissed for several more moments.

Soon, it was time for Faye to leave, and our amazing afternoon was over. She went to change clothes and dry her hair before leaving. Sophia didn't come home early, and Alex never knew Faye wasn't at school. It was another beautiful day of being together.

The ten-week summer semester sped by. We got a great start on the project, and Faye adjusted to graduate school. She performed as I expected she would, and both her academic and research work were excellent. Our group worked well together, and everything went great. It looked as though it would be an exceptional two years ahead for us.

By the time the summer term finished, everyone was ready for a break from work and school. Faye and Alex were planning to visit her family in Nashville for the two weeks we had off. I assumed Sophia and I would take a trip somewhere, but we hadn't planned it yet. When I brought up the topic at home, she seemed disinterested in going anywhere. She explained she was in the middle of a busy time at work and didn't think she could get away. Sophia had always looked forward to our trips together and juggled her schedule to accommodate our plans. This time, she wasn't interested in going anywhere. I realized I'd become somewhat distant, and we weren't as close anymore. I'm sure it had a lot to do with my relationship with Faye, so I understood why she might not want to go. Instead, I planned to stay in Gainesville and play golf, relax at home, and get caught up on my pleasure reading. I also needed to write a research report describing our project plan and beginning efforts, so I'd have extra time to work on the report. And I'd be thinking about Faye, not Sophia.

CHAPTER 14

But You'll Thank Me for It

Faye seldom contacted me when she was out of town during breaks from school, so it surprised me to receive this message from her before she returned to campus for the start of classes for the fall semester of 2008.

*****

Date: Mon, 11 Aug 2008 10:41:13 (EDT)
From: Laura McDonald
To: Phillip Demarco
Subject: Nashville

Howdy!!!

How is my favorite professor doing? I miss you! It seems like forever since I've seen you! Did you finish the progress report? I know you did, but I figured I'd ask, anyway. Were you mad that you didn't get to go anywhere for the break?

I got this strange email this morning from somebody in the dean's office asking if I want to be in some promotional photos for the college? Were you involved in this somehow? I'm sure you were. Why else would they pick me? Anyhow, I told them I would. I hope the photos aren't like the ones you took of me out in the woods that day. But you need to be in them too. People won't know what to think if they see me without you!

We had our family reunion, and there were about sixty people there. I didn't know many of them. This weekend, we're taking my mother to the Grand Ole Opry for her birthday. I only enjoy country music when I'm in Nashville, just like you. But I can't wait to get back to Gainesville. Well, that's all for now, my love.

Your BP

*****

On the first day of classes, I didn't arrive at my office until late because of a dental appointment. Faye heard me come in, and as soon as I sat down, I received a message from her.

*****

Date: Mon, 15 Aug 2008 09:50:32 (EDT)
From: Laura McDonald
To: Phillip Demarco
Subject: You're here!

Hello, handsome,

I just wanted to say how delighted I am that my wonderful handsome prince has returned. I'm on my way over there right now!

Faye

*****

We had our first research meeting that day to get organized. Everyone attended, and it appeared they were all happy to be back. None of the four graduate students on our team were in my class this semester, but they would be in the spring.

In addition to our Monday and Thursday meetings, I was always available to answer questions anybody might have about our project. Sometimes, Michael, Yongsun, or Nicole would come in with questions or needing guidance, which often took a good bit of my time. Whenever that happened, Faye became upset. Michael was the worst of all because he could talk and talk and talk, and any discussion with him was a long-term proposition, which stole time away from Faye. I didn't like that either.

*****

Date: Wed, 3 Sep 1008 16:34:18 (EDT)
From: Laura McDonald
To: Phillip Demarco
Subject: Michael!

If I'm not mistaken, Michael is in your office using up my entire "Faye hour"! Now I have to go to the library. This is terrible!

I know Michael will talk until you kick him out. So goodnight, HP!

BP

*****

My relationship with Faye grew into something neither of us could have ever envisioned. We spent an enormous amount of time together and remained inseparable. My office was her office, and everyone in the department—faculty and students alike—knew it. I could only imagine what thoughts ran through their minds. But nobody ever said anything negative about it to me. I believe it was because Faye was such a pleasant person, and everybody liked her, and nobody could ever blame me for being with her as much as possible. She and I both wanted to be together every minute we could, and we knew we still loved each other. I realized it was harming my marriage, although I didn't know how it was affecting Faye's. I learned that topic was off-limits during our discussions.

Faye was very affectionate and loving whenever we were alone. The days, weeks, and months flew by, and our lives in each other's orbits were fun and exciting.

But from time to time, each of us struggled with our relationship. We both felt guilty for betraying our spouses, and we both became frustrated that we couldn't or wouldn't take it to an even higher level. I always hoped it would happen, but Faye was hesitant. She often "pondered" where it all was going, where it should go, and where she wanted it to go. Sometimes, she needed to back away, but it never lasted long. I didn't feel the same way. I knew we were still in love and still infatuated with each other.

Faye continued to send me enticing—and entertaining—messages, which I always loved to receive.

*****

Date: Sun, 5 Oct 2008 22:47:09 (EDT)
From: Laura McDonald
To: Phillip Demarco
Subject: What I want you to do

Hello!

I am missing you awful this evening! It's too bad you can't come to visit me because then I could tell you what I want you to do to me! Maybe we'll be able to be alone tomorrow if you can go rollerblading. Well, I'll talk to you later, handsome prince. (And yes, you're still my handsome prince!)

Your beautiful princess

*****

It was autumn everywhere in the northern hemisphere, but it wasn't very visible in Florida. Faye loved the multi-colored fall foliage, which was beautiful every year in Tennessee but uncommon here. She missed the leaves changing colors after moving to Gainesville, where only a few types of trees would shed their leaves. One brisk morning, as I was walking through a different part of campus, I passed an old oak tree shedding its brown, yellow, and orange leaves. Since I knew how much Faye enjoyed fall colors, I scooped up a handful of them and slid them into my briefcase. As I walked toward my building, I found Faye sitting on a bench in the courtyard, enjoying the autumn morning. She wore an oversized navy-blue turtleneck sweater and matching knit tassel hat. I surprised her when I opened my briefcase and handed her the leaves I collected. She loved them and appreciated my gesture. I sat on the bench next to her, and as she held up a large yellow leaf in front of her face and playfully peeked at me from behind it, I took out my camera and snapped a few photos for my "Faye Collection."

"HP, you are so thoughtful! I *love* these leaves! You treat me better than anyone has ever treated me before. You are so precious! Alex would never think of doing something like that for me. Thank you!" We sat and chatted for a little while before we headed in. Not long afterward, Faye wrote to alert me she was coming to visit.

*****

Date: Tue, 11 Nov 2008 10:36:57 (EST)
From: Laura McDonald
To: Phillip Demarco
Subject: I'm coming!

What are you doing over there? I'll soon find out because I'm on my way to visit you!

BP

*****

The day, weeks, months, and holidays passed quickly, and before we knew it, we were into the spring semester of 2009. The relationship between Faye and me continued to be loving and satisfying. We remained a big part of each other's daily lives. My focus was on her rather than my marriage or my future with Sophia. But I still didn't see a path forward for me to end up with Faye. We remained inseparable, and she continued to send me messages when we couldn't be together. And we still enjoyed "misbehaving" every chance we had.

*****

Date: Fri, 16 Jan 2009 11:18:50 (EST)
From: Laura McDonald
To: Phillip Demarco
Subject: In a moment

HELLO, HANDSOME!

I'M COMING TO VISIT YOU MOMENTARILY. HOW ABOUT IF WE SHUT YOUR DOOR?

Faye

*****

Date: Mon, 2 Feb 2009 14:48:08 (EST)
From: Laura McDonald
To: Phillip Demarco
Subject Oh my…

That was quite an exciting time on Friday, wasn't it? I believe it was the first time you removed some of my clothing in your office. You're so bad!!!

I am very lonesome today because my favorite professor already left for the day! I'll just need two "Faye hours" tomorrow to make up for it! Don't have too much fun in all those meetings.

BP

*****

Date: Tue, 3 Feb 2009 11:36:38 (EST)
From: Laura McDonald
To: Phillip Demarco
Subject: It's about time

Welcome back, handsome prince! I'll be over there in a minute!

BP

*****

Date: Tue, 3 Feb 2009 17:01:33 (EST)
From: Laura McDonald
To: Phillip Demarco
Subject: Today!

Hola mi amor!

I had a wonderful time misbehaving with you this afternoon too! That's what happens when I'm away from you for more than a weekend! It's terrible, just terrible! Promise me you won't get mad if I ponder things again, okay? As you know, in a few days, I'll start behaving myself again. I know you hate it, but if I don't behave, I always think about you and what it would be like to spend all our time together. Since I'm not with you, it's very hard for me to always do that, knowing it can't happen.

Since you always want to know what I'm thinking, I'll tell you. I was thinking about how wonderful you are. I love being around you, talking to you, and looking at that handsome face of yours! I hope you know that I love you. If not, now you do!

Well, I intended on this being a short letter, and I've been rambling on. I'll see you tomorrow, love of my life!

Faye

*****

That was the first time Faye referred to me as the love of her life. I thought the same about her many times, but never told her so. Perhaps our relationship was moving to a different level, and I didn't realize it.

I had to leave to attend another conference a few days later, this one in Aspen, Colorado. Whenever I visited Colorado in the winter, I always tried to arrange my schedule so I could hit the slopes a time or two during my visit there. Faye expected as much.

*****

Date: Mon, 9 Feb 2009 14:39:40 (EST)
From: Laura McDonald
To: Phillip Demarco
Subject: Your "conference"

Hello, handsome!

How's that "conference" going? I'm sure you're working hard—at skiing, that is! Well, it's a quiet day here. I have no one to talk to at all! Have a fantastic trip and remember to watch out for those trees (and those blonde snow bunnies)!

Your blonde snow bunny in Florida

*****

Date: Mon, 9 Feb 2009 23:39:40 (EST)
From: Phillip Demarco
To: Laura McDonald
Subject: No bunnies

Hello, BP,

My "conference" is going fine, but I miss you awful! And just so you know, I haven't seen one snow bunny yet. I'm having fun, but I'd rather be there with you. I also want to tell you, IWALY! (Try to figure that one out.)

Your bunny-less HP

*****

Date: Tue, 10 Feb 2009 10:45:12 (EDT)
From: Laura McDonald
To: Phillip Demarco
Subject: Abbr.

Well, I figured out your secret abbreviation! And IWALY too! Hurry home!

Your BP

*****

Once I got back to Gainesville, we picked up right where we left off before my trip to Colorado. We spent as much time together as possible, and Faye continued to be demanding of my time, which I didn't mind at all. She thought she deserved immediate access to me anytime she wanted it, and I felt the same way about her. I loved the possessiveness of me she was now taking and revealing in many of her messages.

*****

Date: Mon, 13 Apr 2009 14:56:13 (EDT)
From: Laura McDonald
To: Phillip Demarco
Subject: You're missing!!!!!

Where have you gone? I came back from class, and now you've run away! How terrible! *Adios mi amigo*!

Faye

*****

Date: Fri, 1 May 2009 14:20:11 (EDT)
From: Laura McDonald
To: Phillip Demarco
Subject: Boring

Hello!

It has been a very boring day without you here, and I don't like it at all! From now on, you can't miss any more Fridays unless you're with me!
Your sad little graduate student!

*****

Date: Wed, 24 Jun 2009 12:20:25 (EDT)
From: Laura McDonald
To: Phillip Demarco
Subject: Washer repair guy

What? You're not coming back this afternoon? Those
repair guys are never on time, so now I won't get to see you.
How sad! I'll stay here until 2:00 or 2:30 p.m. in case you call
me. If I'm not here, you can call me at home. Alex shouldn't
be there until after 4:00 p.m. So call me!

BP

*****

Date: Mon, 29 Jun 2009 16:19:28 (EST)
From: Laura McDonald
To: Phillip Demarco
Subject: Stop Talking

If you and Yongsun ever finish whatever you're doing,
why don't you come over and visit me? I may leave at 4:45
p.m. today, so stop talking and come here!

BP

*****

Time was flying by for us. Almost before we could blink,
we moved through the summer and fall Semesters of 2009.
All the while Faye and I remained as close and as much in
love as ever.

We were happy to get back to our regular routines after
the holidays. When classes resumed for the spring semester
of 2010, it would be a semester that was sure to bring about
many changes in our lives. Alex was on track to graduate in

May, and Faye and Nicole would graduate in August with their master's degrees. Once again, I expected my relationship with Faye would end, and we would both move forward in different directions. But the last two semesters with Faye still held adventures and unknowns, one being the exact direction each of our lives would take. One new adventure, however, confronted us right away.

When academic institutions receive research grants, the funding agency requires periodic progress reports. It's common practice for the researchers to write technical papers, which are subsets of those progress reports describing parts of the work, and to present those papers at professional conferences or meetings. Being about halfway through our research grant, we already got some good results, and our group generated three papers about our work. Conference organizers accepted two of them for presentation at a conference in New Orleans during February 2010. Michael, Yongsun, and Charles wrote one paper, while I wrote a second one with Faye and a third with Nicole that she wanted to submit to a physics journal instead of the conference. An important part of graduate education is to give students the experience of presenting conference papers at those professional meetings. Charles and I discussed it and decided that Michael and Faye should be the ones to present our papers, and he and I would attend as coauthors to help answer questions. Charles would inform Michael about our decision, and I would tell Faye.

When Faye came to my office early the next morning, I greeted her by saying, "Faye, I going to ask you to do something you won't want to do, but you'll thank me for it."

She laughed and replied, "I don't think that will happen! But okay, what is it?"

I told her about the papers being accepted and that Charles and I wanted her to present one at the conference in New Orleans. I knew she didn't like to speak in public and wouldn't appreciate the idea at all.

Faye's immediate response was, "I don't want to!"

"I already knew that. But you need to. Presenting your work is part of your education."

"But I'll hate doing that all by myself. What if I can't answer the questions, then I'll look stupid!"

"You won't look stupid. You're a brilliant student, and you'll know all the answers before you go. Besides, if you get stuck, I'll be there to help you out."

Faye responded, "But I don't want…" And she stopped mid-sentence as her jaw dropped and she stared at me. I knew exactly what she was thinking at that instant.

"Yes, BP, we'll *both* be going, without Alex or Sophia, and we'll be staying in one of those fancy hotels and have our own rooms!" She closed her mouth, and her eyes grew wide before a huge smile appeared.

"Do you think we can spend an entire night together while we're there?"

"That would also be a yes," Now I responded with a grin.

"Then great, I can't *wait*… to present our paper!" she said, laughing.

"But just so you know, Charles and Michael will also be there, but we can keep to ourselves as much as possible."

"That'll be perfect. Thank you, HP!"

I replied, "I knew you'd thank me!"

Faye wrinkled up her nose and gave me a "Humph" and walked out.

We spent the next few weeks finishing our paper, making slides for the presentation, and having Faye practice a few times in front of our team. I knew she'd do well since the work she was presenting was her master's degree research. The only trouble Faye had in our practices was she had a tendency to talk too fast because of her nervousness and finish too soon, leaving too much time for questions. Michael had the opposite problem: he talked too long and didn't leave any time for questions.

Conferences always ran from Monday until Thursday, but we planned to arrive on Saturday so we could enjoy the city and attend some preconference social functions. All four of us booked the same flight, so we met on campus in the morning and rode a university shuttle to the airport. Everything went well, and we arrived in New Orleans by mid-afternoon. We took a taxi from the airport to the Hilton Riverside Hotel near downtown, the host hotel for the conference, and registered. Before we left Gainesville, I called ahead to the hotel and requested Faye and I get rooms on the same floor. It turned out her room was only a few doors from mine, which made it very convenient for us. We all met for dinner at the hotel restaurant at 6:00 p.m. and then walked up to Frenchmen Street to find some classic New Orleans music. We heard some great jazz and blues at the Maison, Bamboula's, and the Spotted Cat. We also heard an authentic brass band playing in the street to a large crowd before taking a taxi back to the hotel around 10:30 p.m. Charles and Michael had rooms on different floors, far from ours.

We went to our separate rooms before Faye tiptoed down the hall to mine a short time later. I had given her a key earlier, and she walked in wearing one of the white robes the hotel provided to its guests. After a passionate kiss, the robe somehow fell to the floor. We couldn't find the bed fast enough, and I helped her remove the sexy red nightgown she brought from home. And we got to spend a night together at last, after such a long time of wishing for it to happen.

We didn't get much sleep. We spent most of the time cuddling, kissing, and making love. It was an incredible night of two people exploring and adoring each other. We slept through Sunday breakfast and were tired most of the day, but it was worth it. In the afternoon, we rode a Hop-on, Hop-off tour bus through the Garden District and Uptown to see more of the city. When the bus stopped at Louisiana Avenue, we hopped off to take a walk along Magazine Street and its many shops, galleries, bars, and eateries. Then we walked up Napoleon Avenue to St. Charles Avenue to ride one of the historic streetcars back to Canal Street. We finished our afternoon with a romantic dinner of authentic Creole food at Tujague's on Decatur Street, before returning to our hotel.

We ended up spending all five nights together in either my room or Faye's. We skipped out of the conference social events early each evening so we could have more time alone. Those nights together were even better than we expected, and we came home loving each other more than when we left. One thing we found that we both enjoyed was my brushing Faye's long, beautiful hair before going to sleep. I brushed it at least one hundred strokes every night. Each time, Faye would comment about how much she enjoyed me brushing it for her. I felt as though I was doing it for a real beautiful princess, and I told her so. The hair brushings often led to me giving her a back rub, which evolved into a "front rub". And I did my best to mess up her "haa-ir" before falling asleep with her in my arms.

Faye's presentation went well. She was very professional, spoke without rushing, and answered all the questions. It was her first professional conference, and she impressed those in attendance. I was proud of her!

We both enjoyed the conference and the city, both inside and outside our hotel rooms. I'd been to New Orleans before, but Faye hadn't. She loved the food and the music and expressed an interest in returning when she could stay longer. One highlight of our trip was visiting the original Tipitina's to hear some authentic Zydeco music, which we both loved.

Before we arrived in New Orleans, Faye was worried about our safety there. We'd both heard it was a dangerous city after Hurricane Katrina. But we didn't have any problems at all, nor did we see any crime while we were there. We felt safe the entire time and were both taken by the many charms of such an amazing city.

CHAPTER 15

There's Always a Catch

When we returned to Gainesville after the conference, we all had a lot of work to do. Charles and I had to write another research progress report, and Faye and Nicole had to finish writing their theses and prepare to defend them so they could graduate. If everything went well, both would complete their master's degrees in the summer, so time was becoming short to get everything done. Alex was graduating in about a month and had started job hunting, so once again, it looked as though my time with Faye would end soon.

I had to travel down to the Kennedy Space Center (KSC) to talk to NASA officials about some future research possibilities. My trip coincided with the launch of the Space Shuttle Discovery on Mission STS-131. A former student of mine who worked there invited me to watch the launch from the VIP area about a mile away. I had never seen one so close-up before, and to make it even better, STS-131 was the last scheduled night launch of the Shuttle Program. I wanted to take Faye with me, but it wasn't possible.

*****

Date: Mon, 5 Apr 2010 14:09:21 (EDT)
From: Laura McDonald
To: Phillip Demarco
Subject: Space Shuttle Launch

Hello!

I hope you have a good time down at KSC! I'm sorry I can't go with you. I wish I could! Be careful driving.

Faye

*****

It was an incredible launch to see in person, and it thrilled me to witness it firsthand. The next afternoon, I received this funny message from Faye.

*****

Date: Tue, 6 Apr 2010 14:37:27 (EDT)
From: Laura McDonald
To: Phillip Demarco
Subject: Beware!

Hello!

How was the shuttle launch? I watched it on TV, and it looked beautiful. I'm writing to warn you about things when you get back tomorrow! Nicole found out the paper the two of you submitted to the physics journal didn't get accepted for publication. She claims the reviewers said they didn't think the work was correct or something, but I read the letter, and that's not what they said at all. She's just upset. So now, Nicole has decided she'll never find a job and will end up working as a cashier. I'm the unfortunate person here alone with her when she's in one of her "I suck" moods! It's been a very long day already. Anyway, I hope you had a good trip, and I want you to hurry and come back here. I'm very lonesome without you. Well, I miss you, and I can't wait to see you tomorrow! And remember beware of the mad physicist!

Faye

*****

Nicole had calmed down by the time I returned to campus the next morning. I talked with her before Faye arrived and explained how everybody gets papers rejected; that's the way the system works. We'll make changes and resubmit it. It often takes two or three iterations before a paper gets accepted, and sometimes, it's never published. After I told Nicole I've had a few of those during my career already, she felt better. But she still viewed the rejection as a personal insult, which was how Nicole perceived things. A little later, I received another amusing message from Faye.

*****

Date: Mon, 3 May 2010 10:26:05 (EDT)
From: Laura McDonald
To: Phillip Demarco
Subject: Annoyed

Don't these people know that from 10:25—10:30 a.m. is a Faye five minutes? Won't they ever learn? I'll see you after I get back from my fluid mechanics / "anti-evolution" class. Have a nice seventy-five minutes!

Faye

*****

Faye directed her "anti-evolution" comment toward the professor teaching her class. He was a "Christian" who couldn't keep from proselytizing his religious beliefs to the class. None of his students, Faye included, appreciated it. She wasn't religious at all and often referred to those who were as "church people." If this faculty member only knew how much the students laughed at him, he might reconsider his teaching style.

I wasn't sure what to expect as far as my future with Faye after she graduated. Until one morning when she danced into my office as usual, then said, "I have some news I want to talk to you about," as she plopped herself down in her "Faye" chair.

"Oh? What news, Faye?" I asked, without having a clue what it could be.

"Okay, so you knew Alex is graduating this semester, right?" she started.

"Yes, I knew that" I replied.

"Well, he received a job offer from a company here in Gainesville he wants to accept, but I need to have something to do, too. Plus, I don't want to leave school yet. So I've been thinking about it a lot, and I'd like to stay on and get a PhD if I can. Do you think that would be possible, HP?" Faye asked.

Surprised, I answered, "Well, getting a doctorate is a huge commitment, Faye. It would mean at least three more years of school. And you need to have a great reason for doing it because it's very hard and requires a tremendous amount of work. I believe you could do it, but first, why do you want a PhD?"

"I've thought a lot about that too, and I've decided I'd like to be a professor. I love how you teach, and you've inspired me to want to do it too."

"Thank you, Faye. I think you'd be an excellent teacher someday. And the field of engineering desperately needs outstanding female professors. I'm sure there wouldn't be a problem with you being accepted into the doctoral program.

You have a terrific academic record and have done exemplary work," I said.

"But I'll need funding to continue, and I'd want to keep working with you," she said. "Do you think both those things are possible?"

"Well, yes, Faye. All PhD students receive funding, and yes, you can continue to be my graduate student. It would offend me if you worked with someone else!"

"We have one more year left on our grant, so you can still work on that. Then since you'd like to become a professor, I'm sure Robert would hire you as an instructor to teach some lower-level classes each semester. Teaching would pay you more money, and you could start after the grant ends. How does that sound to you?"

"It sounds *perfect*, HP! I'd love to teach classes here. Thank you for being so supportive."

"It's my pleasure, Faye. I don't want you to leave either."

"But there's something else you should know about Alex's job. It will involve some traveling, so he'll be out of town a few days each month," she said, smiling.

"He will? That sounds perfect too, BP!" I replied laughing. "Okay then, go submit your application, and I'll talk with Robert about developing a funding plan for you. But I don't foresee a problem with your funding, either."

"Wonderful! Thank you! I will *love* staying here with you for three more years!"

"I'll love it too, Faye."

I was speechless after Faye left my office. I hadn't even considered the possibility she might want to stay on for a doctorate since most graduate students leave after receiving their master's degrees. Nor did I consider Alex would take a job in Gainesville. I was very pleased. He started working immediately after graduating in the spring semester, and we were soon into the summer semester of 2010.

The summer was a relaxing one. I was only working on research and not teaching any classes. Faye had finished all her coursework and was finishing up her thesis while also continuing to work on our project. We developed a plan for another project she could use for her doctoral dissertation, which would require at least two more years of research. So during the summer, Faye was very busy, and I wasn't. Alex had to travel three or four days a month for work, besides continuing his Air Force reserve duties one weekend each month. As a result, Faye and I spent many hours together at her house.

I also had time to play golf when I wasn't with Faye or at the office, since Sophia always seemed to be very busy. Faye didn't golf but enjoyed hearing about my adventures on the course. Most of the time, I could only play early in the morning to beat the heat and came to work afterward. I often played with friends or colleagues, and we always had fun. I'm not a great golfer, but I enjoyed playing and getting some outdoor exercise. One day, when I returned, I went straight to Faye's office to say hello. She asked me how my golf game was. I didn't have much good to tell her about how I played, but I told her some funny jokes I heard from my friends.

Faye and Nicole defended their master's theses in the next few weeks. Their presentations were outstanding, as was everything they did during their graduate programs. Faye's performance justified the confidence I placed in her abilities. She finished with a perfect 4.0 GPA and became well known in the department to both students and faculty alike. Everyone liked her a lot. Colleagues often tried to steal her away from me to become their graduate student, but Faye had no interest in working with anybody but me. Both women graduated at the end of the summer, and Nicole's boyfriend, James, received his PhD in mathematics at the same time. James accepted a faculty position at the University of Central Florida in Orlando, and Nicole found a job at Lockheed Martin nearby. As Faye and Nicole's major professor, I sat between them in the floor seating area of the Stephen C. O'Connell Center, while their families sat together in the spectator section. It was a fun day, and there was plenty of laughing and joking throughout the ceremony.

Meanwhile, Faye received her acceptance into the doctoral program, and we solidified a funding plan for her. She'd continue to work another year on our research grant, then become an instructor, teaching lower-level engineering mechanics courses, like the first one she took from me. I'd serve as her teaching mentor and be her major professor for her doctorate.

After graduation, Nicole moved to Orlando with James, and Faye and Alex went on a one-week-long Caribbean cruise out of Miami. Over the break, they flew South to meet up with their ship for a well-deserved vacation for them both. Once again, Sophia and I stayed in Gainesville as she showed little interest in going away. Her travel schedule had increased with more frequent trips back to New York. I was seldom asked to go along, and when I was, I found an excuse to stay at home. I had been to the city many times—too many times, perhaps—and didn't enjoy it much anymore. I felt as though I'd already seen and done everything in New York I ever wanted to see and do, plus I'd rather be in town when Faye returned from her vacation.

I knew my marriage was slipping away, and I'm sure Sophia felt the same way. We weren't as close as we used to be, and I knew it was my fault. But I decided several years before to pursue a relationship with Faye, regardless of its effect on my marriage, and I was still glad I did. I knew the risk involved in doing so, and my feelings about my decision hadn't changed. I still loved Faye, even though I didn't expect she would ever leave Alex to be with me. Although I now realized I was ready to end my marriage to be with her.

Before we knew it, the break from school was over, and we were back for the fall semester of 2010. Faye and Alex enjoyed their cruise, and I had a relaxing time at home. Faye soon started classes, and we got back to our research. After Nicole left, Faye had their office to herself. She and

I were together even more during the day, plus whenever
Alex traveled for work or was on reserve duty. We continued
to have lunch together three or four times each week; I
interacted less with my colleagues and other students, and I
began getting to work earlier and staying later each day.
Every minute spent together was joyous for us both. Our
conversations often ended with our expressions of us being
soul mates, a bizarre concept for two people twenty-four
years apart in age.

During her first year of doctoral study, Faye needed to
take some courses of a broadening nature to prepare for her
PhD qualifying exams the next fall. As a result, Faye didn't
have to take classes from me anymore, but ones taught by
other professors in the department. They all seemed to enjoy
having her in class and would often comment on how lucky I
was to have her as my PhD student. Her sparkling personality
won them all over.

The fall semester blended into the spring semester of
2011, and it would soon be summer. Our grant was almost
over and we began writing the final report, which was due in
late April. We also wrote two more papers for a conference in
San Diego in February, which Faye and I would attend alone
this time. She would present one paper, and I would present
the other. She was much less apprehensive about speaking in
public this time.

We traveled to San Diego on Saturday before the Monday
the conference started. This time, I called ahead and arranged
for us to have adjoining rooms, which I didn't mention to Faye
before we left. I rented a Mustang convertible at the airport,
thinking at some point we could drive out to the beach. But
the California weather didn't cooperate; it was cool and rainy
most of the trip, and we didn't put the top-down once. We
drove around the city and the harbor when we arrived before
heading to the hotel. When we checked in, Faye quickly
realized we had connecting rooms, and she couldn't keep
from laughing, even though she said I was terrible for doing

so. We spent much of our time in either my room or hers and each night together in one of our king-size beds.

Monday was Valentine's Day, so I made dinner reservations at Tom Ham's Lighthouse on Harbor Island. It was a clear night, so we sat outside on the back deck overlooking the water, where we could watch the many boats returning after a day on the Pacific Ocean.

We ordered a chilled platter of oysters, clams, baby scallops, tiger shrimp, and mussels—all of which were excellent—and the setting was very romantic. Many other couples there were also celebrating the night. But looking around, it was easy to see we were the couple with the largest difference in ages, which made me somewhat uncomfortable, but Faye didn't seem to mind. At least she didn't show it. She was joyous the entire evening. After we returned to the hotel, we were sitting on my bed talking, and I gave Faye a gift. Before leaving Gainesville, I stopped in a novelty store and bought her a little girl's plastic tiara, which was silver and loaded with many colored glass chips. I used it to unofficially crown her a "beautiful princess." Faye thought my joke gift was hilarious, but also romantic. I also bought her a small box of chocolate truffles again and a funny Valentine's card, which I gave her after the tiara. She gave me a beautiful and very romantic card to celebrate as well.

Faye's presentation was at 9:00 a.m., and mine was at 3:00 p.m., both on Tuesday. Faye did very well once again and handled all the questions flawlessly, but she felt better when it was over. After her session, we had lunch in the hotel and went back to our rooms to relax before I presented my paper. I tried to give Faye the impression I was a little nervous, although I wasn't. She was sitting on the bed and motioned for me to come and sit beside her. When I did, she kissed me and removed my tie and unbuttoned my shirt. I stretched out and pulled her next to me. As we kissed, I undressed her, and she finished undressing me. We made passionate love and played in bed for an hour before it was time to get dressed again, and head downstairs for my session. My presentation also went well, and I enjoyed speaking with Faye's smiling face in the audience.

The entire San Diego trip was fun and romantic, and I felt spending five more nights together brought us even closer. I was sad for it to be over and to return home on Thursday. Each time, it got harder to leave each other and go back to our spouses.

Our grant was ending in April, and I didn't have funding lined up for the summer for me or for Faye, since she wouldn't start teaching until the fall. One day, in mid-April, I received a call from one of my contacts at KSC. This was the same individual I visited earlier to discuss research possibilities. He called to ask me if I'd be interested in spending the summer there to work on an internal development program. The money was good for government work, about one hundred dollars per hour, so I was happy to accept the offer. During our conversation, I mentioned I was also in need of summer funding for Faye and asked him if he had any ideas. He responded that he'd be happy to have her come down and work on the same project. When I described her capabilities and told him she was a doctoral student, he offered her a summer position, paying fifty dollars per hour. KSC was about a two-hour and thirty-minute drive from Gainesville, but there were no additional funds for living expenses, so we'd have to cover those costs on our own out of our salaries. The arrangement was fine with me, and I didn't think Faye would object either since her summer pay from NASA would be higher than her salary as a graduate student. After ending our phone call, I went across the hall to tell Faye about the opportunity.

As I walked through the doorway of her office, I said, "Faye, guess what?"

"What, HP?"

"Well, you know how we don't have any funding for the summer after we finish working on our grant?" I began.

"Yes, I'm very aware of that fact," she answered with an annoyed look on her face.

"Well, I've got some news," I said.

"News? What news? Tell me, tell me, tell me!" Faye replied.

I explained, "The news is, we were just offered summer jobs down at Kennedy Space Center, working full-time for NASA."

Surprised, Faye said, "Wait, what? What jobs? What do you mean, *we*?"

"Engineering jobs, and if you want to go, we'll be working together on the same project, and they'll pay you fifty dollars per hour."

"What? Are you serious?" Faye responded.

"Yes, I am, but there's a catch," I answered.

"Oh no, another catch! What's the catch this time?"

"Well, the catch is we'd have to live down there all summer and cover our own living expenses out of our salaries, since there's no extra money for that. Does that sound like something you'd be interested in doing?" I asked.

"For fifty dollars an hour? That's a lot more than I get here. Yes, I'll take it! Call them back right now and tell them I accept," Faye directed me.

"Are you sure you want to be away from Gainesville the entire summer?" I replied. "Yes, I'm sure! As long as you're going too! You'll be going too, won't you HP?" she continued.

"Well, I've already accepted it for me, so yes, I'm going. If you're sure, I'll call them right now and tell them you accept too. It will start after school gets out mid-May and last until
mid-August," I explained.

"That sounds perfect!" Faye answered. "Plus, we'll get to be together the whole summer, won't we?"

"Yes, BP, we sure will!" I replied.

CHAPTER 16

The Dancing Princess

When the news about our upcoming summer jobs at Kennedy Space Center sank in, Faye and I realized we needed to quickly arrange for housing in the area. We knew we couldn't share an apartment since Alex and perhaps Sophia would come to visit. After searching for places to live we developed a list of possibilities, most of which were in Titusville, Florida, about a twenty minute drive from KSC. Faye was eager to find a place and wanted to go down to check out the possibilities over the coming weekend. I couldn't get away, so Faye and Alex drove down alone.

Before she left, I teased her and said, "Find one for me too."

On Monday morning, Faye danced into my office wearing a huge smile. When I inquired about how the apartment-hunting trip went, she replied, "Great!" and gave me a handful of papers.

"What's this?" I asked.

"It's the lease information for your new apartment in Titusville. All you have to do is sign them and send them back with your security deposit."

"You found one for me?"

"Yes," she answered. "We looked at several places, and this was the best one. I rented one too, and yours is right by mine! We're on the bottom floor of a three-story building with entrances from an outdoor walkway in the middle. Our doors are across from each other, apartments K1 and K2, in the back of the complex. The location is very secluded. And another great thing is, they're *furnished*, so we won't have to rent furniture! What do you think?"

"That's incredible, Faye, *you're* amazing for doing this! Thank you! And thank you for finding us apartments so close to each other. I'm astounded!"

"You're welcome, HP. It will be great!"

It was about two weeks before we were to start work when Faye began acting oddly. She didn't come to my office unless she needed something; she stopped going to lunch with me and meeting at her apartment, and just acted distant overall. I asked her several times what was wrong, but she would never admit to anything or tell me her thoughts. We discussed what we needed to do to prepare to move, but not much else. Our relationship became strained and uncomfortable, at least for me.

When it came time for us to leave for Titusville, we drove down in separate cars on the Friday before the Monday we were to begin work. We wanted to sign up for utilities, settle into our apartments, and acquaint ourselves with the area before starting work. The layouts of our apartments were mirror images of each other. In mine, a small dining room was on the immediate left after entering, with the living room on the right. Beyond the dining room on the same side was the kitchen. The bedroom was farther down the hall on the right past the living room, and the bathroom was on the same side as the kitchen. White walls and tan carpeting adorned the entire place. It had well-used but functional furniture. A small TV was on a stand against the solid wall closest to the door, and a comfortable large sofa sat across the room from the TV and against the opposite wall. A small table next to the TV was where I placed the desktop computer I brought with me. Faye's unit had similar furnishings, but she brought a laptop computer instead. Since our computers were near each other, Faye could access my Wi-Fi service to save money. I expected Faye and I would spend most of our time together and share many intimate moments. But I was wrong. She remained distant and somewhat reclusive. When I asked her to go to lunch or dinner, go shopping, or spend time together in one of our apartments, she always declined. Something was up, but she wouldn't tell me what it was or even admit to it.

We decided Faye would ride with me to work each morning, so we had that short time together, but our conversations during our drive were nothing more than chitchat. When we arrived at our jobs on the first day, it turned out that we were to share an office with a woman named Terri, who was single and in her early forties. Terri welcomed us and provided valuable tips about working and getting around KSC. I could tell it would be a pleasant summer sharing our workspace with her. The office was very government issued, with old green metal furniture and filing cabinets. Terri's desk was on the far end beneath the windows, while Faye's and mine were on the opposite wall next to each other.

As we got started working, Faye was all business, treating me more as a boss than as a lover, and remaining disconnected from me. I didn't understand what was happening between us, but many thoughts ran through my mind. Perhaps our love affair had run its course, and she didn't want to continue it any longer. Or maybe she was tired of me. Perhaps she realized the obvious: I was far too old for her. And since we had little privacy at work, we couldn't talk about it during the day.

When we arrived back at our apartments after work each day, and as I hoped we could have dinner together, she'd walk to her door, turn, and say, "Okay, I'll see you tomorrow." I was at a loss for words and didn't understand her behavior. I could tell something was different, but I honored her unspoken wishes and gave her the space she seemed to want.

So we got our own dinners each night. I ate out more often, and Faye fixed dinner at home more to save money. We continued to ride to work together and share an office, but for the first two weeks, Faye was nothing more than an acquaintance. She wouldn't talk about it, nor would she spend any time alone with me. I felt lost and very disappointed. We had always communicated well until then. So, I assumed we were at the end of our romance.

I became very frustrated with our situation. On the third Friday night in Titusville, I didn't bother asking Faye to dinner, assuming she wouldn't go. As we reached our apartment doors after work, I unlocked my door and, without looking at her, said, "Well, I'll see you on Monday then!" My words surprised her, and she stood in silence as I disappeared through my door.

I had dinner out alone, and then visited a small club in Titusville to listen to some live music. While I sat at the bar, I met a nice woman named Julie, who was around my age, and we started a conversation. She was a nurse at Parrish Medical Center, and as the evening progressed, Julie became friendlier, and we enjoyed talking to each other. We also danced a few times. When the night grew late and the band finished playing, we didn't want our evening to end. Julie asked me back to her condo for a nightcap, and I accepted, which may not have been a wise thing, but I was enjoying our talk and wanted to continue it. I followed her in my car. Once there, we talked until morning and got to know each other better, but we didn't have sex or even kiss. I would have felt terrible if we had.

It was daybreak before we realized, and we decided some food was in order. We drove in our separate cars to a nearby Waffle House for a classic Southern breakfast. After eating, I headed back to my apartment, arriving around 9:00 a.m. When I did, Faye saw me coming in as she was walking to her car. She could tell from the clothes I wore I was coming in from the previous night. She didn't ask me where I'd been, but she had a very curious look on her face. We exchanged good mornings but nothing more, and I went inside to get some sleep. I slept until the early afternoon, and when I awoke, I had an email from Faye waiting for me.

*****

Date: Sat, 4 Jun 2011 12:24:52 (EDT)
From: Laura McDonald
To: Phillip Demarco
Subject: This is bad!

HP,

You might not want to read this because you won't like it. I know you were out with another woman last night! Why else would you be coming home in the morning looking so guilty? Where were you and who was she? And where did you find her?

I am very upset about this. I realize I haven't been very nice to you since we came down here, but you didn't have to go have sex with someone, did you? But I guess you'll say it's my fault for neglecting you and not wanting to do anything with you this summer. But you told me you weren't having sex with anyone besides your wife, and then you do something like this. I'm very disappointed in you.

HP, I asked you not very long ago if you wanted to sleep with other women, and you said no, which means you lied to me! Have you slept with anyone else other than the woman last night? If so, you need to tell me. This makes me wonder how many other lies you've told me. It upsets me very much that after all this time, you could look me in the eye and lie to me. Now I feel as though I'm only one of your conquests, and I don't feel like the BP anymore. I'm sure you think I'm making too big of a deal about this, but how would you like it if you were in my position? You don't know this, but one reason I never ran off with you was because I was afraid of something like this happening. How could I ever run off with someone who can outright lie to me? When I see you next, I'll only think about how you were with that woman and how you probably touched her the same way you touch me.

HP, I had such a wonderful time in San Diego, and I was, once again, contemplating running off with you, then I got scared. I love you, HP, but I don't know if I can be with you after this. It's hurtful to me when you're out there chasing other women while we're sleeping together. And yes, I've been crying over you once again.

When the summer started, I was ready to spend all my time with you, and then I got scared about running off with you. I should have told you why I was acting so strangely. But now it doesn't seem like you want to be with me anymore. I understand if you might like to go out with other women instead. But if you do, we can only be friends, nothing more, even though that's not how I want it to be. I could not handle only having you on the days you can't find anything/anyone better.

Well, I just wanted to tell you how upset I am. I hope I didn't make you too mad at me. But you need to think about how you would feel if you found out I was sleeping around and lying to you about it. I guess that's it. I'll talk to you later!

Faye

*****

Faye's message upset me, too. She made many false assumptions. But it helped explain why she'd been avoiding me since we got to Titusville. I should have talked to Faye right away, but before I could, I received another message from her.

*****

Date: Sat, 4 Jun 2011 13:33:52 (EDT)
From: Laura McDonald
To: Phillip Demarco
Subject: Disregard my earlier message... please!

HP,

I hope you aren't too mad at me after reading my last message. I know I should have asked you about what you did last night instead of making assumptions, but I got upset. You know I'm jealous of you because I can't stand the thought of you doing anything with someone else. I'm sorry I didn't discuss it with you first, but I only got upset because of the way I feel about you. And yes, I still think about what it would be like to run away with you (now I guess I'd have to ask you). I know we'd be happy together.

San Diego was such a wonderful time, and I enjoyed all our conversations too, especially the ones we had when you were brushing my "ha-irr." I feel like I can tell you more now than ever before. By the end of the summer, I might not keep quiet. I think spending so much time together will be very beneficial to me. Before we came down here, I always wondered if we would still get along as well if we saw each other all the time. I guess I wasn't sure how much we liked each other because we could never do that back in Gainesville. Being with you down here should clear it up for me. I've loved being with you so far, even when I was acting so weird after we first got here.

Well, HP, I wanted to tell you I still love you! And I need to see you as soon as possible, so tell me when I can come over there, if you want me to!

BP

*****

After reading Faye's last message, I felt much better. I wanted to answer before seeing her, if for no other reason than for me to process it all and to put my own thoughts into words.

*****

Date: Sat, 4 Jun 2011 14:11:12 (EDT)
From: Phillip Demarco
To: Laura McDonald
Subject: You'll always be my BP!

Oh, BP, I am so sorry I hurt you and made you feel so bad! Can you ever forgive me? I swear I have never lied to you. You are the most precious thing in the world to me, and I feel awful you think I lied. I met a woman at the bar last night, but nothing happened at all. We talked until late, then we went out to breakfast at the Waffle House. I didn't sleep with her or even kiss her. All we did was talk. And all those things I told you I've only done with you were true. I only want to be with you, and I'd do anything to make that happen. But now I seemed to have ruined any chance I might still have with you. I feel awful, but it's my fault, and I apologize. What I did was only out of loneliness because you were keeping away from me, and I didn't understand why.

Can't we begin our summer over again and put my bad behavior behind us? Please? I know I don't deserve someone as wonderful as you. But I promise you now, if you could ever again consider running off with me, I would *never* want or need anyone else in my life, only you. But after this incident, I'm sure you wouldn't. Once again, I apologize. I want you and nobody else! I miss my best friend in the world! I hope I'm still your HP.

PD

*****

I thought I'd get a quick shower and go over to Faye's apartment. By the time I finished, I had one more message from her waiting for me.

*****

Date: Sat, 4 Jun 2011 14:32:30 (EDT)
From: Laura McDonald
To: Phillip Demarco
Subject: I do!

HP,

I forgive you! I should have talked to you before I got so upset and sent you that first message. It made me very sad to think you'd been lying to me all this time, but now I know you weren't. You don't realize what the statement "...if you could ever consider running off with me, I would never want or need anyone else in my life" means to me, HP. I don't think you've ever said that to me before. I feel the same way about you. Sometimes I still feel guilty when I'm with Alex because I'm always thinking about you.

I want to begin the summer over again too and put those weeks of me being mean to you and this incident behind us. I will still consider running away with you. The BP must be with the HP! Remember, I told you not to read my message because you wouldn't like it? You should have listened to me! Although now you know how I feel about you lying to me. I think we should forget about what happened earlier this summer and begin again. None of this would even have occurred if I hadn't been mean to you when we first got here. I guess I was afraid of what might happen if we spent too much time together or something. Just the thought of you being with someone else made me realize how much I need you. I can't stand you being with anyone but me. Okay, let's start over and forget any of this ever happened. Do we have a deal?

Since I've said too much already, I want to see you now! Remember I love you, and I'll be over there in a minute, handsome!

BP

*****

Well, enough of our emailing. Faye arrived at my door a few minutes later. When she came in, we hugged and kissed each other like we hadn't seen each other in months. We sat on the couch and kissed more, making up for the lost time and showing how much we missed each other. We were both happy about us restarting the summer.

That evening, I cooked dinner for us in my apartment. And we danced. Faye had never slow-danced before and didn't know how. So I taught her. I played some oldies on the computer from a playlist I made, which included songs by Johnny Mathis, Ray Charles, Billy Joel, Dolly Parton, and many others. Most of them were popular before Faye was even born. She caught on fast, and we had a wonderful night of dancing. I even sang into her ear along with the music as we danced. Afterward, she stayed in my apartment the rest of the weekend, and we made sweet, passionate love as much as we could. I think we were both thrilled we got past this rough patch in our relationship. From that point forward, we became inseparable once again. There were some weekends when Alex would visit or when one of us had to go back to Gainesville, but when we were in Titusville alone, we spent our nights and about every minute of the days—both at work and outside work—together.

Monday morning came much too soon. Faye awoke early and went to her apartment to have breakfast and get ready for work. Within an hour, she knocked on my door so we could leave for KSC. Our drive in was more pleasant than when she was being distant, and it was more enjoyable talking about the weekend and the day ahead of us. Once we arrived at our office, I had an early meeting, and Faye stayed behind and wrote me this message, which I read as soon as I returned.

*****

Date: Mon, 6 Jun 2011 08:54:39 (EDT)
From: Laura McDonald
To: Phillip Demarco
Subject: The dancing princess

HP,

You can't even imagine how much fun I had with you this weekend! I loved you cooking dinner for me, dancing with me, making out on the sofa, and everything else we did all weekend long! I can't remember the last time I was so happy. I would spend my weekends thinking about how wonderful it would be to be spending them with you, and now I finally get to do it. I love being with you so much it makes me cry! (I know you're wondering what doesn't make me cry, aren't you?) I fell asleep hearing your beautiful singing in my head. I could have danced with you all night, and I can't wait to do it again. I loved every minute we spent together.

As you know, I need to get back to work, HP. I just wanted to tell you I had a fantastic time this weekend, and I am glad we started our summer over. I'll talk to you in about one second, I'm sure.

Your dancing princess

*****

At my morning meeting, I learned that each year, KSC celebrates the 1969 moon landing. This summer was the forty-second anniversary of that historical event. An engineer (a male) told a joke about it before the meeting started, which I couldn't wait to tell Faye when I got back to the office. His "Manny Klein" joke claimed Neil Armstrong's famous words when he first stepped on the moon were really, "That's one small step for man, one giant leap for Manny Klein." The reference to Manny Klein goes back to arguments Neil claimed to have overheard between his next-door neighbors Manny and Ethel Klein when he was growing up in Ohio. Manny would often ask his wife, Ethel, for oral sex, and her loud response was always, "Only when a man walks on the moon!" So Neil offered his statement as a tribute to Manny Klein.

Faye's response was predictable. "Oh, brother, you men!" She didn't believe the story to be true.

CHAPTER 17

I've Been a Bad Girl

The summer with Faye was turning into everything I hoped it would be before we got sidetracked at the beginning. We loved working together and living across the hallway from each other, except we spent almost every night at my place. We even exchanged keys to each other's apartments. And Faye became more playful, both at home and at work, and very adventurous in the bedroom. She always wanted to try new things and took great pleasure in all our activities there.

*****

Date: Tue, 21 Jun 2011 13:39:00 (EDT)
From: Laura McDonald
To: Phillip Demarco
Subject: Watching you

HP,

I had a lovely time with you last night. I even enjoyed watching you sleep. You don't know this, but when I was in the shower, you fell asleep on the couch. When I came into the living room, I watched you sleep for a while. The best part was, I kissed you on the lips several times, and you never knew. I still adore you, HP. I just don't let you know it all the time. You also looked very peaceful later when you were sleeping with your arms around me.

I have to get back to work now. I'll talk to you/fantasize about you in about one second!

Your graduate student,
Laura McDonald

*****

Date: Wed, 29 Jun 2011 16:41:30 (EDT)
From: Laura McDonald
To: Phillip Demarco
Subject: Later...

When we get home, I want you to ???? me!

One of the two women in this office

*****

The next weekend was long because Monday was the Fourth of July. I had to attend a friend's wedding in Gainesville on Saturday, and then I needed to go to Washington, DC, for some meetings. I'd fly to Gainesville from Melbourne, Florida on Friday, and then I'd fly to DC on Monday before flying back to Melbourne on Thursday. Faye agreed to take me to the airport and pick me up when I returned. I felt terrible about leaving her for an entire week. It would have been fun celebrating the Fourth with her and having three days off work to spend together. Faye would be alone since Alex had reserve duty over the weekend. Our airport goodbye wasn't easy.

During my time back in Gainesville, out of obligation, I asked Sophia if she wanted to come to Titusville for a weekend, but she declined. She replied once again that she had too much going on at work and couldn't get away.

Sophia didn't disappoint me by not wanting to visit. Later, after I got home from the wedding on Saturday afternoon, I received an amazing message from Faye. And a series of messages between us ensued.

*****

Date: Sat, 2 Jul 2011 12:44:38 (EDT)
From: Laura McDonald
To: Phillip Demarco
Subject: Missing you...

HP,

I had such a great time last Saturday (and Sunday too). I would love to do all of it over and over. Well, just as I suspected, it has happened: since I've been spending all this time with you, I want you more than ever (and not only for playtime in the bedroom, although that's always enjoyable too). I now get aggravated with Alex when we talk on the phone, and he doesn't even say anything wrong. I'd just rather be talking to you instead.

As of now, Alex will be down here next weekend. I hope this will change, but I doubt it will. This is terrible to say, but I'm not looking forward to seeing him because it only makes me miss/want you more. I'd rather spend my remaining weekends here with you, my HP.

I hope all the things you've been telling me for the last five years have been true, because the more I'm with you, the more unhappy I am with Alex. I don't know how long I'll be able to tolerate him not treating me the way I want after being with you this summer. When we go back to Gainesville, it will be very difficult for me to sit at home every night and be happy when I know what it could be like if I was with you instead. So, HP, if you were not serious when you said all those things to me, you need to tell me now before I say something to Alex I may regret later. I guess what I'm saying is, for the last two weeks, I have had ever-increasing thoughts (yet again) of running off with you. (I could ask you whenever I'm ready, right?) I'm sure you're skeptical of that. But even before we came down here, I've always dreamt of how wonderful it would be to be with you forever. It doesn't matter how good things are going with Alex; I still wonder if it would be better with you or how much happier I'd be. You somehow know how to treat me and how to make me feel as though I'm the only woman in the world who matters to you. No one else has ever done that. You are the only person who holds the key to that part of me.

I was telling you the truth the other day when I told you I stayed for yet another degree just so I could be around you. I knew I should have left, but I realized it wasn't possible. How could the BP live without the HP? You already know the answer; the BP *can't* be without the HP when she is crazy in love with him.

Well, I hope you read this. If you can't tell, I'm lonesome here without you. I want to kiss you right now. So hurry and get back here! I miss you and love you more than you'll ever realize.

The lonely BP

*****

Date: Sun, 3 Jul 2011 10:11:50 (EDT)
From: Laura McDonald
To: Phillip Demarco
Subject: It's terrible!

HP,

You made my day when you called me this morning. I was hoping you'd call me yesterday, but you never did, so it thrilled me to hear your lovely voice today. It's too bad we couldn't have talked longer. I can't wait until Thursday to see you again, HP. I haven't been sparkling in two entire days!

Last night, when Alex told me he wants to come down here next weekend, he noticed my disappointment, but I couldn't tell him he would interrupt my time with the HP. The other day, he mentioned he might be here a whole week. Can you imagine how thrilled I was with that news? It would be awful!

Not only do I miss you so much it's terrible, but I also miss you being terrible!

Love you,
BP

*****

Date: Sun, 3 Jul 2011 11:20:29 (EDT)
From: Phillip Demarco
To: Laura McDonald
Subject: We belong together

BP,

Thank you for your messages. They're *wonderful* and they've carried me through this trip so far. I'll be very disappointed if you're busy on the weekend. But I'll understand; I won't like it, but I'll understand.

I've thought about you ever since I left. I'm *so* happy being with you and miserable when I'm not. You said so many wonderful things to me in your emails, I only wish I had time to respond to each one of them, but I only have a few minutes right now. I hate being away from you. You are the light of my life! Please remember how crazy I am about you, BP. Everything I said to you over the last five years was true. I'm glad you now realize we belong together!

I better go. Happy Fourth tomorrow! I know you'll enjoy the day off from work. I'll call you from DC on Wednesday. If

Alex isn't there when I get back, we have to spend the night together. I need to hold you and love you all night long! Your HP

*****

Date: Mon, 4 Jul 2011 19:55:57 (EDT)
From: Laura McDonald
To: Phillip Demarco
Subject: No sparkling here

Happy Fourth of July! Now come home, please! I almost can't stand being alone with myself anymore (if that makes any sense). Since Alex will be here this weekend, maybe you and I could take a half day off from work on Friday and spend the afternoon together if you want to. I know it's not a very long time, but it's better than nothing, I suppose.

So, HP, when Alex is here, are you planning to go out with some other woman? This has been bothering me all weekend. I'm not sure I could handle you going out with somebody besides me. I can't help it, HP. I know you could get dates with many women, but I don't want you going out with someone else and holding their hands and kissing them, etc., etc., etc. I'm getting aggravated again just thinking about it! Well, enough of that. You already know how I feel about the topic. I only want my handsome prince to be with me.

I hope we have time to spend more weekends together this summer before we have to go back. I'll hate it if we can't. All I did this past weekend was relive the last weekend we spent together in my mind. I loved it! I seem to love every night I spend with you. But when we return to

Gainesville, you can still come to visit me whenever Alex is away. Or if you can't, just call me late at night and whisper to me.

Well, I'd better go. Hurry and come back. I need to sparkle again. And one more thing, I love you, I love you, I love you, I love you!

Your nonsparkling BP

*****

Date: Tue, 5 Jul 2011 10:40:26 (EDT)
From: Laura McDonald
To: Phillip Demarco
Subject: A BP in search of an HP

My missing HP,

How's it going up there? I have some good news. Alex won't arrive until Friday afternoon. So I can still pick you up at the airport, then we can have one night together. This is great because it would drive me crazy to wait until Monday to get my hands on you...for a hug, ha-ha.

I wish you would call me again, HP; I miss hearing your wonderful voice. I am so ready for you to come back to me. I can't stand being here without you. I have kept myself busy at work today, so it's not too boring. I try not to look at your empty chair, though; it makes me miss you too much.

I want to dance with you again. I liked that, HP!

Love,
The BP with no dancing HP

*****

Date: Wed, 6 Jul 2011 21:43:37 (EDT)
From: Laura McDonald
To: Phillip Demarco
Subject: Your call...

HP,

Thank you for calling me tonight. I loved hearing your voice and the wonderful things you always say to me. I'll see you tomorrow.

Your lonesome BP

*****

I could tell Faye missed me a lot, but I didn't know how much until I received another message from her later that night. Faye had become more sexually empowered with me, which I relished and appreciated because I was much the same way. Perhaps I influenced her, or her me. Either way, it made me miss her even more than I did already.

*****

Date: Wed, 6 Jul 2011 23:48:52 (EDT)
From: Laura McDonald
To: Phillip Demarco
Subject: I've been a bad girl!!!

HP,

I'm so bad! I started missing you so much after I sent my email that I went to lie down in your bed. After a few minutes, I began thinking about the last time we made love. I wanted to be adventurous with you, but you weren't here. These thoughts got me very excited, so I ended up touching myself! Then I thought about what it would feel like if you were inside my ass, which got me even more excited, until (I waited as long as I could) I couldn't wait any longer. I had to make myself cum. Then I thought about you tasting me after I did. I wished you were here to do that so I could kiss you and taste it, too. I needed your services, HP! So think about me lying there, touching myself, and cumming while I was thinking about you, your mouth, and your hard cock, my sweetheart!

Your terrible BP!

*****

Date: Thu, 7 Jul 2011 00:21:29 (EDT)
From: Phillip Demarco
To: Laura McDonald
Subject: You did what???

My dearest BP,

Whew! You don't know what your last message did to me! I could make love to you for hours and hours, doing everything and anything you want to do. You are the sexiest woman I've ever known! I never imagined I could find someone as beautiful and as sexy as you. You are a dream come true for me, and you turn me on so much!

XOXOXOXOXO to the love of my life
Your lonely, very turned-on HP

*****

Date: Thu, 7 Jul 2011 08:54:12 (EDT)
From: Laura McDonald
To: Phillip Demarco
Subject: Sparkling again

HP,

I'm glad you liked me being terrible in your bed while fantasizing about you. Well, I enjoyed doing it! It's too bad you weren't here to watch. I might have even told you a very, very naughty story.

I loved everything you said in your email, HP. I love what our relationship has become, and I don't see how it will ever change, except to get better. I'm sure you can tell from my last message I'm much more open with you now. I used to always want to write/say those kinds of things, but I was afraid. Now it doesn't bother me at all since I know how much you like it.

This is my last day of work without you, thank goodness! It is boring when you aren't here. I can't wait to fetch you at the airport after work today; I'm not even going to go home first. And since Alex won't be here until tomorrow, we can spend the whole night together! I am sparkling as I'm writing this message. Just the thought of you makes me smile. I'll see you soon, my love!

BP

*****

Having Faye pick me up at the airport in Melbourne was fun! I felt as though my wife was meeting me, and we were going home together. On the way back to Titusville, we stopped and had dinner at a small Italian restaurant. When we got to my apartment, I put on some music, and we danced again. After a few songs, I gifted her a pair of golden earrings I bought in Washington to show her how much I missed her. We spent the night together and made up for the time we lost when I was in DC. We were both hungry for each other's touches, kisses, and love. We fell asleep melting into each other.

Besides the fact Alex would be in Titusville over this weekend, it turned out Faye needed to go to Gainesville over the next one. I wasn't happy when I heard that news, but neither was she when she told me about it.

*****

Date: Fri, 8 Jul 2011 08:20:12 (EDT)
From: Laura McDonald
To: Phillip Demarco
Subject: Your beautiful self!

HP,

I am so glad you have come back to me. I hate being apart from you anymore. Not seeing you on the weekends used to be bearable, but now that I've gotten accustomed to being with you, I'll hate it this weekend and next! I don't want to be away from my HP anymore. I promise to make it up to you! I'm sorry I won't be with you for the next two weekends. I can tell you aren't happy about it, but neither am I. Remember, though, even when I'm gone, I'll be thinking of you, as I always do.

I think I've realized (it only took five years), I need you, and we should be together. Spending the summer with you has made the world of difference to me. I'm so glad we got to come down here, although it didn't start off great. Now I want to spend every minute with you, even if they are minutes spent sleeping next to each other.

Well, HP, I guess I should get back to work. Okay, we'll talk in about two seconds.

Love,
BP

*****

CHAPTER 18

The Most Handsome Prince

The following Friday, before Faye drove to Gainesville, we took the afternoon off from work. I packed us a lunch, and we went to Chain of Lakes Park for a picnic. It was a hot day, in the mid-nineties, and humid. We found a picnic table in the shade to eat, then went for a walk on one of the many walking paths. Even though it was hot, it was fun getting to spend the afternoon with Faye before she left. I knew I'd miss her very much. And I promised to avoid talking to other women in bars. I couldn't wait until she returned on Sunday night. It was unfortunate though because when she did, Alex came with her again to stay for a few days, which was a surprise to both of us.

*****

Date: Mon, 18 Jul 2011 14:11:16 (EDT)
From: Laura McDonald
To: Phillip Demarco
Subject: Mr. no-emailer!

HP,

I sure missed you this weekend, HP. I hated leaving you on Friday. I had such a wonderful time, as I always do. It's unbelievable how we can have fun walking in ninety-five degree weather, but somehow we do. I thought about you all the while I was gone; I know we'd have had a great time if we were together.

I knew I'd get upset in the car driving to Gainesville, and I did. Remember how on Friday, before we left the park, I said I didn't want to go, and you replied, "Then just don't go?" I wanted to say, "Okay, let's run off together instead." HP, I've been contemplating running off with you, and I realize how wonderful it would be and I know we'd be happy.

I guess Alex realizes there's a problem between us, but I don't think he has a clue how to fix it. At one point, he asked if there was someone else, and I considered saying yes, but then I would have had to tell him who it was and I didn't want to get you in trouble. Well, at least he knows I'm not as happy as I should be. Maybe it's sinking into his head at last. You have spoiled me rotten, HP. I love how you treat me, and nobody else treats me the way you do. That's why he wanted to come down here this week since he was off work. I'm sorry he's here. I wish he wasn't!

Well, HP, I guess I'll go for now. Your blue eyes keep peering over at me as I'm typing this. I can't wait to get my hands on you again!

Love,
BP

*****

Faye asked me to go to dinner with her and Alex that night. I wasn't eager to go because I don't enjoy seeing them together. I agreed to join them, but only because she wanted me to, and I'd do anything for her. I knew it would be a challenge for me to make it through the night.

Dinner wasn't easy. Both Faye and I tried to engage Alex in conversation, but he resisted. He talked a little, but was quiet throughout the evening. I could tell he didn't appreciate me being there, and I wondered what he thought. At one point, I asked Alex if he wanted to hear a blonde joke. He gave a sideways glance at Faye to see her reaction, then turned back to me and replied, "Sure."

Faye looked at me and said, "Oh no, not another blonde joke."

"Okay, here goes," I said. "I heard this one over at KSC. If you don't like it, you can blame those guys."

I told them the one about the blonde who wanted to go on a mission to the sun, but to avoid burning up, she planned to go at night. Alex laughed and Faye didn't, but it was a good icebreaker. We somehow made it through a rather tense evening and I paid for dinner, which helped.

*****

Date: Tue, 19 Jul 2011 13:35:08 (EDT)
From: Laura McDonald
To: Phillip Demarco
Subject: Groupie

HP,

You look marvelous today, although you'd look better with my hands inside your pants. Thank you for going to eat with us last night; I realize it wasn't easy for you. I love being with you even if we're not alone. It was hard for me to not stare at you the entire evening. I missed you very much after we got home. I don't enjoy being with Alex when I know it would be more fun if I were with you.

Love,
Your HP groupie

*****

Date: Wed, 20 Jul 2011 15:07:32 (EDT)
From: Laura McDonald
To: Phillip Demarco
Subject: Your treatment...

HP,

Since Alex is leaving in the morning, we can be together tomorrow night, and then I can get my hands on you at last! I can't wait! Have a great evening and behave yourself if you go out (please!)!

Love,
The BP who needs her HP's treatment (if you know what I mean)

*****

Since Faye and I would spend Thursday night together, I arranged for us to take Friday off work. It turned out to be a wonderful idea. We slept in and enjoyed the morning. Later in the day, I received this message from her.

*****

Date: Fri, 22 Jul 2011 14:14:01 (EDT)
From: Laura McDonald
To: Phillip Demarco
Subject: All those things

HP,

I loved waking up with you wrapped around me this morning. I liked it when we were lying on our sides with your arms and legs all over me. And yes, HP, I feel contented and safe when I'm with you. Just the thought of you makes me

happy. I want (and love) everything we share. I can't imagine my life without you. I love you, HP, and I want you…
I love and want you,
The sparkling BP

*****

After one more wonderful weekend with Faye, our time at KSC was close to being over. Even worse, on Tuesday, I had to leave for another meeting in Washington, DC, on Wednesday. I'd only be away two nights and back on Thursday, but Faye was not happy about me leaving again, and I wasn't looking forward to going either.

*****

Date: Tue, 26 Jul 2011 13:36:14 (EDT)
From: Laura McDonald
To: Phillip Demarco
Subject: I can't stand it!

HP,

Please don't leave! I can't stand to be away from you for two more entire nights! I'll be very lonesome without you here with me. You must make it up to me when you get back.

I love spending the night with you, HP. I don't even have trouble falling asleep next to you anymore. I used to not sleep very well with you before, but I have no problem anymore! It must be because of all the time we've spent together over the past couple of months. Our dancing was marvelous last night too, and so was your singing. I could have danced with you all night long. But it always makes me cry because dancing and having you sing to me reminds me of how much I love you. I want to dance with you every night. But I know it's not possible, for now, at least. That's what upsets me the most.

I'm dreading you leaving me already. I'll try not to be too terrible in your apartment while you're gone, although I can't make any promises. I might think about me ????? and ????? you and may just lose control of myself! Well, thank you for the wonderful evening last night. I'll miss you so much while you're gone!

BP

*****

Date: Tue, 26 Jul 2011 17:40:40 (EDT)
From: Laura McDonald
To: Phillip Demarco
Subject: You're terrible!

HP,

I wish you were here! I'm going to hate going back to school, the land of two separate offices, fewer lunches together, late afternoon goodbyes, etc., etc., etc. I need to be with the HP always, not just a few minutes here and there. I'll hate it!

You were so terrible today before you left. First, you told me about wanting to kiss me after (well, you know) and then how you wanted to take me into a stall in the men's room. You are just terrible! What other little things are there that you might like to try but have been hesitant to tell me? I would love to hear about them if you have any others, HP. I'm planning to be very, very naughty tonight. It's a shame you won't be here to watch me! So hurry and get back here!

BP

*****

Faye had become much more sexual with me, both in her actions and her words. I've always found sexual openness to be a very attractive quality in a woman. I felt very lucky to have her in my life, and I knew I wanted to keep her there forever.

Having written Faye some erotic stories in the past, I often told her she needed to write one for me, not thinking she ever would. She teased back that she might try it someday. But she surprised me with the email she sent the night before I came back to Titusville. She was being bad again.

*****

Date: Thur, 28 Jul 2011 00:41:16 (EDT)
From: Laura McDonald
To: Phillip Demarco
Subject: Wishing you were here…

HP,

Guess what I'm doing at this second? I'm lying in your bed and touching myself with the tips of my fingers. It's too bad you aren't here to do it for me, but you aren't, so I'll just take care of it myself. I want you now, HP. Do you know what else I'd do if you were here with me? Well, if not, I'll tell you…

As you're sitting on the couch, watching TV, I sneak into the living room without you knowing. I slip up behind you and place a blindfold over your beautiful blue eyes. Then I bend down and begin kissing the back of your neck and ears, and while I do, my hands slide down your shoulders and chest until they reach the top of your pants. When I look down, I see you're already very excited. And the sight of your cock bulging out gets me very excited, too. Next, I grab your hand and lead you to the bedroom. I unbutton your shirt and kiss your chest as I work my way downward. I push you toward the bed and then remove your shirt. I force you to sit down, and I massage your legs with my hands. I move my mouth against your hardness, which makes me want to lick and suck you. Then I unbutton and unzip your pants. I stay on my knees and make you stand up and remove the rest of your clothes. Then I lick the top of your cock as I'm kneeling before you. A droplet of your pre-cum falls on my tongue, which drives me crazy. I can't help but put your long, hard cock all the way inside my mouth. My pussy is so wet I have to touch myself. I get wetter and wetter as I rub my pussy while sucking you. You moan and you tell me you want to lick me. Before I let you, we must play a game. I'll give you permission to lick me if you can watch me pleasuring myself without touching yourself. You agree, and so I remove the blindfold and force you onto the bed. I'm standing before you naked with my nipples already hard. I lay down in the opposite direction of you so you can see my pussy close-up. I want your dick inside me, but I can't have it yet, so I use my finger on myself instead. You see my juices glistening on my finger. But I think we should be more adventurous. Your cock is so hard, and it would feel so good inside my ass. Since we are still playing my game, you watch me pull out my favorite little beads, which I hid under the pillow. While fingering myself with one hand, I insert the beads one at a time into my tight ass with my other hand. The sight of your hard dick is now driving me crazy, but I still can't have it. Me fingering myself and playing with my ass is making you so excited you must touch yourself. You're a naughty boy since you broke the rules of our game and must now be punished. I take my finger out of my pussy and put it in my mouth to taste my juices. It tastes so sweet, and you want to taste it too. But I must punish you first. I make you place your knees around my head and bend over, and you do as you're told. I can see all of you, only inches from my face, and you can see my wet pussy and the beads trying to pop out of my ass. I begin your punishment by licking and sucking your balls, and I wrap my hands around your cock and pump you. My hands move away from your dick, and you feel a finger in between your legs. As I stroke and lick your balls, my finger moves around to your ass and begins rubbing. My tongue is soon right below your ass. As I lick around it, I move my hand back to your cock. After licking your ass for a few minutes, my finger enters you, and you can't help but moan. I love seeing my finger move in and out of you. I order you to pull the beads out of my ass so I can replace them with your hard, throbbing cock. You do as you're told because you can't wait to thrust yourself deep into me. After the beads are out, I take my finger out of your ass and give you one last long adventurous lick. You stand up next to the bed, and I get on my knees in front of you. I reach around and grab you and say, "Fuck my pussy and put your finger in my ass first." You thrust your dick inside me, and you can feel my excitement. I'm so wet for you, and I love your finger in my ass so much I almost can't stand it. I yell to fuck me harder. I love having your cock all the way inside of my dripping wet pussy. After having my pussy fucked long and hard, I turn around, bend over, and put your wet cock into my mouth. I suck all my juices off your cock, and then I look up and tell you to fuck my ass now. I kneel in front of you again and your throbbing cock pushes into me. You go faster and deeper than ever before until you shoot your hot cum inside of me. We both moan with delight as you remove your cum-soaked cock from my ass. I stand up and turn around and give my naughty professor the most sensual kiss ever.

Now wouldn't you rather be here with me tonight, my handsome prince?

Love you,
BP

*****

I read Faye's message when I woke up in the morning and before I left for Reagan National Airport and my trip home. It was a long flight with me rereading Faye's incredible story several times. She may be a natural at writing erotica.

*****

Date: Thu, 28 Jul 2011 06:36:22 (EDT)
From: Phillip Demarco
To: Laura McDonald
Subject: Who are you?

I'm speechless! Who are you, and what have you done with my BP? I love you more than you could ever imagine! I'll be home soon, so stay "warm" for me!

Your HP

*****

Date: Thu, 28 Jul 2011 13:24:39 (EDT)
From: Laura McDonald
To: Phillip Demarco
Subject: You are soooooooooo bad!

HP,

I want your hard cock in my pussy right now!!

Your BP

*****

When I returned from Washington, I went straight to my apartment. Faye was still at work. As I walked in I found a card on the counter from her, addressed as follows:

To: The most handsome prince in all the world's kingdoms
From: His beautiful princess who misses him terribly

The front of the card read: "I'm no poet, but when I look into your eyes, I see every dream I've ever had. I see the sun rising and the moon shining. I see all my tomorrows captured in a single moment. But most of all, I see..." Then on the inside it read, "...me! Yeah, I can see me right there in your eyeballs! And damn, I'm looking good! I'm hot, I tell ya! I'm...oh, yeah, sorry; I was supposed to be talking about you. So, Okay...dreams and sun and all my tomorrows, blah, blah, blah... Anyway, love those eyeballs!" It was a funny card, so typical of Faye's sense of humor, but on the inside of the card, she wrote the following:

> To my dearest handsome prince,
>   What did you expect, a serious card from me? I miss you very much! I miss you every time you're gone. It's odd; I even miss you when I'm sitting beside you at work. If I can't be right next to you, then I'm not happy. I've had a wonderful time this summer. Spending all this time with you has made me fall in love with you all over again. I knew I loved you before, but I didn't realize how much. I am crazy in love with you, and I could never live without you. You were right, HP, after five years I admit it, we are soul mates, and we belong together always. You don't know how many times I have wanted to say, "Let's run away

together." I so want to run away with you, HP, but I'm not sure how to go about doing it. You are the love of my life, and I will love you always. Who would have ever thought you and I would get along so well together? You are the perfect prince for me! Not only are you terrible, but you also enjoy going to Target with me. It isn't any fun going there without you anymore (the same as everything else). It's amazing how much fun we can have together, no matter what we're doing. I don't even mind getting up early now since I get to see you first thing— the highlight of my day. Just hearing your voice makes me sparkle. You are a marvelous man! I don't know what I'd ever do without you. I've enjoyed every second we've spent together. *I love you Phillip Demarco*!!! (And don't you ever forget it!)

♥The beautiful princess

CHAPTER 19

You'd Better Not

We were now approaching our final week working at KSC. Our supervisor, Richard, a very nice man in his early sixties, invited Faye and me to an end-of-summer cookout at his home in Cocoa Beach on Friday night. It was a small party of about ten people, including a few of the interns in our group; their supervisors; Richard, and his wife, Emily; and Faye and me. Richard grilled out steaks, and Emily made the rest of the dinner. It was a beautiful starlit evening, and we ate on the back deck of their house overlooking the Banana River. After dinner, we stayed outside and had drinks, talked, and told stories.

Faye rode to the cookout with me, and we got back to Titusville around 10:00 p.m. By the time we did, Alex had already arrived for the weekend again and was waiting inside Faye's apartment. Before leaving the car, we kissed for a few minutes, and we both wanted to make love. But she knew she had to go inside to see Alex. It was a disappointing end to a very pleasant night out together. The next morning, Faye sent me a message.

*****

Date: Sat, 6 Aug 2011 09:09:49 (EDT)
From: Laura McDonald
To: Phillip Demarco
Subject: Those looks

HP,

I wanted to tell you, last night at Richard's house (after they lit the candles on the deck), I kept looking at you. You looked so handsome with the glow from the flames on your face. I could have stared at you all night. Whenever our eyes met, I just about went crazy! I love when you give me those little "I wish everyone else would leave so we could be alone" looks. You know how to drive me out of my mind without even saying a word. Nobody has ever done that to me before, except you.

It killed me to not spend the night with you. I guess I won't get to see you until Monday or tomorrow night if Alex goes home, which I hope he does.

BP

*****

It turned out Alex wasn't leaving until Tuesday, so I didn't see Faye again over the weekend until she knocked on my door at 7:30 a.m. on Monday for us to go to work. During our drive in, we talked about beginning our last five days at KSC. Once we arrived, we remembered Terri was on vacation for the entire week. It was fun sharing an office with her. We said our goodbyes to her on Friday, but it didn't hit us until we found ourselves alone in the office for the first time all summer.

We worked with the door wide open, and there were many colleagues nearby, so we had to be careful about our conversations, even with Terri gone. Being creative and adventurous, Faye began writing me little messages on Post-it notes (sometimes, it took several). She would write something, slide it across her desk to me, and I would answer the same way, no different from what elementary school children might do, but it was still fun. This continued throughout our last week of work. Many of our written conversations were very sexual, and all were playful, and we even described some of our fantasies. Faye had become very good at expressing herself sexually and overcame most of the inhibitions she had when we first met. That fact was obvious in our notes during that last week, some of which we wrote in secret code.

*****

Faye: I ♥ the HP! I want you right now!
Phillip: I ♥ the BP! What do you want me for?
Faye: To take advantage of you in every way possible!
Phillip: Give me an example, and perhaps we'll leave early for lunch.
Faye: Okay, e.g., I want to lick *every* part of your body! Phillip: You are so *terrible*! But all right, let's go!

*****

Faye: I want you, HP!
Phillip: What for BP?
Faye: Bad things, what else?
Phillip: But tell me what kind of bad things (it will keep me going through the day).
Faye: *terrible* things!
Phillip: How about a hint at least?
Faye: Well, I might make you watch me pleasure myself with my toys and not let you take part, or I could force you to lie down and close your eyes. And when you open them, you'll find "me" right in your face, trying to get your attention. Or I could suck you

while my little fingers are exploring, or perhaps my tongue will explore you in a very sensitive area. Can I crawl under your desk, unzip your pants, and suck your cock? This would be a surprise for you, so you wouldn't be hard yet, but I would feel you getting harder as I sucked on you. I would keep sucking you until you came. How would that be?

Phillip: I'd love it, BP! But you're wrong about one thing. I'm already hard from reading your last message! Come over here and crawl under my desk right now!

*****

Faye: HP, you look great today (but I picked your clothes out this morning, after all). I'm crazy about you, HP! I'm glad I quit being as stupid as I was when we first came down here. I would have regretted it forever if I had neglected you the entire summer. Although now, because of my silly behavior earlier, we're much closer than we were before. And just so you know, you are the love of my life!

Phillip: ILY, BP.

Faye: ILY2, HP. I'll love you forever regardless of what happens. You are my soul mate. Now I'm sure you won't want to go, but Alex and I are going out to dinner tonight. You could come with us. I would love it!

Phillip: Thanks, but I'll pass. I doubt either Alex or I would enjoy me going with you again. I'd be afraid I'd say something wrong. I might call you BP or rub his leg under the table instead of yours.

Faye: Okay, I understand. I know going to eat with Alex is about as much fun for you as getting a root canal. Well, it's an open offer if you change your mind. We'll go around 7:00 p.m. or so.

Phillip: Thanks, BP, but I don't think I'll reconsider. I can't wait until Alex leaves so we can spend the rest of the week together.

Faye: Neither can I, HP!

*****

Phillip: You were wonderful last night, and *very* much the BP! I missed you after you went to take a shower this morning. All I wanted today was to stay in bed with you all day and kiss you, touch you, hold you, and play with you. I'm so crazy about you, Ms. McDonald!

Faye: HP, you were wonderful too! I love how you always want me next to you and put your hands on me every second (even if it's not in a "terrible" way). I wish we could spend a whole day in bed doing those things. You still drive me crazy too, Dr. Demarco, as you already know. I ♥ you!

Phillip: Our time together just isn't enough anymore. I love being close to you all the time; I love when you touch me, and I love being inseparable from you! I need to always be next to you. Last night, I felt everything was how it should be when we were in bed. I was happy and contented, and I don't need anyone else. You are the only one I want. The more I'm with you, the more I realize it. I'm so glad we spent the whole summer together, but it has only confirmed what I already knew: we're perfect for each other, and we *are* soul mates. Nothing will ever change that or how I feel about you, BP. You're marvelous!

Faye: You are wonderful, HP. I'm also glad we spent the summer together. Now I realize how much I need you to be with me. Although I hate to admit it, you were right all along, and we *are* soul mates! Somehow, you and I have a magical connection.

And tonight, you will be the recipient of me doing something terrible because of it!

*****

Phillip: You were *so much* fun last night... I loved it!

Faye: So were you, HP. I love it when you get behind me and say terrible things to me. I think we should roll around in your bed for a few hours tonight, too. I might even tell you a story. I will have HP withdrawal next week since I won't get to spend any nights with you. I'll hate it!

Phillip: Hmmm, I'm looking forward to going home today to partake in that activity! I'll have BP withdrawal after we go back to Gainesville, too. What kind of story are you talking about?

Faye: A story requiring very graphic language and involving me and another woman playing with each other while you're watching us. You'd end up doing more than just watching in the story because I'd want you to ???? me too!

Phillip: BP, you are the sexiest woman I have ever known! It's such a turn-on for me when you tell me stories and use graphic language.

Faye: Why, thank you, and you are the sexiest man I've ever known! I can't wait to come over tonight and play with you again. You look so handsome today. I wish I could kiss you. You are a marvelous HP. I love you so much!

Phillip: Thank you, BP. I adore you!

*****

Phillip: BP, do you want to try some things we've never done before?

Faye: And what might you be referring to? If you explain
            them to me, then I may be interested in trying
            them.

Phillip: Well, many possibilities exist. One would be
            something neither of us has done with anyone else.

Faye: I don't know what you're thinking about, so why
            don't you give me a few more details?

Phillip: I was thinking about something you're curious
            about but wouldn't try unless it was the perfect
            situation and I was there too, and you could just
            enjoy yourself.

Faye: Perhaps if it was the perfect situation! I'd get
            very excited knowing you were there watching (or
            doing more) and seeing you so turned on!

Phillip: Nothing could get me *more* turned on and excited!
            Watching you would be the most erotic thing I
            could imagine. And nobody has *ever* gotten me as
            excited as you do!

Faye: And what would you be doing while you were
            watching? And what would you enjoy seeing? (I'm
            sure you wouldn't enjoy watching me and a woman
            licking each other, now would you?)

Phillip: What I'd be doing while watching you would
            depend on what you were doing with her. I'd love
            to see a woman kissing you, running her fingers
            through your hair and touching your face. I'd also
            enjoy watching her undressing you and kissing
            each part of you as she does. And it would drive
            me crazy to watch her lick your pussy, knowing it
            would be your first time. If you licked her too, I'm
            sure I couldn't keep from cumming during such
            an incredible event.

Faye: I'd like you to be inside me this minute! And just
            so you know, my panties are soaked as I write this!
            It would be the perfect time for you to put your

tongue inside of me. Then I'd have to kiss you afterward so I could taste myself too.

*****

Phillip: This conversation is making me very hard. I'd love tasting your soaked pussy right now. I'm sure a woman would enjoy licking you as much as I would. I'd also like to have you sucking my hard cock, but I might not hold back for very long. If something would end up in your mouth, then I may just have to kiss you. You wouldn't mind that, would you?

Faye: I'd love for you to kiss me after you cum in my mouth, which would get me very excited! Then I'd need to have you in my pussy. I think we should be adventurous tonight. I want to feel you going where no one else has been. I'm sure we'd both love it, don't you agree?

Phillip: I'm interested in doing *anything* that gets you excited, BP! And yes, I agree with you about being adventurous. So are you interested in doing *anything* that gets me excited too?

Faye: Now when you ask about "anything that gets me excited," do you have anything specific in mind? And yes, I'd love doing those things.

Phillip: I'll admit I'd love to see you with another woman; it would be such a turn-on for me. Anything you could think of that you might enjoy, I would too. Are you still turned-on?

Faye: Yes, my panties are drenched! Let's make a plan using your "another woman" idea! If you were present, I couldn't let you just sit in a corner by yourself, you'd have to take part! If she was licking me, perhaps I could suck you, and you could watch both of us. This sounds interesting and exciting, and tonight, you can give me more details about it!

Phillip: Your version of my idea is much better. And perhaps I could be inside of you while you licked her. I am thrilled you'd consider it. You are just wonderful to me and I adore you!

*****

Faye: You're lucky I'm not riding in the car with you on the way back to Gainesville. I couldn't wait to get there to have your hard cock in my mouth. So, can I ride to Gainesville with you, please?

Phillip: Sure, let's go! But think about this tonight. I'd like to cum inside your mouth and then kiss you. Would that excite you?

Faye: Yes, but would I have swallowed your cum or what? This is a very interesting thought!

Phillip: You needn't swallow.

Faye: Then I must have to spit it out, right, or are you being a very naughty professor?

Phillip: I'm being a very naughty professor!

Faye: You are *so* bad!! We can try that anytime you wish, HP. Just the thought gets me very excited!

*****

Phillip: I ♥ U!

Faye: I ♥ U2! IWURN!

Phillip: IW2TURN!

Faye: Okay! IW2TURN2!

Phillip: Where?

Faye: Somewhere very hard or very sensitive, or wherever else you so desire.

Phillip: All those places would be perfect! When?

Faye: Anytime is fine for me! I'll think about it tonight when I'm lying in your bed with you, under the c overs, touching myself while you're watching.

Phillip: Great! Can we watch each other? I hope you get excited enough to be very naughty tonight.

Faye: I'm sure I'll get very excited since I'll be watching you too. So you want me to bring my toys over so we can play with them again? You like it when I'm adventurous with my toys, don't you? My little beads are fun, but I'd rather you be inside me!

Phillip: Yes and yes! And I wouldn't mind at all if you used your beads in my bed. Anything you'd enjoy is fine with me. I wish I were inside of you right now.

Faye: How about if we go home for lunch today so I can take advantage of you? I'll make you touch me, lick me, and fuck me very hard!

Phillip: It's a deal! I'm not hungry (for lunch) anyhow! I promise to fuck you very hard and very long! Plus, I'm looking forward to putting something into your filthy little mouth. (I love it when you talk dirty to me).

Faye: And just what are you going to put in my filthy little mouth? I hope it's something long and hard. You are amazing!

Phillip: Perhaps it will be something that goes in long and hard and comes out soft and slimy. And no, it won't be a stick of chewing gum. You are amazing too, BP!

Faye: Okay! Let's do it *now*!

*****

Phillip: BP, remember that after work today, I'm going out for some beers with those guys down the hall. They invited you too, but I didn't think you'd want to go. Do you? If not, you can drive my car home, and they can drop me off afterward.

Faye: No, I don't care to go. But I'll be eagerly awaiting
            your return!

*****

Faye: Thanks for coming home early from drinking beer
            with those guys. I hope I showed you how much I
            missed you.
Phillip: Yes, you did, BP. Thank you!
Faye: HP, I did something I didn't mention to you.
Phillip: You did? What was it, BP?
Faye: Well, after I made dinner and before you came
            home, I was very lonesome for you. So I got my
            toys out and went to lie down in my bed. I was very
            horny and needed to make myself cum.
Phillip: Hmmm, well, did you?
Faye: Yes, I did! Somebody had to since you weren't there.
Phillip: What were you thinking about when you did it?
Faye: Well, it was about being adventurous with you. I
            may also have thought a little about your idea of
            me with a woman. I wish you could have been there
            with me. I was lonesome, and your "friend" was wet
            and ready to play.
Phillip: Oh my, BP! But tell me more about what you were
            thinking last night. We could leave a little earlier
            than usual today.
Faye: Well, I was thinking about you and this woman
            undressing me together. While I was being
            undressed, you were both rubbing your hands all
            over me. Then she started kissing me and went
            down toward my chest, then down a little farther.
            She moved her hand up my thigh and rubbed in
            between my legs. By now, I was very excited by her
            touching me and by watching you play with
            yourself. Next, we all lay down on the bed, and
            she started kissing and licking my body. This time,

she was teasing me by touching my pussy with her tongue and mouth. She spread my legs all the way apart and began moving her tongue all over me and putting it inside of me. While she did, I needed you inside of my mouth, and I sucked your hard cock. Then I went down a little further to suck on your balls! While I did, she put her fingers inside my pussy while she licked me. Her fingers made me want to have you inside me. You asked me to turn over and get on my knees and then you entered my dripping wet pussy from behind and then… (I'll let you continue from here).

Phillip: …after I slid my hard cock into your dripping wet pussy, she moved up on the bed and opened her legs on either side of your head so your face was inches from her pussy. When she began fingering herself, I pumped you from behind. With each thrust, your face moved closer to her pussy. You watched her finger herself as she got wetter and wetter. Then she moved her hands to her nipples to play with them. As I fucked you hard, her wet pussy was glistening, and you put out your tongue. During my next thrust, your tongue reached her. You loved her taste, so you slid your tongue in further. Then you licked upward toward her clit in slow but steady strokes. She was moaning as you enjoyed your first taste of another woman's pussy. As I watched from behind, I got even harder. When you moved closer to her and inserted your fingers into her, I slid my finger into your ass as you moaned with delight. Then the three of us reached wonderful orgasms together.

Faye: Oh my!!!

*****

Phillip: BP, I love all these little notes we've been
           exchanging this week. I'm saving them all for my
           book about us too, okay?

Faye: Okay, HP, but you'd *better not* use my real name now
           for sure!

*****

CHAPTER 20

What My Behavior May
Lead You to Believe

The summer was a productive one work-wise as we finished our project and presented the results on our last day. To do so, we scheduled a 9:00 a.m. seminar. I introduced the project, discussed our goals, and gave a summary and our conclusions, while Faye provided the technical details of our analysis. KSC management liked our work very much, and afterward, our workgroup took us out for a farewell luncheon. We were pleased about twenty coworkers attended. These were outstanding people, and we enjoyed our time working there. We spent the rest of the day visiting and saying goodbye to everyone we met and worked with during the summer.

On our last Friday night in Titusville, we had dinner at our favorite Mexican restaurant before going back to my apartment for dancing, playing, loving, and being "terrible" with each other. It was yet another marvelous night together, and we were both very sad knowing it was our last one for a while. With everything that happened between us over the summer and everything we said to each other, I was confident Faye and I would somehow end up together. I even let myself consider the possibility of having children with her if we did. This was something I didn't allow myself to think about since I met Faye for fear it would never happen. Now

I felt it could. That night I asked her if she wanted to have children. She answered, "Yes, but not right away." Then she asked me, "Didn't you ever want kids?"

"Well, Faye, yes, I did. It was Sophia who never wanted kids because she was more focused on her career. I've always thought I'd like at least one child of my own and have felt cheated by not having any. And it would be fun to have children with you." Perhaps that was something I shouldn't have said, but it was on my mind.

"Well, HP, if we end up together, we can talk about it, but I wouldn't want kids right away if we did."

Faye's comments surprised me and left me a little disappointed since I was much older and waiting might make me too old to be very helpful raising a child. But I didn't have any kids with Sophia anyhow, so I wouldn't be losing anything.

We were planning to leave Titusville on Saturday morning, but by the time we cleaned our apartments, packed our cars, and turned in our keys, it was early afternoon. Faye would follow me back to Gainesville in her car. As we were leaving town, I drove over to Merritt Square Mall and parked in front of Macy's department store. When I got out of the car, Faye said, "What are we doing here, HP?"

"Well, BP, I wanted to show you how much I appreciated all the hard work you did on our project this summer, so I'd like to buy you a new outfit."

Faye's jaw dropped, and she replied, "What? You don't have to buy me anything."

"I know I don't, but I want to, BP. Please let me?"

"Okay, HP! Thank you!"

Faye picked out some very nice clothes I know she wouldn't have bought for herself. She did great work on our project, even with all the emailing and note writing, and it made us both look good to NASA. So it was a small thank you for her significant contribution.

I told Sophia when I'd be getting home, but when I arrived, she wasn't there. Instead, I found a note on the kitchen counter that read as follows:

> Phillip, I'm sorry I wasn't here when you got back. I went to New York for the weekend and will be home on Sunday evening. I'll see you then.

I knew Sophia and I didn't see each other or even communicate much throughout the summer, and I was sure it was my fault because I was so focused on Faye. But it surprised me she wasn't home since she didn't mention her trip to me when I talked with her earlier in the week. My first thought was not that I wished she was home, but that Alex wasn't so I could spend more time with Faye. After an entire summer together, I still wanted more. Regardless, Alex was home, so I couldn't see her. Sophia returned home Sunday evening as she said. She was friendly, but she wasn't welcoming or affectionate. I assumed she was distant because we'd been apart for three months, so I just let it go. Classes for the fall semester of 2011 began on Monday.

Robert assigned Faye to teach two undergraduate courses, and she got busy right away preparing for them. Before long, we were back in our old routine of having offices across the hall and seeing each other much less than we were used to. We found it difficult to arrange any intimate time at all, but we were still together a lot at school and had lunch several times a week. We also "played" in my office when we had an opportunity. But it wasn't the same, and I missed our closeness and our intimacy. I could tell she did too.

*****

Date: Wed, 24 Aug 2011 20:22:26 (EDT)
From: Laura McDonald
To: Phillip Demarco
Subject: I'm lonely for your face, etc.!

HP,

I'm so lonesome without you. I wish you could be here with me right now. I have to see your beautiful face again (I also need to touch you once or twice, or more). I can't stand being away from you. I want us to still be in Titusville, and I wish I wouldn't have wasted those first two weeks of the summer. We missed out on two weekends because of me. Well, it's too late now, but I'm sorry I acted the way I did. That's all my love. I'm looking forward to seeing you tomorrow! I miss you, and I love you.

BP

*****

Faye's teaching was going very well, and she enjoyed it. As her mentor, I sat in on several of her lectures to critique her performance. It didn't surprise me she was a natural in the classroom. And I was proud to see a lot of my lecturing style in hers. She came a long way from her days of being afraid to speak in public. The students in her class liked her very much—especially the males. Most of the questions she had for me about teaching were how to handle excuses for students not doing the required work. Overall, she was doing an excellent job.

The semester moved along fast, and Faye was very busy preparing for her doctoral qualifying examinations scheduled for November, doing her research, and teaching her classes. It was a hectic time for her, and we didn't get to be alone often. Then one day, I received this unexpected message from her.

*****

Date: Thu, 27 Oct 2011 20:57:33 (EDT)
From: Laura McDonald
To: Phillip Demarco
Subject: You'll never guess what Nicole did!

HP,

First, let me say I enjoyed your surprise this afternoon in my office. You should surprise me more often!

Now back to the main point here. A few weeks ago, I called Nicole to ask her how she was doing, and she asked how school was and stuff and about the financial situation here, etc., etc., etc. During this conversation, I mentioned I might have to find a job for next summer because there may not be any teaching funds until the fall, so I would have no money at all. A few days after our talk, she emailed me and said she talked to her boss at Lockheed Martin and told him I'd be available in May. Then her boss asked for my resume, so I sent it to her to give to him, even though they weren't looking for anybody right now. (Keep in mind, I *never* said I was leaving Gainesville in May, and I wouldn't make that kind of decision without talking to my number one adviser, the HP). Well, tonight I got an email from Nicole saying her boss is interested, and they want me to come down for an interview on November 15! So how in the world am I supposed to handle this situation? You know how Nicole wants me to leave here and get a job down there, so I don't know what she said to her boss about me. She may have told him I'm moving to Orlando in May. So, HP, the question is what should I tell her? I need your advice on this, even though I know you don't like the topic. Please help me, HP!

Love,
BP

*****

Date: Thu, 27 Oct 2011 21:16:52 (EDT)
From: Phillip Demarco
To: Laura McDonald
Subject: Nicole did WHAT???

BP,

Wow, I'm stunned! I'm not sure what to say. If you want a job, I guess that would be a good place for you to go. But if you leave, it will be very difficult for you to finish your PhD, just so you know.

If you don't want to leave, then you need to tell Nicole and her boss you would only be available for the summer until after you were finished with school. They should accept that reason to keep you interested in working for them after you graduate.

I guess you are at yet another of many inevitable crossroads in your life. But this is something you must decide for yourself, either way. You need to be up front and honest with her boss about your intentions to help keep your future options open. The best reason for not being interested right now is your desire to finish your degree. Any manager in any company should accept that reason. If not, then it's not somewhere you'd want to work anyhow.

I must tell you, BP, it would crush me if you left. I doubt we'd ever see each other again, which I would hate. But perhaps we're just getting to that point sooner rather than later. I don't want you to go anywhere, ever! But I'm sure you already know that.

Love,
HP

*****

Date: Fri, 28 Oct 2011 08:40:26 (EDT)
From: Laura McDonald
To: Phillip Demarco
Subject: How could I?

HP,

After I read about how it would crush you if I left, I got upset (once again). I shouldn't have said anything to Nicole! I should have known better. I know I said I might need a job, but I didn't mean a permanent one! I can't go. It would kill me if I had to leave you here. I couldn't ever walk out of your office knowing I wouldn't be able to come in and see you sitting in there every day (even if you were in one of your "aggravated with Faye" moods). I can't imagine going for days/weeks/months/years without seeing you; that would be terrible! Thinking about this once again made me realize how much I love you. I wish we could have gone home together today. I need your arms wrapped around me. I miss you, HP. You're always on my mind! Well, I guess I'll see your handsome face tomorrow. I still love you more than you know!

Love,
BP

*****

I needed time with Faye again, too. In an unusual twist of fate, the heavens smiled on us on a Wednesday night. Alex was out of town for work, and Sophia wouldn't be home until late after a day of meetings in Jacksonville. After we left school, we had dinner at the Olive Garden again before I drove her home. Once we were inside, we couldn't get undressed fast enough, and we made passionate love on the living room floor. Then we moved to her spare bedroom and spent a few hours with our bodies intertwined.

It was difficult leaving and reminiscent of our early days together when we began falling in love. Later that night, Faye wrote me this sweet message.

*****

Date: Wed, 9 Nov 2011 23:48:37 (EDT)
From: Laura McDonald
To: Phillip Demarco
Subject: Again and again...

Hello, my dear HP,

I had a wonderful time with you tonight! We need to repeat that again and again and again. My having a good time when I'm with you isn't a big shocker, though; I always have fun when we're together. I've missed you kissing and touching me so much. It's easy to tell how much we both care from the way we touch each other.

I almost kissed you when we were sitting in your car after dinner, but there were too many people nearby. It was driving me crazy when you kept licking your lips! You were being terrible! HP. You still know how to get me excited, even after all these years! I guess some things never change! Well, that's all for now. Thanks for a great evening; I enjoyed it so much.

And just so you know, I am still in love with you regardless of what my behavior may lead you to believe.

Love you,
BP

*****

Faye's comment about her behavior was about the impression she gave me by being distant again—not always, but sometimes—which bothered me a lot. She would deny it when I brought it up, but she was acting like the way she did at the start of our summer in Titusville.

The big news for Faye was she passed both her written and oral doctoral qualifying examinations. Since she already finished her coursework, all she had left to finish was her research and writing and defending her dissertation. Not that it would be easy in any sense, but she had a great start, and her goal for finishing her PhD became May 2013.

Before we knew it, the semester was over and the holidays arrived, and all the while Faye and I were spending less and less time together for a variety of reasons. It would have been easy to rationalize it away, but our relationship was changing. I knew we couldn't keep the intensity of our summer in Titusville, but I still didn't like what was happening. When Faye came back after the holidays and school started up again in the spring semester of 2012, things between us were definitely different.

I was in a sentimental mood one night, remembering our wonderful summer together and the times we spent dancing. I made Faye a CD containing a playlist of the songs we slow-danced to in Titusville. It contained about twenty-five songs, most of which were oldies, and when I gave it to Faye, I attached the following note.

*****

BP,

I made this CD for you over the weekend. It has many of the songs on it we danced to (and I sang to you) last summer. But it's more than that. It's about you, it's about me, and it's about us.

The CD tells a story through its songs. It describes how I felt about you when we first met, how we fell in love, the marvelous summer we spent together in Titusville, and how, for whatever reason, we now seem to be drifting apart. The story is a wonderful and romantic one, as our relationship has been wonderful and romantic from the beginning. It's both a happy and a sad celebration of the love we've shared over the years.

Listen to the lyrics and try to follow our story as I'm trying to tell it. You may not like all the songs, but a part of each one has a special meaning to me about you or us. I hope you enjoy it and that it reminds you of our time in Titusville. I loved making it for you!

Love,
HP

*****

Date: Wed, 18 Jan 2012 21:55:38 (EDT)
From: Laura McDonald
To: Phillip Demarco
Subject: This CD!!!

HP,

I have three words for you... I *love it*! You were right (as usual). I sat here crying almost the entire time I was listening to it; I also had a smile on my face, if that makes any sense, just like I did last summer. I appreciate you making it for me/us. I will treasure it always. I love all the songs; I don't know why you thought I wouldn't.

I liked the second song the most; you may not remember why, so I'll tell you again. The first morning I was home with Alex after spending the summer with you. For some unknown reason, I woke up right as that song started playing on the radio. I got so upset by it because you had sung it to me the night before. I wanted to walk across the hall and ask you to run off with me. Ever since then, every time I hear that song, it reminds me of all the things we said and did together in the summer.

HP, I want you to know that even though I might not always show it to you, I still love you more than you'll ever know. And you're my best friend, and I wish we could be together always. I realize it would be perfect! Please understand that even if I don't see you as much these days, I'm still thinking about you, missing you, and wanting to be terrible with you. You are my soul mate, and you always will be. You only have to give me one of your looks or touch me to remind me of that "small" fact. So, the next time you imagine that I'm trying to distance myself from you, please remember you are in my thoughts and in my heart because, as the last song says, I will always love you!

Love,
BP

*****

The second song on the CD Faye referred to was 'She's Got A Way', by Billy Joel, a beautiful song of love from his first solo album, *Cold Spring Harbor* in 1971. It was as if he wrote the lyrics with Faye in mind. They gave a perfect description of her to me, the last line in particular, which said, "But I know that I can't live without her, anyway." I knew that lyric was true for me now. The last song on the CD Faye also referred to was the song Dolly Parton wrote in 1973 as a farewell to her former singing partner, Porter Wagoner, called 'I Will Always Love You'. The last line of that beautiful song was the same as the title of the song, something I told Faye and sang to her many times.

*****

Date: Wed, 18 Jan 2012 22:40:5:11 (EDT)
From: Phillip Demarco
To: Laura McDonald
Subject: Storybook relationship

BP,

I'm glad you liked the CD. It's something I will also treasure because it reminds me of all the things we've done together over the years.

I made the CD for several reasons. One was to commemorate our amazing summer together in Titusville. But also because I've been missing you, and making it helped me to feel closer to you again.

But the real reason I made it was to remind you again of the marvelous relationship we have and how wonderful our lives would be if we were together, like they were this past summer. It's rare for a person to find their soul mate, and since we've been lucky enough to find each other, I know we'd both be much, much happier if we could spend our lives together.

Most people would give anything and everything to find the love of their lives, to have someone who adores them, to have a romantic storybook relationship, and to have the most perfect life imaginable. I will always love you too!

HP

*****

If I were truthful, I'd admit I made the CD for Faye because it felt as though I was losing her, and I wasn't sure why. If it was true, I could come up with several explanations, the most probable being our age difference. But she never gave me the impression it was a problem for her, although it was the easiest and most understandable explanation I could accept. From my viewpoint, I wouldn't want a beautiful and vibrant fifty-six year-old forced into a life of caring for an octogenarian. That was not a life she'd choose for herself, nor should she have to make such a choice.

CHAPTER 21

Everybody Needs a Love Story

Before we got very far into the spring semester of 2012, Faye and I established our routine, which was much like the one for the past fall semester. Faye was busy again teaching two classes and working on her dissertation research. As the semester progressed and we headed toward summer, she received more good news. Instructional funds became available for her to teach in the summer, so she wouldn't have to take a temporary job with Nicole in Orlando.

We moved through the summer semester and the fall semester of 2012 and into the spring semester of 2013 in what seemed like record speed. Faye was busy trying to finish writing her dissertation while also being a conscientious and caring teacher, which she was.

Things were still not going well between us. We were spending much less time together, and we appeared to be drifting even further apart. Alex wasn't traveling anymore with his job, and he left the Air Force reserves, so we had few opportunities to be alone. Even her visits to my office didn't occur as often anymore. After much thought and contemplation, I decided if I ever hoped to win Faye, I needed to make a move before she graduated, and it became too late. I was no longer in love with Sophia, and I doubted she was still in love with me. The way I viewed it, I had to pursue Faye now or lose her forever. For that to happen, I had to end my marriage. Since Sophia and I had been married for twenty-one years now, I knew it wouldn't be an easy thing to do. I couldn't go on without Faye any longer; she was the one I loved. But even if my efforts failed, I'd be content with the time I had spent with both Sophia and Faye. The prospect of living life alone from that point forward didn't frighten me or make me uncomfortable. It was worth the risk to me.

I planned to tell Sophia I was no longer happy, and that I was in love someone else. I was prepared to explain everything that had happened with Faye and why. As a strong and independent woman, I knew she'd be fine without me, perhaps even better. Sophia made a higher salary than I did as a professor, plus her trust fund was significant, so money would not be a problem for her. And I had no interest in claiming any of her money in a divorce.

I intended to tell Sophia and then surprise Faye with the news, hoping she'd be happy. Perhaps it wasn't a great plan, but at least it was a plan. After another mundane, uninspiring weekend at home, I thought I'd talk with Sophia after work on Monday and then tell Faye on Tuesday morning.

Preoccupied and nervous most of Monday, I didn't see much of Faye. When I got home, Sophia wasn't there yet. I waited for her in the living room and sipped a cold beer until she came home. When she arrived about an hour later, she tossed her sweater and purse on the sofa and sat down next to them across the room from me. She had an odd expression on her face.

Not knowing how to begin, I said, "Sophia, we need to talk."

Before I could say another word, she replied, "Yes, Phillip, we do. I have to tell you I'm tired of living in this small town, and I'm moving back to New York. Today I received a job offer from Morgan Stanley, which I've accepted. I'll be starting there in a few weeks."

"Oh? I didn't realize you wanted to go back," I responded. "But you know, I'm not interested in moving," I continued.

"Well, Phillip, I'm not asking you to. I know you love your job. It's just that I've been here long enough, and I need a new challenge, and I want to live in a big city again. Besides, I've met someone up there, and I'd like to spend more time with him."

"Okay, I understand. I realize we've been drifting apart for a while now, and our connection isn't as strong as it once was, but I'm sure it's my fault."

"Let's not try to assign blame, Phillip. I'm at fault too. I do know you've been seeing your graduate student, what's her name, Laura? And she went to Titusville with you last summer, didn't she?"

"Well, she didn't go *with* me, although she was there working at NASA too. How did you find out about her?"

"Phillip, you can't pee in this town without everybody knowing about it. That's how small towns are. It's one thing I don't like about living here. But it's okay. I'm not upset with you. I've seen her. She's gorgeous, and she must be very smart. I see why you'd find her attractive. Maybe she can give you the son you've always wanted."

"I can't envision a child being in the cards for me with anybody. I'm sorry, Sophia. I never meant for you to learn about it that way. I wanted to discuss it with you tonight before you told me your news. I hope we can get along and not hate each other because of it."

"Oh, Phillip, I don't hate you. I realized a good while ago our marriage had run its course. I'm sure you knew it too. We had some great times together. I just want us both to be happy. If it means living separate lives, I can accept it, and I hope you can too."

"Yes, I'm fine with it, Sophia. I'll always be grateful for everything you did for me and for the sacrifices you made to come to Florida with me in the beginning. So where will you live up there? And how should we split up the house and all our stuff?" "Stop right there, Phillip! I've rented a townhouse in Chelsea. It'll be close to work, and it's where I want to live in

Manhattan. Plus, Morgan Stanley is doubling my salary to move there, and with my trust fund, I'll have plenty of money. Please don't worry about me. I'll take my personnel belongings, but I don't want any part of the house, the furniture, or anything else we shared. You were very good to me for a long time, and I'd like for you to have it all. I don't need any of it. I'll be happy with my clothes, my car, my other stuff, and some of our photos. Besides, I'd like to start over with all new things, anyway."

"That's very generous of you, Sophia. Thank you! Please let me help you in your transition. Just let me know what I can do."

"OK, Phillip, I will. Now let's have some wine to celebrate the good years we had together and toast the new lives ahead of us both. And I'm glad we don't hate each other."

"I am too, Sophia! Red wine or white?"

"Red, please," she answered.

As we toasted each other, we both said, "I love you." We had one last night together and shared some intimate moments that reminded us of the days when we were in love. A part of me would always love her, we just needed to find different lives now.

I felt relieved, and I could tell Sophia did too. We knew it was the best thing for us both, and she'd be happier in New York. Since we didn't have any children, splitting up would be easier than if we did. I was glad we would have an amicable breakup. I thought we were being fair to each other, with Sophia not wanting her share of our house, and me not seeking any part of her trust fund in a settlement. That was something she had before we married, so in my mind, I had no claim to it anyhow.

Soon, I began looking forward to the possibility of being with Faye forever, as we teased about so many times. I hoped she would welcome my sudden availability, but I wasn't sure if she would or not. I often thought back to our first night together in my car when she said she wasn't sure our relationship could go anywhere. I guess now I'd find out if it could.

I got to work early Tuesday morning, long before Faye. Soon after I heard her arrive, she came across the hall and walked through my open door. As she approached my desk, I could see her eyes were red and that she'd been crying. Without saying a word, she began waving her hands up and down on each side of her face to help dry her tears like she always did when she cried.

"BP, what's wrong?" I asked.

All she answered was, "Things aren't going so good at home," and she walked out of my office and back to hers.

For a moment, I wondered what could have happened between her and Alex. Did he find out about us? Did they argue about something else? I hoped he wasn't abusive to her. Then my thoughts turned selfish, and I thought, what if, by some coincidental karma, she told Alex she wanted to be with me? I couldn't wait to hear, so without hesitation, I went across the hall to find out what had occurred. When I entered, Faye was sitting at her desk, dabbing her eyes with a tissue.

"Faye, what happened at home?"

"I'm not sure if I can tell you," she answered.

"Please tell me, maybe I can help," I replied.

"Well," she started, "things aren't so good because I told Alex I met someone else, and I wanted a divorce."

All I could say was, "You did? You told him that?"

"Yes, I did, Phillip. His name is Patrick, and I met him at the gym back in December."

Faye's news hit me like a brick! All I could bring myself to say was, "Oh? So you're leaving Alex for someone else?"

Faye replied, "I'm sorry, Phillip. I feel terrible about this, but I just had to tell you and didn't know how."

I was in shock! After everything we'd been through, did together, and said to each other, she was getting divorced, but not to be with me. It was difficult for me to process what she told me. I could have done a lot of things, but I wasn't sure what to do. I probably should have told her about Sophia, although what good would it have done after hearing her news? She felt bad enough, and I knew telling her would have made her feel even worse. I loved her and wanted her to be happy. If she'd be happier with Patrick, then that was where she should be.

I said, "I'm sorry too, Faye," and I walked out of her office and back into mine. I closed and locked my door like I'd done so many times to be with her and was now doing to be away from her. I needed to ponder what had just happened between us. I always knew it was a long shot to get her to run away with me. From the beginning, I realized our age difference was problematic; Faye was now twenty-seven, and I was fifty-one. She warned me when our love affair started, so her news shouldn't have shocked me. This was the only practical outcome for her. Faye needed to move on with her life without me. I rationalized years ago that having the chance to be with Faye, even if it was only temporary, would be worth any price I had to pay. Now it was time to pay that price. And even though our relationship cost me my marriage, it was still worth it to me. *Faye* was worth it to me. I knew I'd never love this way again, and I would crave her forever. I'd never let go of those feelings and the wonderful memories of everything we did together. But everybody needs a love story. Faye was mine, and I thought I was hers. Perhaps I was wrong, and Patrick was her love story, not me. If so, I'm glad she found it.

If the problem wasn't my age, I couldn't imagine what it was. I thought our relationship was perfect. I guess I was wrong, and I didn't know why or when it went bad. I pondered many things during the weeks ahead. Could our relationship have become too sexual? Did Faye just use me the entire time? Didn't she mean the things she said to me? Perhaps I read too much into her actions, and she was teasing me all along? Or was I just an overzealous old man somehow thinking a beautiful young woman would want to be with me? Not knowing why was the worst part. I suppose I was just being foolish all along.

We didn't speak at all over the next few weeks. Then we only spoke about her dissertation research or when she had a question about teaching. Our conversations were just in the sense of a true professor/student relationship. She stopped coming in to chat, and we quit going to lunch together. I noticed her a few times in the courtyard outside our building, crying while talking to Alex. I never saw her with Patrick, nor did I ever meet him. She mentioned to me in passing one day that she had moved into an apartment by herself across town. I still couldn't bring myself to ask her more about her situation, and I doubt she'd want to tell me anything else anyhow. So I was unaware of what was happening between her and Alex and Patrick.

At one point, I told her I'd understand if she wanted to replace me as her major professor, but she declined. After everything, she still intended to finish her doctorate with me. I was pleased she did.

Sophia moved back to New York, and we both cried the day she left. It didn't take long for us to get a "no contest" divorce, and as we hoped, our split was amicable. She even invited me to visit her in Chelsea. I didn't tell her what happened with Faye, and I never told Faye about Sophia. I didn't feel sorry for myself like others may have done if this happened to them. I felt lucky to have had two incredible women in my life, even though neither relationship lasted. Many men never get to have even one.

I adjusted to living alone in a big house. I worked more, dated now and then, and often pondered looking for a new job in a new city or retiring altogether.

I also began writing that book about Faye and me. As I promised, I saved all her emails and notes during our time together. I thought they were very entertaining, and I believed others might also find them interesting. Although I wouldn't use them without her permission. As the weeks and months passed, we were cordial but impersonal. One day, I was joking with her and asked, "Faye, is it still okay with you if I use your old emails and notes in that book about us?"

She answered, "Yes, Phillip, but you still can't use my real name when you do!" Then she joked back, "But shouldn't I be a coauthor since you're using the things I wrote? After all, there wouldn't be a book without me!"

I replied, "I agree, Faye, but how about if I just give you half the profits instead, if there are any?

"It's a deal," Faye said.

In order for Faye to schedule her defense, I had to approve her dissertation as her major professor and adviser before she could distribute it to her examining committee. That required me to study it and give her any comments I might have, which she needed to address before giving it to the other committee members. The day she gave it to me, I thought I'd have a little fun with her.

When she handed me what she considered her completed dissertation, I said, "Faye, did I ever tell you about the graduate student who gave her dissertation to her adviser to read for the very first time?"

Faye responded, "Oh, no. Do I want to hear this?"

"You might not, but I'm telling you anyhow," I answered.

"Well," I started, "she was a doctoral student in a different department here at UF. She finished writing her dissertation and gave it to her adviser for his approval before scheduling her dissertation defense. A few days later, her advisor returned it with a single note on the front, which read, 'Needs work!'" So she made some minor changes and resubmitted it several days later. Again, her adviser returned it with another note, reading, "Needs work!" This time, she pored over it for days, reread every word, added every reference she could find, and reformatted the entire document to make it more readable. A week later, she walked into her adviser's office, handed it to him, and proclaimed, "I've done everything I can to improve this dissertation. In my mind, it's perfect!" The adviser took it from her and said, 'Okay, I guess I'll read it this time.'"

Faye didn't laugh but gave me a piercing stare and, in her best scolding voice, said, "You'd just better not do that to me!" I spent the following weekend reading every word of Faye's dissertation. It was an excellent piece of work, as I expected it would be, and I was happy with what she produced. I returned it to her early the following week, with only a few minor comments. She scheduled her defense for the middle of April, and if she passed, she would graduate in May. I knew Faye wouldn't have any problem defending her work, and she was also very optimistic. Her experiences presenting papers at conferences and teaching classes paid off as she developed self-confidence in her ability to speak and answer questions in front of groups. I was very proud of the professional she had become.

When the day of Faye's dissertation defense arrived, she did very well and passed with flying colors. She impressed her committee with both her work and her presentation. All she had left to do was make a few small editorial changes, but nothing difficult or anything that would take much time. Faye made the suggested corrections in a few days, obtained all the required signatures, and submitted her final dissertation to the university before the deadline. She had nothing more to do! After she finished, other than teaching her classes, she became scarce around the department, and I didn't see her at all.

Graduation day was Saturday, May 4. About a week before, she appeared at my office door. As she stood in the doorway, she knocked and said, "Phillip, may I come in?"

When I looked up and saw her, I answered, "Yes, Faye, you needn't ask."

"Well, I didn't know," she answered.

Then she began, "I wanted to thank you for everything you did for me over all these years. It was so much fun. Plus, I came to apologize to you for what happened between us."

"You're welcome, Faye, and there's no need for you to apologize for anything. I enjoyed every minute of it!" I hesitated before I asked, "So, what are your plans now?"

"Well," she said, "we haven't talked about any of this, and a lot has happened in the last month. First, I'm not seeing Patrick anymore. After our divorce, Alex confronted him and scared him off. He sure wasn't what I thought he was. Now Alex has accepted a new job in Miami and wants me to go with him."

"Are you planning to go?"

"I hate Miami, and I'm still not happy with Alex. But what are my options since I don't have a job anywhere yet? I guess I could go to work with Nicole in Orlando. I don't like Orlando either though, and I don't want to go to Miami. Patrick is out of the picture, and I messed things up with you so bad. I just don't know what to do, Phillip!"

"What would you like to do with your PhD?"

"I still want to teach, Phillip, like you!"

"Well, you could stay here. Robert already told me he'd hire you if you didn't want to leave Gainesville. You didn't mess things up with me, either. When I said I would always love you, I meant it!"

"How could you, Phillip, after the way I treated you? I was awful! You can't forgive me for that, can you?"

"Sure I can, BP, I'd forgive you for anything. And you've been nothing but wonderful to me, far more wonderful than I deserved."

"Oh, HP, I've never stopped loving you either. The thing with Patrick was a huge mistake. I'm so sorry it happened. I shouldn't have rejected you. I got scared because of our age difference, but I'm over that now. Plus, I didn't think you would ever leave your wife to be with me."

I pointed to "Faye's chair," next to my desk, and said, "BP, have a seat, there's something you should know…"

*****

"HP, why didn't you tell me sooner?"

*****

On the day of Faye's graduation, we sat together during the ceremony, and I walked her to the stage when they called her name. There, in the O'Connell Center, I had the honor of hooding a new PhD. I was very proud of her and thrilled to hood her. Once again, Faye's family traveled from Nashville to attend. This time, though, Alex was missing. After the ceremony, I took Faye and her family out to dinner to celebrate at Ember's Wood Grill on SW Thirty-Fourth Street, the best steak house in Gainesville. Since Faye was the first family member to graduate from college, let alone earn a doctorate, a celebration was certainly in order. It was a wonderful evening.

Later that night, after I got home, Sophia surprised me with an unexpected phone call.

"Hi, Phillip, this is Sophia. We were once related by marriage, remember?"

I laughed and said, "Yes, I remember. Hello Sophia, how are you?"

"I'm good, Phillip. I'm in Orlando on business and wondered if I could drive up to Gainesville tomorrow to see you if you aren't busy."

"Sure, Sophia, that would be great! Come up for lunch, and we'll spend the afternoon together. Is everything okay?"

"Yes, Phillip, everything's fine. I love living in a city again, although my job at Morgan Stanley isn't what I expected. I'll tell you all about it tomorrow. It will be good to see you, Phillip!"

"Likewise, Sophia! Until tomorrow then and drive safe."

Sophia arrived around noon. I knew she'd enjoy spending time at the house, so rather than going out to lunch, I grilled fresh salmon and vegetables on the deck by the pool. And we had wine, white this time. And we talked and talked.

During our conversation, Sophia said, "Living in Chelsea is great, although I don't enjoy my job as much as I enjoyed teaching finance at the community college. I've been thinking perhaps I should teach full-time now instead. I saw how much you always loved it, and I might too."

"Well, there's still time if it's what you want," I replied. "I'm sure you could teach finance at many schools."

"But it's more than that, Phillip. I may have made a big mistake not wanting children, or at least us not adopting later on. It may be my biggest regret as I get older."

"You shouldn't have regrets, Sophia. Looking back, I'm not sure having children would have worked for us," I responded.

Then I asked, "Are you still seeing the same guy in New York?"

"Well, yes, but we're only friends. The romance part didn't work out. And if I may ask, what about you and Laura?"

"Our relationship didn't work out as I thought it might either," I answered. "She graduated but isn't sure what she'll do next or where she'll be. She also ended up getting a divorce, although it wasn't because of me."

I knew Sophia could read between my words. All she said was, "I'm sorry, Phillip."

We spent the rest of the afternoon catching up on news about family and friends and reminiscing about our years together and our many trips. It was clear we both still loved and respected each other, and we shared some tender moments, but we both knew the spark we had once was gone. Before Sophia left to return to Orlando, I promised to visit her in Chelsea, which I looked forward to doing soon, perhaps even in the next few weeks before school resumed.

It was wonderful to see Sophia again, but I never made the trip to New York.

*****

It was a warm spring morning in New Orleans, one that would soon give way to the inevitable sultry summer ahead. I was sitting on a bench in the section of Audubon Park known by locals as The Fly. Overlooking the Mississippi River, I watched as a tugboat pushed its barge downriver on its next journey, something I did often to ponder my life and reflect on past events and their unexpected outcomes. The peacefulness of the slow-moving water and the many magnificent live oak trees peppered throughout the park provided the serenity necessary for such thought.

I retired and left Gainesville several years earlier and escaped to this wonderful city with my wife when she accepted a faculty position at Tulane University. We purchased a classic Southern home on State Street in the Uptown section of New Orleans near Audubon Park and within walking distance to campus. Our home was a raised center hall cottage style, two stories tall, with double balconies and white columns in the front. It was close enough to the river and Port NOLA that foghorns and train whistles were more than common at all hours of the day and night. Having lived in a small college town for many years, the robustness and excitement of New Orleans provided an opportunity for new lives for us, which we adjusted to and embraced quickly. The exceptional food and unique musical culture drew us in without the slightest bit of hesitation. There was something special about this city, all of it welcoming, and much of it romantic.

As I enjoyed the quiet, lazy morning, I typed on my laptop and worked on the final chapter of the book I was writing about Faye and me. As I did, a young child's voice from the open field behind me broke the silence.

"Hey, Dad, come play catch with me!" Hearing those words brought an immediate smile to my face.

I turned and shouted, "I'll be right there, Daniel!" As I moved to get up, a single finger pressed against the back of my hand as it rested on my leg and stopped me.

"I just needed to touch you once before you left."

"You know, I'm almost finished writing the book about us." Then I added, "You told me many times you didn't want me to use your real name. So what name should I call you?" She giggled, and her warm smile widened into a slight laugh as she looked down and returned to grading the exams she'd given the afternoon before.

As I picked up my old, worn baseball mitt and began to walk over to play catch with our son, she answered, "Phillip, it doesn't matter anymore what you call me in the book. So, just call me Faye!"

www.ingramcontent.com/pod-product-compliance
Lightning Source LLC
Chambersburg PA
CBHW031250170626
46807CB00001B/74